PRAISE FOR MELANIE RAABE

PRAISE FOR *THE TRAP*

"Intricately constructed . . . nicely done twists and turns."
—*Kirkus Reviews*

"Suspenseful . . . taut storytelling."—*Publishers Weekly*

"You won't be able to resist."—*Elle UK*

"*The Trap* had me hooked from the start. Linda's story unravels so cleverly, and Raabe keeps you questioning what's fact and what's not right to the end, ratcheting up the tension at the same time . . . A genuinely gripping debut: I had to keep reading until I was finished!"
—Debbie Howells, author of *The Bones of You*

"A page-turner with a plot that surprises . . . The storm that *The Trap* generates is as big as its charm."
—*Die Welt* (Germany)

"A smart and enthralling psychological thriller . . . splendidly entertaining."
—*WDR* (Germany)

"A fascinating psychological thriller."
—*Bild* (Germany)

PRAISE FOR *THE STRANGER UPSTAIRS*

"What more could you want from a story than complete, unrelenting tension and creepiness to the point that you are nearly terrified to find out what is going to happen? That, in a nutshell, is *The Stranger Upstairs* — this absolute rollercoaster that makes you question everything you thought you could trust." —*Magnolia Reads*

"Full of suspense, right up to the final paragraphs . . . An edgy thriller." —*AU Review*

"Another unsettling and slippery psychological thriller that keeps you guessing up to the last page." —*Readings*

"A classic domestic noir . . . Generates sustained psychological suspense that gets under the skin." —*Age*

"The fear is palpable . . . You'll be engrossed every step of the way." —*Better Reading*

"Raabe cleverly sets up her story, inserting twists and red herrings so that the reader is kept guessing until the final, staggering reveal. Flawlessly translated from German by Imogen Taylor, this page-turner is even better than Raabe's debut." —*BookMooch*

"Raabe once again delivers an enjoyable, page-turning, high concept domestic noir thriller." —*PS News*

"This psychological thriller will keep you guessing until the end." —*Daily Life*

THE
SHADOW

MELANIE RAABE

Translated from the German by Imogen Taylor

SPIDERLINE

First published in German as *Der Schatten* in 2018 by btb Verlag, a division of Verlagsgruppe Random House GmbH, Munich, Germany
First published in English in 2020 by The Text Publishing Company, Australia
First published in Canada in 2021 and the USA in 2021 by House of Anansi Press Inc.
www.houseofanansi.com

House of Anansi Press is committed to protecting our natural environment. This book is made of material from well-managed FSC®-certified forests, recycled materials, and other controlled sources.

25 24 23 22 21   1 2 3 4 5

Library and Archives Canada Cataloguing in Publication

Title: The shadow / Melanie Raabe ; translated by Imogen Taylor.
Other titles: Schatten. English
Names: Raabe, Melanie, 1981- author. | Taylor, Imogen (Translator), translator.
Description: Translation of: Schatten.
Identifiers: Canadiana (print) 20200273507 | Canadiana (ebook) 20200273590 |
ISBN 9781487008635 (softcover) | ISBN 9781487008642 (EPUB) |
ISBN 9781487008659 (Kindle)
Classification: LCC PT2718.A22 S3313 2021 | DDC 833/.92—dc23

Cover design: Adapted from the original by Text
Cover images: Walter Jarolim/EyeEm/Getty and iStock
Typesetting: J&M Typesetting

House of Anansi Press respectfully acknowledges that the land on which we operate is the Traditional Territory of many Nations, including the Anishinabeg, the Wendat, and the Haudenosaunee. It is also the Treaty Lands of the Mississaugas of the Credit.

 Canada Council for the Arts   Conseil des Arts du Canada    ONTARIO ARTS COUNCIL CONSEIL DES ARTS DE L'ONTARIO an Ontario government agency un organisme du gouvernement de l'Ontario

We acknowledge for their financial support of our publishing program the Canada Council for the Arts, the Ontario Arts Council, and the Government of Canada.

Printed and bound in Canada

 FSC www.fsc.org   MIX Paper from responsible sources FSC® C103567

THE SHADOW

In the desert
I saw a creature, naked, bestial,
Who, squatting upon the ground,
Held his heart in his hands,
And ate of it.
I said, 'Is it good, friend?'
'It is bitter—bitter,' he answered;

'But I like it
'Because it is bitter,
'And because it is my heart.'

'IN THE DESERT', STEPHEN CRANE

Prologue

She would simply disappear. The ice would crack and give way beneath her feet and she'd be pulled swiftly under—no flailing and thrashing to stay above water, no struggle, just down, down, down into the darkness and silence.

When she was little, she had often walked on the frozen pond that lay between the edge of town and the fields. It didn't occur to her back then that it was possible to fall through.

To think that such a place existed—a small lake in the middle of the wood, overhung by trees, their branches weighed down by snow as if they were mourning. The tips of her fingers were numb, her toes so cold that they hurt. She swung the torch to and fro. There was nobody here but her. They hadn't come. And yet there were tracks. Had she missed them? Was she late? She glanced at her watch. No, she wasn't.

She switched off the torch. Inching her way along the forest path, she had needed the grainy beam of light, but now that she'd stepped out from the shadowy trees, she could do without it.

The stars were bright out here, far from the city. Frosty leaves crunched underfoot. The night glistened. For a moment she forgot what she was doing here in the middle of the night—forgot about the betrayal and the anger and the pain.

She stepped out onto the frozen surface, stopped, listened. The ice creaked, a living being, stirring in a dream.

She listened more closely, looked up at the sky, closed her eyes. The silence sang in her ears.

Strange, she thought.

A wind got up, sharp as a knife and smelling of fresh snow. She hunched her shoulders.

The stars gleamed milkily. She had the feeling she shouldn't be here.

Then she saw something on the ice. She hesitated. Stooping to get a better look at whatever it was, she reached out a hand to it. When she realised what she was looking at, she recoiled. A dead bird, dark against the white snow, not yet frozen.

She stiffened and turned away abruptly, breathing fast. She believed in signs.

There was nobody there.

She wheeled round—nothing, nobody, just her and the night. She looked up at the stars again. Then she made up her mind.

She would do it. She would destroy them, all of them. But the one she really wanted to destroy was Norah.

1

Norah loved goodbyes. She loved moments of transition: the minutes between night and day, winter and spring, one year and the next. She loved new babies and weddings. Another life, a second chance, rebirth. A clean slate and a new pencil.

Then why are you crying?

The road stretched endlessly before her. The woods were black and impenetrable, the sky bruised by the night. Norah stared into the darkness, and in the rear-view mirror her old life receded, growing smaller and smaller, almost unreal—her job, her boyfriend, her home, the dog.

The disaster.

Norah wiped away her tears. One day she'd get over what had happened in Berlin. Life wasn't fair, she knew that; she'd survive. The anger and bitterness would never entirely disappear, but they would fade like an old tattoo. The heaviness of the last weeks and months was beginning to lift even now, with every mile she put between herself and Berlin. She'd been right to leave.

Norah had a good six hours' drive ahead of her. She slowed the car and rounded a bend, taking care not to cut the corner. She switched on the radio and electronic music poured out of the speakers. It was some time since she'd passed a car going the other direction and she liked it that way—liked the sound of the asphalt under the tyres, the soft music, the woods, the peace, the feeling of starting over. The last light faded. The pine forests on either side of the winding road seemed to grow denser. She steered the car around another long drawn-out bend and stepped on the accelerator. When she looked up, the sky was suddenly full of stars—a handful at first, then dozens, thousands, myriads.

A glance at the sat nav told her she had almost five hundred kilometres to go. So what? She wasn't in a hurry. She slowed and pulled over, switched off the radio, engine and headlights, and sat and stared at the sky.

Then she got out of the car, walked to the middle of the road and threw back her head. The stars were painted with the finest of brushes. She smiled and for a moment she just stood there, looking up. She felt the cold on her cheeks first, then in her fingertips, through the thin leather of her gloves, then in her toes. She tried to remember why stars twinkled, but she'd forgotten. *What was that?* A cracking noise. She turned and stared into the darkness. Forest sounds. Norah laughed at the sudden thumping of her heart.

Forest sounds, her own breath. A dead straight road ahead, and above her the sky. Nothing to be afraid of. She got back in the car without hurrying, switched on the headlights, started the engine. Her handbag lay beside her on the passenger seat; a few belongings were piled in the back. That was all. The hastily packed removal boxes were waiting for her in Vienna. She was starting over; she was free. Norah turned the radio on again and changed stations. Then it was just her and the road and the music.

2

When Norah woke up in her new flat in Vienna the next morning and walked barefoot to the window, the grand facades of the houses opposite were already bathed in the milky light of the winter sun. She opened the window and stood there, enjoying the crisp chill on her face as the city stirred to life below. A group of children was crossing the road, their shouts almost drowned by the noise of the traffic. Norah took a deep breath, then closed the window and looked about her.

How little there was to her life. Her bed was only a roll of slats and a few pieces of wood, strewn over the parquet of her bedroom like a disjointed skeleton—she'd spent the night on a camping mat, feeling the hard floor beneath her whenever she'd moved. Then there were the removal boxes, forty-eight of them. That was as much of her old life as she'd brought with her into the new.

She opened one of the boxes at random. It was labelled *Clothes* and contained summer things—flip-flops and the white bikini she'd bought for the previous year's holiday in Sardinia, where they'd celebrated her thirty-fourth birthday.

She'd packed too hastily, desperate to leave the flat in Berlin. Alex had looked on in bewilderment, knocked sideways by what was happening. He didn't know what to say and she wouldn't have listened if he had.

Norah shut the box again, then opened another and another and another: bedclothes, diving gear, blankets, shirts, T-shirts—but no warm jumper anywhere. She shivered. It was cold in the flat; the radiators barely gave off any heat. Sighing, she threw down a black blouse, then stretched and looked about her again. The removal men had stacked the boxes at random all over the flat. Piled up against the backdrop of bare white walls and high ceilings, they looked like installations in a museum of modern art.

Only a few things were already in place: her desk in the study, her sofa in front of the TV in a corner of the living room—she could leave the TV on, if the silence got too loud for her—and the coffee machine in the kitchen. The rest was a desert. No, she thought, not a desert—a blank sheet of paper, waiting for the first brushstroke.

Norah found herself smiling.

When she went out a little later, locking the door behind her, the communal stairs smelt of damp carpet and filter coffee. She was about to head down when she heard a low noise and, glancing up, she saw a small black cat eyeing her shyly from the stairs above.

'Hello,' said Norah. 'Where have you come from?'

She crouched down and reached out a hand. The kitten stared. Then, timid at first, but gradually bolder, it started towards her. Norah stroked the little head gently. She'd always wanted a cat as a child, but her mother hadn't wanted a pet in the flat, and by the time Norah was old enough to make her own decisions she was working twelve hours a day in an office and didn't have the time.

The cat, forgetting its initial caution, pushed its head against the back of Norah's hand, arched its back and began to purr.

'Katinka?' said a voice from the next floor up. The cat raised its head, clearly uncertain whether to respond to the call, or stay and be stroked a little longer by its new friend. It didn't hesitate for long; when Norah stood up, it began to rub itself coquettishly against her legs.

'Hello,' Norah called up the stairs. 'If you're looking for your cat, it's here.'

There was a laugh, then footsteps. The voice said, 'Well, Katinka? Pestering the neighbours again?' And then to Norah, 'Sorry, she must have given me the slip. I'm Theresa, by the way. From the third floor.'

Norah froze for a moment, staring at the almost almond-shaped eyes, the blonde lashes, the small curved mouth that looked as if it had been painted with a single flourish, the freckles...

'Are you okay?' asked the young woman, but Norah barely heard her.

So similar...

'Don't you feel well?' the woman said.

At last Norah managed a smile.

'I must have been dreaming,' she said. 'I'm sorry.'

She took the hand that was held out to her.

'Norah,' she added, 'from the second floor.'

'Cool,' said the woman. 'Nice to meet you.' She glanced over her shoulder. 'I'd better try and catch the little devil.'

Norah stepped slowly down the stairs to the ground floor.

Don't you feel well? the woman had asked. *Well?* How were you supposed to feel well, when you'd seen a ghost?

3

Vienna was giving Norah the cold shoulder. When she'd visited with Alex in the summer, she'd been enchanted; it had seemed to her a city with a mind of its own, unlike anywhere she'd been before. That felt like light years ago.

Everything seemed so bleak—a Munchian vision of a city; a dark, urban forest, warped and menacing. The gloom pervaded Norah's empty flat and the dingy streets. Passers-by stared grimly at their phones; melancholy coated everything like a film of grease. And it was fucking freezing.

Norah bought an Austrian paper, a German paper and a packet of cigarettes in the newsagent's across the road, and sat down with them in the corner bistro. By the time she took her first sip of coffee, the shock of memory aroused in her by Theresa had subsided a little, and she could turn her mind to the day ahead.

Although Norah's job wouldn't officially begin for two weeks, her new boss had asked her to go and meet him that morning. They'd talked at length on the phone, but this would be their first real meeting, and Norah was looking forward to it; she couldn't wait to get back to work, even if she was a little nervous. She knew she was a good journalist; she'd won prizes for some of her features, and there had even been attempts to headhunt her. But all that had been before what she secretly thought of as *the disaster*. Coming after that, the job offer from Vienna had seemed too good to be true; she was almost afraid it would turn out to be a cruel joke.

Mira Singh, the publisher, had rung her in person. Norah's feature on women soldiers in Afghanistan had caught her interest; she'd gone on to read all Norah's latest work and been impressed by her keen eye and her choice of topics. Mira was involved in setting up a new weekly magazine in Vienna and wanted Norah on board. The idea, she explained, was to forget about trying to keep up with the internet and publish an old-school high-quality magazine headed by an outstanding team of editors and filled with well-researched articles by prestigious writers.

It sounded perfect to Norah. Where was the catch? Did Mira realise Norah was lumbered with a lawsuit? Mira only said that she'd read the article in question. She was looking for a woman with attitude and thought she'd found one in Norah. Not wanting to sound overeager, Norah had asked for a day to think it over. Then she'd accepted. What else could she have done?

And here she was.

The magazine offices were in the touristy part of town, not far from St Stephen's Cathedral, on one of those big shopping streets lined with fast-food outlets and clothing chains that sell more or less the same things the world over. Norah knew the area from one of her previous visits to Vienna; it was packed from early till late with tourists and those who lived off them. There were tour groups on their way to the cathedral, con artists, buskers, teenagers taking selfies on their phones, and here and there an exasperated local who actually wanted to get somewhere. And there were beggars and homeless people, their calls echoing through the streets like the cries of ghosts. The living

9

shuddered at their voices, but pretended not to hear them.

Some years ago, Norah had wanted to write a feature on homeless minors, but hadn't been able to persuade her boss. Maybe it was time to give it another go. She lit a cigarette and walked down the street, thinking hard. Her tongue probed a molar that was throbbing dully, as if the tooth couldn't make up its mind whether or not to ache properly. That was the last thing she needed. She wanted to go to the shops that evening, not the dentist.

Outside H&M, a nondescript girl was sitting cuddled up to an Alsatian with a sign in front of her. *I'm hungry*. Early twenties at most, reddish-brown hair under a black beanie, military parka, chewed fingernails. Next came a man of sixty-odd with finely drawn features behind a pair of glasses, and then a guy with blond dreads—presumably the local psycho—who sat there, mumbling away to himself and scrounging off the passers-by, occasionally turning on a passing woman and hurling obscene abuse at her with astonishing inventiveness and persistence.

Then Norah saw the woman—an elderly woman, with striking wrinkles and clear, bright blue eyes. The kind of face that won photographers prizes, if they were lucky enough to spot it in a remote mountain village.

She wasn't sitting or kneeling on the ground like the other beggars, nor was she at the edge of the street. She was standing right in the middle of the pedestrian precinct with a small brass dish in her hand, apparently unfazed by the milling crowd. It was incredible. This woman—a good six foot, Norah guessed—stood in everybody's way, and yet nobody bumped into her; the bustle of the city washed over her like water lapping a river island. Now and then a couple of coins chinked in the dish, but she didn't say thank you, she just stood there motionless—upright and forbidding in the steady flow of people. A rock, a black tower. Only her eyes moved. Norah wondered what story she had to tell.

•

Sebastian Berger, Norah's new boss, was a tall, strongly built man in his fifties, with still-dark hair combed back off his face. He was wearing jeans and a tweed jacket that made him look rather donnish. What really struck Norah, though, was his expression. It said, *You are not the way I imagined you.* But she was used to that. With her fine-featured face and petite figure, she was regularly mistaken for the rookie, even now, in her mid-thirties. When she'd had photos taken for the various web portals where her writer's profile was posted—photos that Sebastian Berger had presumably seen—she'd deliberately worn dark clothes and a serious expression, and then chosen the pictures that made her look the most grown-up. In real life, of course, such tricks were no use to her, and she'd realised early in her career that if she wanted to be respected, she had to be tougher than most, and work harder. Berger, to his credit, soon regained his stride. He offered Norah coffee and they resumed the conversation they'd begun on the phone about potential topics for articles. When Norah took the lift down two hours later, her mind was whirling with ideas. It felt good to be going back to work.

Outside, it had warmed up a little. Norah had planned to go and get Austrian number plates for her car and, if that didn't take all day, to look for some furniture afterwards. She unbuttoned the grey winter coat she was wearing over a black woollen dress. It was mild, almost springlike; the sun shone in a deep blue sky. All was brightness in this city. No shadows anywhere. She paused for a moment to watch the crowds of people ploughing their way down the pedestrian precinct, lured out by the glorious weather.

Norah soaked it all in: shoppers, tourists, police, neon signs, pigeons, cigarette ends, paper cups, the smell of deep-frying, the clatter of heels. A man touting roses, the distant clip-clop of hoofs from the tourist carriages, fountains, balloon-sellers, ice-cream cones and popcorn, smartphone zombies and con artists. She could feel herself being swallowed up and tried to get along more quickly, but it was useless; an enormous tour group even pushed her back a little. Norah abandoned all politeness and began to elbow her way through, holding the bag with the vehicle papers close to her body. She dodged a rickshaw cyclist who, for reasons best known to himself, seemed to think it a good idea to chauffeur his passengers through this mayhem. Then she realised that her phone was ringing. She fished it out of her bag and gave a start when she saw the screen. *Alex.* They hadn't spoken since Norah had moved out—she'd stayed in a hotel for a few weeks before coming to Vienna, and neither of them had made any attempt to get in touch. Norah stared at the screen, feeling cold. Should she pick up or wait for her voicemail to kick in? Then it was too late; Alex had given up. Norah slid her phone into her coat pocket and raised her eyes.

The old woman she had seen begging earlier was standing right in front of her, so tall that Norah had to look up at her. She reached into her bag and pulled out her wallet to put a few euros in her dish.

'You bring death,' the woman said, her husky voice calm.

Norah frowned. 'What did you say?'

The woman seemed not to hear.

'Flowers wither,' she said. 'Clocks stop. Birds fall dead from the sky.'

Her grave stare was still fixed on Norah. Her hair was darker, her eyes brighter and her wrinkles deeper than Norah had realised. The pale turquoise of her irises was flecked with specks of red, like the tiny particles of blood in the yolk of an egg.

It suddenly occurred to Norah that the woman was mentally ill.

'On February 11 you will kill a man called Arthur Grimm in the Prater,' the woman continued. 'With good reason. And of your own free will.'

Norah didn't know what to say. She had just opened her mouth to speak when someone or something rammed into her from behind, making her stumble and drop the papers she was carrying. A few loose sheets slipped to the ground and she stooped to pick them up.

By the time she had straightened back up, the woman had vanished. Norah looked about her in bewilderment. A group of Chinese tourists shoved past her, then a young couple with a pram. Where had she gone? Desperately scanning the street, Norah pushed her way between two football fans in Rapid Vienna scarves. The woman was so tall she ought to have stood out above the crowd, but she was nowhere to be seen; it was as if the earth had swallowed her up. Shame, thought Norah, she looked like a woman with a tale to tell.

But it had been slightly unnerving.

4

A supermarket, a bookshop, a university building, a drugstore, restaurants, antique shops, a dolls' hospital, a shop selling guns. On a house wall, a row of posters, each printed with a single huge letter, spelt out the words: *ARE YOU SURE?* Norah tried to fix everything in her memory. This was her neighbourhood now—this was home. But it would be a while before she stopped feeling like a tourist.

She looked up. The tram wires cut through the blue of the sky, making beautiful geometric patterns, like shattered glass. The houses were grand and imposing, just like all over the city. What was going on up there, behind those windows? Were people arguing? Watching TV? Cooking? Watering their flowers, committing adultery, committing murder?

As a child, she had often wished for x-ray eyes so that she could see through walls and find out what was happening on the other side—what kind of people lived there and what they got up to. These days she was sometimes glad not to have to know the distressing details—to see only the gleaming facades.

Her new flat was big and empty. No Alex, no dog—only echoes and shadows and bare walls. She'd tried to call Alex back, but hadn't got through. Part of her was glad. She clapped shut her laptop, unable to concentrate on the notes she'd been trying to make. An old, dark thought had been stirring in her all day, and now there was no ignoring it.

She decided to ring her friend Sandra. Back in Berlin, Norah would simply have dropped in on her; she'd lived only a few streets away. And in the years before Berlin, Norah would have numbed the thought with drugs. But all that was a thing of the past; she'd been clean for ages.

Sandra didn't pick up. Norah let her eyes wander over the moulded ceiling, the spotless parquet, the cardboard boxes, her few belongings—and all of a sudden she noticed a buzzing sound. She felt it rather than heard it, somewhere between her diaphragm and her breastbone, and it was a moment before she could put a name to it. These last few years she'd been alone so little she'd almost forgotten the feeling. It was loneliness—deafening loneliness.

She had to get out. Out into life. That always helped when gloom threatened to descend. Norah glanced at her phone and wondered who else she could ring. In Berlin it would have been easy to find someone who'd go out for a drink with her, but it was different in Vienna, where there was really only her best friend Max and his husband Paul—and her old mate Tanja, of course, but she was in Hamburg just now. Max had been thrilled when Norah had told him she was moving to 'his' city. She tried his number. Voicemail.

She thought of going out by herself, but didn't have the nerves to face the comments and pick-up lines that a woman alone in a bar would be bound to attract. Her chest felt as if it were about to burst. She sat down, checked Facebook and Twitter, and tweeted.

Anyone else out there who can't sleep?

#sleeplessinVienna

She waited for a few minutes, but no one replied.

Then she gave up and zapped her way through the TV channels until she found a documentary about indigenous foxes that she liked the look of.

Norah sat up with a start. She couldn't have slept for long—the same documentary was still showing on TV—but she felt that vague confusion that comes over you when you wake from a deep dream. Dazed, she sat up, wiping sweat from her forehead. Floorboards creaked overhead; her upstairs neighbour was still awake. What was her name again? That's right, *Theresa*.

How strange life was. Norah had left everything behind to start over in another country, and the past had caught up with her on her very first day in the new city.

Rubbish! It was only a stupid coincidence that her new neighbour looked the way she did. Didn't people say that everyone has a doppelgänger somewhere? And how often in the past years had Norah thought she'd seen *her*, in a passing train, an airport lounge, a pavement cafe?

But it wasn't only the similarity between Theresa and *her* that had made Norah think of her on and off all day. It was also the words spoken by the woman with the begging bowl.

On February 11 you will kill a man called Arthur Grimm in the Prater. With good reason. And of your own free will.

On February 11, of all days...

Norah went over to the window, thinking hard, and looked down onto the street. On the other side of the road, someone was trying to squeeze a black station wagon into a ridiculously small parking space. Norah heard the muted laughter of a passing couple through the double-glazed windows.

Given what the woman had said, it seemed only sensible to conclude that she was mentally ill. Norah didn't know anyone called Arthur Grimm. And she certainly wasn't intending to do anyone in. But the date. That fucking date. It had to be a coincidence.

Norah decided it was the discrepancy between the woman's

16

appearance and her words that was troubling her. She hadn't seemed mentally ill, she'd seemed lucid and controlled. Norah had never come across anyone quite like her before; her interest was piqued. There might be something exciting behind it. She resolved to go in search of the strange fortune teller the next day—to find out who she was and what her story was. Norah was good at that kind of thing; it was her metier. In the meantime she could google the name the woman had mentioned.

Arthur Grimm. Norah screwed up her eyes, trying to think. No, she didn't know anyone by that name. And yet it rang a bell. Or was she imagining things?

A fraction of a second later, the search engine spat out images of a face so handsome and yet so unnerving that Norah gasped.

5

Norah had dreamt she was alone in an empty world where there was no sign of life—only the occasional bird flying past, far away, out of reach.

Then the birds fell down.

Norah woke on her back in the dank cold of her flat. She was breathing heavily and when she opened her eyes, she had the impression that the ceiling had dropped to no more than a couple of feet above her face. It had rained in the night, staining the road dark and covering the city in a grey haze. Everything looked blurred at the edges, as if the cold and wet had attacked the very substance of things, watering them down to produce grubby pen and ink washes. Inside, Norah felt the same.

Somehow or other she managed to get up and make her way, shivering, into the shower, where she washed off the uneasy feeling with hot water.

Out on the stairs, she was met once more by the smell of mouldy carpet. At the letterboxes, she bumped into the ground-floor neighbour, a small, thin man with suspicious eyes and a crumpled face. She said good morning, but got no reply.

By the time she entered the corner bistro to fortify herself with a cappuccino, she was beginning to feel better.

Three elderly ladies were sitting at the window table over the first coffee and cigarettes of the day. There was a blonde, a redhead and a brunette, like in a bad joke, and they had worn heels, mangy fur coats and broad Viennese accents. Norah sipped her cappuccino, licking the froth from her lips, and stared out at the street, listening to the women's scathing remarks as they bemoaned the state of the world, the decline of moral standards, the appalling dress taste of passers-by, and the smoking ban—not that they seemed to heed it. Norah was about to ask for the bill when her eye was caught by a young woman walking past the bistro. She was staring at the ground, as if she thought she might just get through life unscathed if she didn't look at anything or anyone. Her dark blonde hair was tied in a ponytail and she was wearing tight jeans and a pink puffer jacket that accentuated her enormous girth. She looked oddly beautiful and heartrendingly sad, and if Norah had been any good at painting, she'd have liked to paint her portrait—oils on canvas, something classic.

'It's Marie!' one of the old ladies cried. 'Haven't seen her for a long time!' The other two nodded silently.

The couple at the table behind Norah had also noticed the young woman.

'It's a wonder she can still fit through her front door!' the man said, and his girlfriend giggled. Norah glared at them, but they took no notice. Norah's friend Coco popped into her head. Not that Coco looked anything like the young woman, but she, too, made people turn and look. Thinking of Coco made Norah think of Berlin and the disaster, and soon her good mood had evaporated.

When she left the bistro, it had begun to rain again. The houses seemed to be bracing themselves against the wind and weather, and the street, with its shuttered shops, closed grilles and darkly clad figures carrying umbrellas, looked almost hostile. Norah stopped, fished her phone out of her bag and opened Instagram. She took a photo, tagged it *#winter-invienna* and *#melancholia*, and posted it. She'd been so caught up in events these last months that she'd neglected her social media channels and her blog. No wonder no one had replied last night. She'd better start posting more regularly; this beautiful, lonely city certainly offered enough material.

The underground station smelt of sadness and cement. Norah heard snatches of a melancholy eastern European air, the fruity cough of a homeless man, the ghostly echo of heels. She got on a train and stood wedged between strangers—headphones, lowered gazes, steamed-up windows, the dull noise of a throat being cleared. People's bodies were pressed up close to hers, but the distance between them was unbridgeable. Berlin had been the same—cold and bleak and unwelcoming, though in a different way. The train stopped, the doors opened and people poured out, carrying Norah with them.

The old fortune teller she had come in search of was nowhere to be seen. In fact, the cold, damp weather seemed to have driven the beggars from the streets altogether. Maybe Norah would have better luck later in the day. She was determined to talk to the old woman again. The date was probably pure coincidence. Norah was probably just imagining that the name Arthur Grimm rang a bell. But *probably* had never been enough for her.

In the magazine offices Norah felt like a ghost, almost entirely ignored. Although her job didn't officially start for two weeks, she'd already moved into one of the shared offices overlooking Kärntner Strasse. Berger had shown her around and introduced her to everyone, and she had found her new colleagues polite but aloof. That was fine by her; she'd always tended to keep her social life separate from work, and apart from Werner, she had no journalist friends. Norah knew Werner from her Hamburg days. He was an excellent reporter, but he and Norah had something else in common, too; there had been a time when he'd taken even more drugs than she had. Hard to believe that they'd both been clean for ten years; it was as if they'd been given a second chance. Norah certainly had no intention of straying from the straight and narrow again.

She shared her Vienna office with Aylin, a taciturn, wiry woman in her mid-forties who had positive slogans and photos of palm beaches pinned above her desk and took herself off to yoga in her lunch breaks. She was the anti-Werner.

Norah desperately needed caffeine, or nicotine, or both. She had per-suaded Berger to let her write a series of features on Vienna's homeless scene, and was wondering what tack to take. As usual, she decided to follow her gut instinct and focus on her own interests—though without stretching the remit of the magazine. Thanks to an old press contact in Berlin, she had another job lined up, too: in a few days she would be interviewing a film star. Berger had been thrilled—little sold as well as a real live Hollywood star—and Norah herself was looking forward to the interview, though she knew she would have to be well prepared; the actor had a reputation as a tough nut. Norah was an excellent interviewer. She had a sixth sense for knowing how to make people open up to her—whether to provoke or flatter or take the offensive. Most importantly, though, she had understood very early in her career that an interview, like everything in life, was based on reciprocity. If she wanted to get something out of her interviewees, she knew she had first to offer them something, and so she never inter-viewed anyone without revealing some small secret about herself. She had amused an American pop star in the Kempinski Hotel by showing him the unsuccessful tattoo on her hip. She had softened a neurotic French film director by telling him about one of her recurring night-mares. And she knew exactly how she would get this actor to identify with her and trust her. She was smiling to herself as she entered the office kitchen.

Mario and Anita turned round when they heard her. Anita, a boyish woman from southern Austria with short bleached hair, whom Norah had immediately taken to, was complaining to Mario (who reminded Norah vaguely of her friend Sandra's brother) that just because she happened to be friends with the niece of the new Burg Theatre director, the boss had charged her with getting an exclusive interview with him. As if it made any difference; everyone knew the man refused to give interviews. Norah just nodded to her colleagues, not wanting to intrude, and returned to her own thoughts as she busied herself with the espresso machine. It was a shame she hadn't been able to get hold of Sandra, when she was such a fan of this actor she was interviewing. But she knew what she'd say to win him over. It was easy. Everyone knew he'd been pursued by a stalker for years, so if she could manage to work it into the conversation, she'd tell him about her own stalker, a man who'd followed her everywhere until she'd managed to shake him off by moving to Berlin. That was good common ground. Norah would start the conversation with innocent questions about his latest film which he'd come to Europe to promote, and then gradually—

'Arthur Grimm,' she heard Anita say. 'But as far as I know, nobody's really aware of it.'

Norah stopped in her tracks. Had she heard right? Slowly she turned around. She saw Anita fish a teabag out of a mug and drop it in the bin.

Norah must have made a mistake. It would be too much of a coincidence.

'Do you need any help?' Mario asked, and Norah realised that she had frozen mid-movement next to the coffee machine.

She cleared her throat, flicked down the *On* button and the machine sprang to life, gurgling and hissing like a mythical beast stirring from sleep.

A thought flashed into her mind. Was this whole fortune-telling thing an elaborate joke on the part of her colleagues? Rubbish, she told herself. Who'd do a thing like that?

'No, thanks,' she said. 'I can manage.'

THE WOMAN

My happiest childhood memory isn't celebrating Christmas or going camping in the summer, but watching a boxing match. I went with my father, although in those days it was unusual for children to be taken along. We sat right at the front, by the ring, and I could hear the sound of flesh slapping against flesh. The place smelt of blood and adrenaline, and whenever a boxing glove smashed against bone, I saw a spray of sweat and saliva dancing in the air like dust motes in a beam of light. It wasn't a championship or anything, and I couldn't even say for sure what weight class the boxers were. They were both giants to me, and they went at each other like wild beasts.

There was no knock-out, though I'd hoped for one, if only to see a man that size crash to the floor like a felled tree. The fight went the distance and ended in a draw, which disappointed me, not that I knew which of the men I wanted to win; I suppose it just seemed unsatisfactory to me that something as dramatic as a boxing match could end in something as banal as a draw. When my father told me some days later that one of the boxers had died after the fight, I was fascinated. I suppose, in a way, that was my first encounter with death.

For some reason I was reminded of that evening the first time I saw her. God knows why. I'll never understand how my brain jumps from one thing to another. It fires salvos of associations at me and I just take them as they come.

I saw her in a bar the other day. I didn't follow her in, but I watched her for some time. She was sitting alone, drinking a colourless drink from a thick-bottomed glass and smoking a cigarette, and when the barman alerted her to the smoking ban, she rolled her eyes and stubbed out the fag in a corner of silver paper torn from the packet. Soon afterwards, a man came to her table—tall, with short dark hair, dressed in jeans and a white shirt. I saw him only in profile and couldn't hear what he said or what she replied, but I saw that the exchange lasted only a few seconds and that the man, who had been smiling as he walked to her table, was no longer smiling when he left it. Perhaps one should admire the arrogance with which such women go through life. But for some reason I can't.

In my experience, there are women you get round with flattery and women you get round with insults. But this woman, I feel, would laugh in your face, whichever you tried.

I have spent a great deal of time trying to work out what it is about her that interests me. She looks fragile, but moves as if she owned the world. One day she chain-smokes, the next I see her out jogging. There is something dainty, almost girlish about her, and yet you get the feeling that it would be a mistake to mess with her. She is strangely beautiful, but cynical and aggressive; she rarely smiles, never bows her head, and constantly interrupts others. All that repels me. But there is unquestionably something dark about her, and something vulnerable, too. That interests me. That's what I want to get at.

6

An icy chill, a clear blue sky, a weak morning sun giving no warmth. Business people and joggers, braving the cold. Cyclists, their faces wound about with scarves.

Walking to work with hunched shoulders and the east wind whistling around her ears, Norah thought of the people who lived on the streets in this weather. She had decided to structure her series on Vienna's homeless around four or five particularly fascinating stories, but she didn't want to write mere feature articles; she also wanted to inform her readers about what they could do to help the homeless. For two days she'd been working like a woman possessed. But she hadn't managed to track down the fortune teller. You'd think there was a jinx on her.

Although it was still early and bitterly cold, the girl with the Alsatian had already claimed her patch. Norah took a twenty-euro note out of her wallet and put it in the girl's hat. The girl immediately whipped it into the pocket of her parka, as if afraid that Norah might change her mind.

'I'm looking for someone,' said Norah, crouching down. 'The woman who was standing over there with a begging bowl the other day. A tall woman, at least six foot. Fairly old. Dark hair in a plait, and very bright eyes. Kind of creepy. Do you know who I mean?'

'Don't think so.'

'She was standing just there.' Norah jerked her chin towards the middle of the street.

'Dressed in black,' she added.

The girl shrugged.

Norah stared at her, trying to work her out. How could she sit there all day and not notice what went on around her? Norah stood up and turned to go. Then she stopped.

'It's cold,' she said. 'Tonight it'll be even colder. Do you have somewhere to go?'

The girl hesitated for a moment, then nodded.

'Sure?'

More nodding.

Norah gave her another hard stare, then rummaged in her bag for her notebook. She jotted down her phone number, tore out the page and held it out to the girl.

'If ever you need somewhere warm to sleep, just give me a call, okay?'

The girl frowned at her. She didn't take the piece of paper. Norah left it on her blanket.

'And if you see the woman or come across anyone who can tell me anything about her, then let me know. I urgently need to speak to her and I'd be happy to pay for it, okay?'

This time the girl replied. 'Okay.'

As Norah walked away, she thought she felt someone looking at her, but when she glanced back, the girl was rummaging intently in a plastic bag. Norah could see nothing out of the ordinary, but she couldn't shake the feeling that she was being watched until she was safe in the office.

•

She left work early that afternoon. She was hungry and there were a few things she needed to sort out at the bank, so she bought herself takeaway rice noodles and ate them on the way.

She could still taste the spices as she queued up in the bank. She hadn't made an appointment. The grimly clinical foyer was deserted apart from two bank clerks behind the counter—a man and a woman—and four customers in two lines. The female clerk was middle-aged, the man quite a bit younger, maybe in his mid-twenties, and so short and slight that he'd probably look like a fourteen-year-old even when he was ready for retirement. Norah got in his queue; he'd just finished serving a white-haired man in a checked suit. This elderly gent thanked him politely but, as he turned to go, he cast a glance of irritation at the woman waiting behind him. The boy at the counter, too, seemed troubled by the woman, so Norah had a closer look at her. She was tall, with slim legs in skinny jeans, and long black hair worn loose over a smart, navy-blue coat. It wasn't until she spoke that Norah realised what had been bothering the two men: the woman was trans. Angered, Norah watched the gawping old man leave the bank. She thought of her friend Coco and their recent walk. Norah had talked her into going into town although her face was such a mess, and soon regretted it when she saw the way people stared.

She resolved to call Coco that evening and find out how she was and, coming back to the present, she heard the clerk asking the trans woman for some papers or other. Norah registered with annoyance that he was talking much louder than before, as if she were deaf.

'Mr Gruber,' he read out from the papers.

The woman said something that Norah didn't catch.

'Well, I'm sorry,' the clerk replied, still talking in an unnecessarily loud voice, 'but it clearly says *Mr* here, doesn't it?'

Norah's tooth began to throb.

The man glanced at his colleague for approval. Norah saw her suppress a grin and felt herself growing hot. She couldn't catch what was said next, but she saw the trans woman shrink under the bank clerk's gaze so it wasn't hard to guess. From the snatches she heard, she gathered that he was demanding extensive documentation from the woman, although all she wanted was to open a basic account.

'Then I'm afraid I can't help you, *Mr* Gruber,' the clerk said condescendingly.

Fury seethed in Norah. Since what had happened in Berlin, her rage was never far off the boil, ready to bubble up at a moment's notice. Why did people have to be so fucking unpleasant?

The woman stood at the counter for a few seconds longer, then turned to leave, defeated.

'Have a nice day, *sir*,' the bank clerk called after her with a grin, as she went out, hanging her head.

'Pervert,' he added, catching his colleague's eye.

'I mean, isn't she?' he asked, when she didn't reply. 'Honestly, that kind of thing makes me want to vomit.'

His colleague smiled noncommittally; the man she was serving snorted in amused agreement, but nobody said anything. Norah watched the woman go. Through the glass doors, she saw her cross the road and walk away, so fragile, despite her large build.

'Next, please.' Norah heard the clerk's rasping voice and wheeled round.

'Hello,' she said in a loud voice. She threw a last glance over her shoulder, but the woman had vanished.

'Hello,' the clerk replied. He saw the look on Norah's face and misinterpreted it.

'Ridiculous, isn't it, the kind of people on the loose these days?' he asked, grinning stupidly at Norah, half obsequious, half conspiratorial.

Norah smiled and, leant forwards slightly. The man grinned back and leant towards her. Norah saw thick plaque on his teeth; she could almost smell it.

'A contract killing costs about twenty thousand euros,' she said in a low voice. 'It's an urban myth that you can have someone murdered for two or three grand; I've looked into it. Twenty thousand is more like it.'

The man behind the counter blinked.

'Pardon?' he said.

'I'll be honest with you,' Norah said. 'I don't have that kind of money.' She pushed her hair off her forehead. 'But a shot in the kneecap starts at about three and a half, and I think I could manage that.'

The clerk stared at her.

'I'd just have to go without that holiday in the Seychelles in November,' she said.

There was a pause, while the man processed her words.

'Are you crazy?' he stammered out eventually.

Norah waited for a moment before replying.

'Now you listen to me, you fuckwit,' she said softly. 'I don't care why you're the way you are. I don't care if you had a deprived childhood, or if you have complexes about your microscopic dick—though I assume you do. None of that interests me. But if ever I see you treat that lady or anyone else like that again, I'll hire myself an Andrej or a Giancarlo or a Ditmir, or whatever those reliable Albanians are called, and after that, you can count yourself lucky if you can hobble into the bank on crutches.'

Norah gave the man a dazzling smile, which threw him into even greater confusion.

'Got that?' she asked.

'You're joking,' the man said with a laugh, but he must have noticed how hollow it sounded. He pulled a face.

'You sure about that?' Norah asked seriously.

The man said nothing.

Norah took a closer look at him—the faded acne scars on his pasty face, the gelled hair, the yellowish teeth. He withstood her gaze for a while, then looked away.

Norah nodded. 'I thought as much.'

The woman clerk wasn't serving anyone and Norah could feel her looking at them.

'I'll just have to try another bank,' Norah said, her voice louder again. She turned to go. 'Thanks all the same!'

Before leaving the foyer, she threw a last glance over her shoulder.

'I expect the Seychelles are overrated anyway.'

29

7

'You know what that's called in court?' Norah's friend Sandra asked, when they spoke on the phone that evening.

'I'm sure you're about to tell me.'

'Impulse control disorder.'

Norah rolled her eyes. 'The guy was a bastard. You should have seen the way he treated the woman.'

'I can imagine,' Sandra said. 'Still, you can't do stuff like that all the time, Norah.'

'What do you mean, *all the time?*'

Sandra sighed, and Norah wondered whether her clients ever got to hear her sigh like that, or whether it was something she reserved for recalcitrant friends. Sandra had been working in a solicitor's office for five years, although she was currently on maternity leave.

'One of these days you'll get into real trouble,' Sandra said.

'Aren't I already?' Norah asked.

'There are worse things in life than libel charges.'

Norah saw Coco's cut-up face.

'I know,' she said softly.

'How is Coco, by the way?' asked Sandra, as if she'd read Norah's thoughts.

'I don't really know,' said Norah. 'But not great.'

Sandra said nothing. Then she said, 'Take care of yourself, won't you?'

'You know me,' said Norah.

'I know you all too well.'

Alone in her flat later that evening, Norah stood at the window, watching couples and small groups of people cross the square on their way to a restaurant or cinema or theatre. After talking to Sandra, she'd sent SOS messages to Max and Paul and Tanja, but got no reply. Her eye fell on the orchid she'd brought with her from Berlin—the only other living thing in the flat. She took up her phone again, then put it down in disappointment. No messages. She went into the kitchen, opened the fridge and stared helplessly at the food she'd bought that afternoon.

The trans woman's face popped into her mind; their eyes had met for a moment and Norah hadn't forgotten the look in them. Then her thoughts moved to the bank clerk—his grin, his conspiratorial wink, his nasal voice. Just as she was closing the fridge door, the news came on in the living room. She went and plumped herself down in front of the TV and let the announcements rain down on her; it was like being pelted by the stones of an angry mob. War, greed, drownings, rape.

Norah's mind began its usual downwards spiral. She thought of all the dictators and arms dealers in the world, of a boy in her primary school whose father had hit him so hard in the face that he'd gone blind in one eye, of a girl she'd been friends with in her teens who'd woken up on a motorway car park one Sunday morning, bleeding and half naked, after someone had spiked her drink. She thought of the concept artist who mutilated unstable young women with a scalpel and called it art. She thought of the head of a weapons company she'd once seen playing the philanthropist at a charitable gala while, in other parts of the world, her weapons destroyed lives. She thought of the bankers in their glass towers, of hunger and thirst, bombs and fire and—

Norah jumped. Someone had rung her doorbell.

'Hi Norah,' the young blonde woman said cheerfully, when Norah opened the door.

'Hi.'

It was the upstairs neighbour, Theresa. Norah forced a smile. 'Is anything wrong?' she asked, after a silence, and immediately realised how rude she sounded.

'No. I just wanted to say hello.'

It took Norah a moment to understand that she was expecting to be asked into the flat.

'Sorry,' she said, 'I'm being really unneighbourly. Would you like to come in?'

Theresa smiled and followed Norah into the living room.

'Can I get you something to drink?'

'That would be lovely.'

'I'm afraid I only have tap water. Or white wine.'

'Tap water's great.'

Norah went into the kitchen, filled two glasses and returned to the living room.

'How are you liking Vienna?' Theresa asked, taking a sip of water.

'Yeah, it's nice,' said Norah.

'Where did you live before?'

'Berlin. But—were you wanting anything?'

Theresa cleared her throat, evidently thrown by Norah's determination to sabotage her attempt at conversation.

'Oh,' she said, 'I just wanted to ask if you felt like coming up to dinner later. I've invited a few friends over and I thought since you've just moved here, it might be nice to…'

Her words tapered off.

'That's really sweet of you,' said Norah, 'but I've already got plans for this evening.'

'Shame,' said Theresa. 'They're a nice bunch of people. But if you like, we could do something together tomorrow.'

'I've got plans for tomorrow too.'

Theresa raised her eyebrows.

'Okay. Maybe next week?'

Norah stared at the floor.

'To be honest, I really don't have much time at the moment. I've got a lot of work and…'

An awkward silence set in.

'Sorry,' said Theresa. 'I didn't want to force myself on you.'

'You haven't.'

'When I moved here, I found it really hard to get to know people, so I thought…'

'That's really nice of you, Theresa,' said Norah, cutting her short. 'It's just…'

She faltered.

'You don't like me,' said Theresa.

'We've only just met. What reason could I have not to like you?' Norah knew she sounded stilted.

'So what's wrong?'

Norah searched for the words. Opened her mouth. Closed it again. Started over.

'You remind me of someone,' she said eventually. 'And the memory's painful.'

8

This time it wasn't a dream that woke her, but music and laughter from the flat above.

Norah sat up with a groan and groped for the lamp on the bedside table. Then she remembered that she'd left both lamp and bedside table in Berlin. She got up and switched on the ceiling light. A glance at her watch told her that it was soon after midnight. Was it too late to ring Max and Paul? Max had always been a bit of a night owl, often working long after everyone else had gone to bed—but, no. She couldn't cling to them just because they were the only friends she had in the city. She was too old to carry on like that. You've only just got here, she told herself. You'll soon know more people. In different circumstances she'd already have made friends with the woman upstairs. But the memories that Theresa had stirred in her were too fraught, it was all too—

No, she didn't want to think about it. She looked for her phone, but couldn't find it and switched on her laptop. Two new emails were waiting in her inbox: a reminder of her dentist's appointment the next day from a practice she'd found online, and a note from a friend in Berlin who'd had a baby a few months back and been too busy to see much of Norah since. It was a short email; Francesca came straight to the point.

Norah, my dear,
Sorry not to have been in touch for so long. Hope things are okay with you. I saw Alex yesterday afternoon when I was out pushing the buggy. He was with a woman, but it wasn't you, and I suddenly realised how long it is since we last spoke. I didn't even know you'd split up. Do hope you're well.
Lots of love, Francesca

Norah read the email twice, then shut her laptop. Alex hadn't lost much time, had he? Cue toothache. The pain was real enough now; she had to get out.

The streets were empty, which probably had more to do with the cold and rain than the time of day. Dark, shimmering asphalt, shuttered shop fronts. A little way past the Paulanerkirche, Norah stopped and took a photo for Instagram, but discarded it as too gloomy. She passed an elderly couple—the man long and thin like an exclamation mark, the woman plump in a fur coat and hat—then a young girl in a far-too-thin leather jacket walking a far-too-large dog. Norah crossed the road, wandering aimlessly. If she got lost or walked too far, she could always hail a taxi. She fell to thinking; she always found it easiest to put her thoughts in order when she was walking. Anita's words in the office kitchen came back to her. Had she really mentioned an Arthur Grimm, like the woman with the begging bowl?

The face Norah had seen on the internet popped into her head— the piercing eyes, the narrow lips, the square chin. What was it that made that handsome face look so menacing? Why the ominous feeling in the pit of her stomach?

It was strange. She was sure she didn't know him. She had an excellent memory for names—maybe it was being a journalist—and if she had ever heard the name Arthur Grimm, it must have been a very long time ago. But something about him unnerved her.

The traffic lights changed and Norah crossed the road. A man passed her on a bike. It had stopped raining, but the damp cold was stubborn and insidious and found its way in, however well wrapped up you were. Norah drew in her head and put her numb hands in her coat pockets. Not a soul anywhere now.

The next street sign told her she was in the seventh district. All at once, the cold seemed unbearable. Then the tiredness kicked in. Norah walked faster, desperate to be back in the warmth. There were no taxis in sight. She took a left, then a right, meaning to retrace her steps, but soon realised she was lost. How stupid that she'd misplaced her phone. Norah stopped to think for a second, then on a sudden impulse she took a left and found herself in a street she knew. It was wide and slightly sloping; if she followed it uphill and turned right, she'd come to that lovely cafe where, in another life, she'd once had breakfast. She knew her way home from there.

The street ahead was lined with embassies. Enormous flags—Norah recognised Brazil and Turkey—hung from the facades, billowing in the night like the sails of a ghost ship in a storm. To Norah's left was a high wall, the rendering crumbling in places and daubed with inexpert graffiti. She wondered what was behind it. A private garden? A park? Something made her stop. Bare trees stretched to the sky on the other side of the wall. The road and pavements were deserted. Life had gone out like a lamp, people were in their beds, sleeping like the dead, but Norah had a feeling that someone was there, very close. She looked about her. There was no one in front of her or behind her, no one on the other side of the road, no one at any of the windows. It was quite quiet. But then it hadn't been a sound that had startled Norah; it had been a smell, at once exotic and familiar, sickly sweet. She wasn't imagining things—she was sure she wasn't. As if in slow motion, she turned to face the wall. Someone was there, silent and unmoving, on the other side. Someone was standing very still, holding their breath, like Norah.

A car sped past, and Norah wheeled round just in time to see a taxi disappearing out of sight. Fuck. She returned to staring at the rough rendering of the wall, as if she didn't dare turn her back on whoever was on the other side. She stood and listened for a long time. No, there was no one there. Who knew where the smell had come from. But as Norah was about to go on her way, she heard a noise behind the wall.

Gravel. The crunch of footsteps on gravel. There must be a path or drive on the other side. Norah's heart was pounding. Whoever had been lurking there was walking away with slow, deliberate steps. The crunch of gravel grew softer and softer. Before long there was only a faint smell of pipe tobacco hanging in the air.

9

Even before she opened her eyes, Norah knew she wasn't alone; there was heavy breathing coming from the other side of the bed. She almost groaned out loud when it came back to her—the bar, the gin and tonics, the man. She girded herself to have a look. He was lying with his back to her, a broad swimmer's back, tanned skin; he must have been somewhere exotic—or in the solarium. His hair was light brown. She had no recollection of his face.

Norah's mouth tasted as if she'd been gagged with an old cleaning rag for several hours, and she knew her head would start aching if she so much as stirred. She sat up and felt the hangover kick in. She had a drink from a bottle of water next to the bed, got up, threw on an old T-shirt and staggered into the bathroom. There was a used condom in the toilet bowl. That was something. Norah flushed the chain, went into the kitchen and made two cups of coffee.

Half an hour later she left for work, dressed for an expedition to the South Pole. It was sunny and so bitterly cold that her fingers immediately turned numb.

Deciding to walk to Karlsplatz and get the underground from there, she set off at a brisk pace to get warm. Some of the people she passed were trying to warm themselves on takeaway coffee cups, but most of them scurried by with hunched shoulders. Several had scarves wound around their mouths and noses, making them look strangely creepy, almost faceless.

Norah passed the Volkstheater. A big banner strung across the front of the building read: *Don't forget: if you can touch it, it can also touch you.* In the underground station, she took the juddering escalator down, down into the bowels of the earth and caught her train.

Over coffee, the man in her bed had told her he was studying sport; then it had been time for her to go to work and she'd thrown him out. She had no idea what had induced her to bring him home, but it could have been worse: he was quite cute and made no trouble about leaving. 'You've got my number,' he'd said, after giving her a sleepy kiss on the cheek and thanking her politely for the coffee, and she'd nodded, without knowing what he was talking about.

The train wobbled along under the city and Norah gingerly felt her tooth with her tongue. She wasn't in real pain, but she was glad to have got an appointment so quickly.

The straps swung back and forth on either side of the carriage, performing a minimalist ballet—left, right, left, right, left, right. People stared mutely at their phones, or books, or hands, or out of the window—not that there was anything to see except underground shafts, endless-seeming streaks of black and grey. How old was the Vienna underground? What stories did it have to tell? Was there enough material for a feature? Norah reached for her phone to do a bit of spontaneous internet research, then remembered that she didn't have it. The train stopped and she threw a panicked glance out of the window, but it was only another station. A group of teenagers got on, along with a young, heavily pregnant woman, who was holding a little boy of six or seven by the hand; the woman and the boy sat down opposite Norah. The train started up again and Norah closed her eyes.

When she opened them, the little boy was staring at her.

'Hello,' she said, with an attempt at a smile. 'You all right?'

The boy didn't answer or smile back—just looked at her with big eyes. She glanced at his mother who stared back blankly. Norah shrugged and was about to turn away when the boy mumbled something.

'Sorry?'

The boy said nothing.

'What did you say?' Norah asked.

No reply.

'Leave him, won't you?' his mother said.

'It's all right,' said Norah. 'I'm sorry.' She got up, glad that they were drawing into the station where she had to change trains.

The dentist's practice was in a lovely big old house with a cream stucco facade. Norah rang the bell, told the voice on the intercom her name and entered the building, then stopped when she realised that the voice hadn't told her what floor to go to. She looked about, trying to get her bearings. Next to the letterboxes were four plaques.

First Floor—Huber Architects
Second Floor—Goldberg Solicitors
Third Floor—Dr Bernhard Schlick—Dentist

Norah was on her way to the lift when she realised what she'd just read. Impossible—she must have made a mistake. She turned back and read the fourth plaque again. Her short, sharp laugh echoed in the hallway. Something she'd read somewhere popped into her mind: *Chance is the only legitimate king in the world.* Wasn't it Napoleon said that?

Fuck you, Napoleon, she thought. This is too much to be mere chance.

The dentist was a nice man of about fifty with short, pepper-and-salt hair, elegant glasses and slender hands. Norah usually hated going to

40

the dentist, but this time she was far too distracted to feel distressed. All she could think about as Dr Schlick replaced the filling was the person in the rooms above.

When she left the practice half an hour later, she ran up to the fourth floor. The door revealed nothing; there was no name anywhere, and if Norah hadn't known better, she'd have thought she was standing outside a private flat. She rang the bell and waited. Nothing happened. She rang again, longer this time, then gave up, disappointed.

Strange—but maybe it was for the best. She didn't know what she'd have said if someone had come to the door. Her thoughts were racing as she walked down the stairs. Back in the hall, she stopped again in front of the plaques.

There it was, in dark, elegant letters on a brass background:

First Floor—Huber Architects
Second Floor—Goldberg Solicitors
Third Floor—Dr Bernhard Schlick—Dentist
Fourth Floor—Dr Arthur Grimm—Engineering

10

Norah didn't believe in fate or predestination; she believed people created their own luck, by their own efforts. She believed in chance, but not to this extent. Who was this Arthur fucking Grimm? Why was she confronted with his name at every turn? It was too much for her.

Norah emailed her old friend Werner, the best investigative journalist she knew, and asked him to dig up as much as he could on any Arthur Grimms living in Vienna. She, meanwhile, would try to catch Anita on her own sometime and see if she could get something out of her. She was determined to get to the bottom of all this—though it was important not to let anyone notice her unease. It seemed unlikely that anyone was playing a joke on her, trying to provoke her into reacting—but if they were, she was going to make them wait.

Norah spent the rest of the morning looking into the various forms of help for the homeless on offer in Vienna. When she went into the office kitchen for a glass of water, she found her colleague Luisa there with Tom, one of the freelance photographers who sometimes worked for the magazine. Norah immediately realised that she'd interrupted some kind of tryst; there was clearly something going on between them, although Luisa was married. Tom was standing at the window, fumbling cigarettes out of his pocket; Luisa was taking a smoothie out of the fridge, trying hard to act natural. Norah thought of healthy-living Alex who had weaned her off her diet of coffee, cigarettes and fast food—then felt a pang of guilt as she remembered the man she'd taken home last night. She helped herself to coffee (fuck the water) and went and stood at the window next to Tom. Thinking of Alex had left a lump in her throat and she took a big gulp of coffee to wash it down.

'Hey,' she said, as casually as she could, 'has either of you ever noticed that strange beggar out there? Quite an old woman, quite tall, *very* sinister. Dark hair, piercing blue eyes. Kind of beautiful in a weird way.'

'Here in Kärntner Strasse?' Luisa asked. She took a sip of her smoothie and licked her lips. 'Doesn't ring any bells.'

'Really? She's pretty conspicuous. And very tall.'

'What about her?' Luisa asked. 'Has she stolen something from you?'

'God, no,' said Norah quickly. 'I'm just curious. She looks as if she has a few stories to tell.'

'I think I know who you mean,' said Tom, stubbing out his cigarette. 'Stood there in the middle of the street with a begging bowl. Didn't speak, didn't have a sign or anything—just stood there like a statue. Seriously creepy.'

Norah felt a rush of adrenaline.

'That's the one. Have you seen her lately?'

Tom thought for a second, then shook his head slowly.

'She wasn't around for long. She was different from the others. Most of them have their patches, their fixed times—you get to know them, give them something now and then. But she moved on quite quickly.'

'I'm surprised I didn't notice her,' Luisa said.

43

'She was only around for a day or two,' said Tom. 'Maybe you were skiing. Yes, I think you were. It must have been round about when Norah started.'

Luisa finished her bottle and threw it in the bin.

'Almost as if you'd brought her with you,' Tom said to Norah with a grin, and he and Luisa sloped out of the kitchen.

Norah stared out of the window. The bright blue sky had clouded over. She poured the remains of her coffee down the drain; apart from anything else, she had heartburn. Then she went to the toilet. When she was drying her hands, she noticed that her skin was chapped from the cold and the overheated rooms. She caught a glimpse of herself in the mirror and thought of the little boy on the underground.

You look like Death, he had said to her.

Back at her desk, Norah concentrated on making calls and writing emails, but after a while she couldn't resist googling the name *Arthur Grimm* together with the word *engineer*. Then she added the address of the lovely old house where she'd been to the dentist that morning. The search yielded nothing. She ran her hand through her hair and closed the browser. She had some hard thinking to do.

When Norah saw her colleague Anita heading for the lift that evening, she grabbed her things, threw on her coat and hurried after her. She caught up with her in front of the lift. Anita was alone—perfect.

'Hello,' said Norah.

'Hi.'

The lift arrived and the two of them got in. Norah pressed the button for the ground floor and for two or three seconds she did what people do when they're in a lift with a near-stranger: she watched the descending numbers. Anita did the same. Then Norah rummaged in her bag, as if she were looking for her phone and said, so casually and naturally that she was surprised at herself, 'By the way, Anita, who's this Arthur Grimm you mentioned the other day?'

Anita frowned.

'Arthur Grimm?' she asked. 'Who's that? When was this?'

'Yesterday or the day before, in the kitchen. You were talking to Mario and mentioned someone called Arthur Grimm.'

'Hmm,' said Anita. 'I don't know anyone called that. Maybe you misheard?'

Norah nodded thoughtfully.

'Yes, probably,' she said.

'Why do you ask?' Anita said.

Norah studied Anita's face. Had she lied to her? There was a beep and the lift doors opened.

'Just curious,' Norah said and slipped through the doors.

11

It was a hectic morning. Norah had been up late the night before, researching Vienna's homeless scene—life on the streets, winter shelters, the various charities that provided help. Then Werner had rung to say he was happy to investigate Arthur Grimm for her. Typically for him, he didn't ask why she wanted the information. Norah smiled to herself. Werner was as thorough as a taxman and as tough as a pit bull; the Arthur Grimm matter couldn't be in better hands. If there was anything worth finding out, Werner would find it. But by the time Norah got to bed, it was only a bare two hours until her alarm clock was due to go off.

When it did, she was exhausted. The only good thing was that, for once, the flat wasn't cold; the heating seemed to be working now. Norah peeled herself out of the sheets and crawled to the shower.

She dressed carefully in black designer jeans, a blue blouse and red lipstick—her classic interview outfit. Blue inspired more trust than any other colour. She made herself coffee, drank it far too hot, and clattered down the stairs in her high heels, almost colliding with her old neighbour. As usual, there was no reply to her greeting. She still hadn't worked out whether he was rude or deaf.

A bare hour later, Norah entered the Hotel Imperial. With every step she took, the real world seemed to recede; she felt as if she were floating, light and noiseless. Her office colleagues, the strange woman with the begging bowl, her cheerless, empty flat—all that suddenly seemed miles away. She did, however, find herself thinking of Alex. Why did the interview have to be here, in the very hotel where she and Alex had stayed when they'd spent a weekend in Vienna a few years ago?

Norah reported to reception and sat down to wait in the lobby. There was an almost solemn hush, the only sound the soft creak of the revolving door, steady and soothing as the breathing of a sleeping baby. Gold and pomp everywhere, marble and chandeliers—and through the door, the busy street was visible, but at one remove, like mute projections on a screen.

She'd never liked the phrase 'shut out the world'. The world was everywhere; you couldn't shut it out. But on the two nights she and Alex had spent here, it really had felt as if they'd left the world outside when they stepped through the revolving door after an evening out and went to their room. Later they'd wandered hand in hand down the corridors, admiring the wallpaper, the marble columns, the paintings, until they'd found a small bench to sit on.

'Do you think there's a hotel ghost?' Norah had asked.

'Do you believe in ghosts?'

Norah shrugged.

'No. Do you?'

'Not sure,' said Alex. 'But if I were a ghost, I'd definitely haunt this place.'

Norah laughed.

'We ought to die in the Imperial,' she said.

'What, now?'

'When we're very, very old. We'll take a room and die there. Then we'll stay on and haunt the hotel.'

'Great plan!' said Alex. 'I like it.'

It had been Alex's idea to stay here, although it was way beyond their budget. He knew Norah loved places like the Imperial, not so much for their beauty or lavishness, but for the stories they held. He'd even managed to arrange a guided tour of the hotel, just for the two of them. A charming old man had shown them the grand reception rooms, then led them down a warren of stairs and passages to the underbelly of the hotel, where rooms opened off a spotless red-and-yellow tiled corridor. It was a mysterious in-between realm where the linen was stored, the staff fed, the famous Imperial gateaux baked. Down there, a kind of magic was worked to ensure that, a few floors up, the guests could lean back and forget their worries.

Norah returned to the present to see a woman standing in front of her, and a few seconds later she was following her along a corridor to the suite where the interviews were being held. A television crew passed them, laden with cameras and sound equipment, and Norah said good morning, feeling like an outsider. In Berlin she'd have known who was having an affair with whom, which of them would be up for a drink after work and which had to hurry home to their children. Now she'd left that small, cosy world behind her and was in a new world, full of strangers. Norah thought they looked stressed, but couldn't have said why. Had the interview gone badly, or was there some other reason?

The door to the suite was closed, but Bernadette Schill, the press officer who had organised the interview for Norah, was waiting outside for her.

'Good morning, Norah. It's lovely that you could come.'

'Thank you for arranging it.'

Bernadette was very conservatively dressed in a black suit and pearl necklace, but she had a naughty smile that made Norah like her at once. Here was someone she could talk to.

They shook hands, while the assistant hurried back to the lobby to welcome the next journalist. Interviews with Hollywood stars were always tightly packed, but Norah was glad to have a slot at all.

'The ORF people are on their way,' Bernadette said. 'You're next. It shouldn't be long.'

'Where am I on the list?' Norah asked.

'The seventh this morning, and the second-to-last before the break.'

'Is he on his own?' Norah asked.

Bernadette nodded. She glanced at her watch and seemed to hold back a sigh. The Hollywood star was evidently ruining her carefully planned schedule.

'What's he like?' Norah asked, lowering her voice to a conspiratorial whisper.

'Oh, he's just wonderful,' Bernadette replied sarcastically. 'Absolutely wonderful.'

'Great,' said Norah. The two women exchanged a knowing smile. Somewhere in the hotel, a piano was being tuned.

Then the door opened.

There was something almost surreal about seeing the actor in person. Norah often got to meet famous people, but the strange familiarity she felt when first confronted with them in person never failed to unnerve her. Film stars always seemed less real to her than other people; it was as if she had to see them in the flesh to understand that they existed—that they walked around and ate and drank and had showers and scratched their heads. Most of the stars she met were slightly shorter than she'd expected. Alarmingly, they were also better looking. So she was forearmed when her interviewee switched on his roguish smile.

'Michael,' said Bernadette, 'may I introduce you to Norah Richter?'

Norah felt strangely light when she headed out of the Imperial half an hour or so later. The piano had gone quiet, but a whiff of pipe tobacco hung in the air, sickly sweet. She quickened her pace, impatient to get to her desk and type up the interview—it had been a good one, maybe even really good. She'd know as soon as—

Norah stopped. She'd almost trodden on something lying on the floor. A playing card—no, a tarot card.

She picked it up and turned it over. *Death* stared out at her from empty eye sockets.

THE MYSTERY OF FASCINATION

When I was little, I was fascinated by freak shows. They had, of course, long since died a death by then, but my grandmother sometimes talked of them, and I would listen, rapt, as she told me about bearded ladies and giants and dwarves and two-headed girls. One of my earliest memories is of sitting with my grandmother as she told me stories—plenty of fairytales, of course, but more macabre things, too. For a time I collected old photos of freak shows. Later I fell in love with *Freaks*, an American horror movie from the thirties, which is (except, perhaps, for *Vertigo*) still my favourite film today.

But it is, even now, a mystery to me what I found so intriguing. I was repelled by the freaks, but at the same time, I was fascinated. There's no explanation—that kind of thing isn't meant to be explained. We can't choose who we are. We can't choose what we are repelled or attracted by.

Circus freaks were my first obsession. After that came natural disasters, Medieval witch burnings, the occult, Aleister Crowley and, eventually, serial killers. I see beauty in horror and horror in beauty; it is a gift. It probably explains why I am drawn to *her*: something in her appeals to me and yet at the same time I find her strangely unappealing.

But it is not my job to interpret my obsessions. My job is to pursue them. I begin by finding out all there is to know. Luckily she has made this easy for me.

She grew up in a small town in northern Germany. After leaving school, she studied journalism and art history, then began to work as a journalist. She has lived in various German cities and was also in London for a time. (Source: biography on her blog www.norahrichter.de)

She loves meat and hates fish. She likes red wine, especially Malbec. (Source: Instagram)

She supports Médecins Sans Frontières and Reporters Without Borders. (Source: Twitter)

Her most traumatic experience was the suicide of a sixteen-year-old friend in 2000. (Source: blog post about depression and suicide, 30.05.2014)

She is single, having recently split up with her partner Alexander Bauer, a 39-year-old surgeon who lives in Berlin, the son of a German mother and an African-American father. (Source: Facebook)

In the last six months, she has been to the cinema seven times and attended five concerts—Arcade Fire, Nick Cave, Sigur Rós, Soap&Skin and Amanda Palmer. (Sources: Instagram and Twitter)

Her best female friend is called Sandra, her best male friend is Max. In spite of these social ties, she calls herself an 'introvert' and a 'part-time social outsider'. (Source: blog post on the difference between shyness and introversion, 17.11.2015)

Her greatest fear is to be responsible for someone's death. (Source: feature on gun freaks in Germany, 04.08.2014)

She describes herself as a feminist. Her favourite holiday destination is Florence; she loves Renaissance art—Leonardo da Vinci, Michelangelo, Raphael, Botticelli. She likes wearing black. (Source: Instagram)

She almost died of a drug overdose in London, but got clean with the help of her friends and extreme sports. She speaks openly of her addiction. (Source: Facebook post, 31.12.2015)

She almost studied law, but soon realised that 'law and justice [didn't] have much to do with each other' and switched to journalism. Injustice drives her 'wild'. (Source: her blog, passim)

I'm getting there, moving closer. I'm enjoying myself. I have a feeling it might turn out to be easier than I thought.

12

Norah surveyed her hosts' dining room, a glass of champagne in her hand. Some flats were so perfectly fitted out that they gave you the impression you were in a museum, but although Max and Paul's apartment looked like something out of *Architectural Digest*, they'd managed to give it a warm, homely feel. Paul was preparing food in the kitchen; Max was frowning at the shelves of records, trying to decide on an album, and Lolita, the British bulldog, was snoring on the rug in front of the sofa.

A lot of white, a lot of grey, a lot of brown leather. The high moulded ceilings were newly painted, the parquet recently sanded, the walls hung with modern art. Lush yucca palms and monsteras grew in big pots, and in the middle of the spacious living-cum-dining room stood an enormous mangowood table that Paul had designed and built himself. Norah examined one of the pictures, a painting so rich with gold that it seemed to give off heat. She reached for her phone to take a photo, then remembered, not for the first time that day, that she'd lost it. She'd spent a good half hour searching, but with no luck. Norah turned to a drawing of Max asleep. It was a fine piece of work that had something almost fairytale-like. Max's flat cap had been thrown down next to the bed, his glasses were on the bedside table, his light-brown hair slightly tousled. He looked as if he were dreaming.

'Who did this?' Norah asked.

Max smiled and pointed at Paul, who was coming into the room carrying two steaming bowls.

The Thai food, beautifully served on elegant white china, smelt so deliciously of chilli and coriander and beef and coconut and lemongrass that Norah felt properly hungry for the first time in weeks. Max and Paul had rung her to apologise for not having been in touch earlier and then asked her to dinner that evening.

Norah fell on her food. 'I thought the papaya salad was good,' she said, 'but this beef is out of this world. How did you make it?'

Paul grinned.

'Nine two four nine, three eight zero eight,' he said.

'I don't understand.'

'That's the delivery service number.'

Norah laughed.

'How are things going at the magazine?' Max asked.

'Good.'

'Good. Is that all? You must have something to tell us. No psychopathic boss, no scheming rival, no good-looking colleague, no hot gossip?'

'Nope, sorry.'

'Ah well,' said Paul. 'Here's to your new job.'

He raised his beer.

'Cheers,' said Max.

'Cheers.'

They clinked bottles.

When they'd finished eating—Norah had put away more than Max and Paul together—Max opened one of the big living-room windows and lit a cigarette.

Norah breathed in the cold air with relish.

'You don't smoke anymore,' Max said—a regretful observation, rather than a question.

'Yes, I do. I've started again.'

Max raised his eyebrows.

'Well, in that case…' he said, handing her a cigarette.

When Norah looked up from lighting it, she saw Max and Paul exchange glances.

'It's getting too big,' said Max.

'What?'

'The elephant in the room.'

Norah sighed.

'We only want to know if you're okay,' said Paul. 'You and Alex were together for such a long time. It was so sudden.'

'I'm okay,' said Norah.

'Did anything happen? Did Alex do something?' Paul asked. 'We don't want to be nosey—we just want to know if we ought to hate Alex.'

He scratched his dark beard thoughtfully.

'You know we like Alex; we liked him right from the start. But we like you more.'

'No,' Norah said. 'Alex didn't do anything bad.'

'Okay,' Paul began, 'but—'

Norah interrupted him. 'He proposed to me,' she said. 'Or rather, he was planning to.'

'How do you know?'

'I found the ring.'

Max and Paul looked blankly at Norah.

'He did what?' Paul asked, eventually, with feigned indignation. 'He bought you a ring? That's unbelievable. How dare he? No wonder you cleared out at the first opportunity.'

'Too right,' said Max. 'Any woman with a smidgen of self-respect would have done the same.'

'Are you taking the piss?' Norah asked, but she grinned in spite of herself.

Max looked at her thoughtfully.

'I'm sure you had your reasons,' he said in the end, and Norah nodded, grateful that the interrogation was over.

'I'm going to powder my nose,' said Paul, vanishing into the hall.

For a while, Norah and Max drank together in comfortable silence.

'Oh, shit,' Norah suddenly said.

'What?'

'I completely forgot—I meant to call a friend.'

'Sandra?'

'No, nobody you know. I met her recently when I was researching for a feature. You'd like her, but she does have a few…issues.'

'What kind of issues?'

All kinds, Norah thought.

'She's quite lonely,' she said. 'Somebody knocked her about a bit and—oh, it doesn't matter. But I used to meet up with her at least once a week in Berlin, and we never missed a Thursday evening.'

'I see,' said Max. 'How old is she?'

'A year or two older than me?'

Max frowned.

'What?' Norah asked.

'Nothing. I just imagined her older for some reason.'

'She'd be disappointed,' Norah said.

'Who'd be disappointed?' asked Paul, reappearing.

'Just another of Norah's social projects,' Max said. Norah elbowed him in the ribs.

'I see,' said Paul. 'More beer?'

'Yes, please,' Norah and Max said in one voice, and Paul disappeared again.

'Give her a quick ring,' Max said. 'It's all right.'

'I can't. I've gone and left my phone somewhere.'

'Landline?'

'I don't know her number. Doesn't matter. I'll ring her when I get home.'

They drank in silence again.

'I always thought Alex was the one,' Max said at length. 'Mr Right.'

Norah shrugged helplessly.

'You loved him, didn't you?'

'I—' she said and felt her throat seize up. 'I don't want to—'

'You don't want to talk about it,' said Max. 'I know.'

More silence. Then Max got up. He went over to Norah, bent down and gave her a hug. It wasn't a long hug; he knew Norah couldn't deal with mawkishness any more than he could.

'Maybe you should talk to Dr Snitsch about your commitment phobia,' he said, sitting down again.

'Oh, shut up,' said Norah, 'I don't have commitment phobia. And who the fuck is Dr Snitsch?'

'Dr Snitsch is Max's lady therapist,' Paul said, appearing in the door with more beer. 'I never thought a woman would come between us, but I've been proved wrong.'

'Dr Snitsch is wonderful,' said Max. 'I won't let anyone say a word against her. Everyone should have a Dr Snitsch.'

'What I love is the fact that she's called Dr Snitsch,' said Paul. 'It's such a great name.'

'I can't believe you go to a therapist,' Nora said. 'I thought you were an atheist.'

'What's that got to do with it?'

'Aren't therapists a bit like gods who answer?'

'There's something in that.'

'Here's to gods who answer,' said Paul, raising his beer.

'To Dr Snitsch,' said Norah. 'And to the two of you.'

'And to our newly Viennese friend!'

They clinked bottles. Then they drank another beer. And another.

Then the beer was all gone and one of them suggested calling a cab and going to a bar, and the night opened at their feet like a trapdoor, and they tumbled down into lights and neon and smoke and vodka and tequila and strangers' faces and rock music, and stayed until the sun went up.

13

When Norah got home and switched on the light and the TV, she tripped over a small white cuddly rabbit. For a moment, she stood there, waiting for the ceiling to stop spinning. It was time she got round to unpacking the boxes and stopped chucking everything on the floor. She sighed. The bunny must be Alex's. He was always buying presents for his niece; she'd probably packed it by mistake in her mad rush to leave. At this rate, she'd never get over him.

'Hello,' she said to the rabbit, 'you all right?'

It didn't reply.

'How rude!' Norah said, laughing when she realised how drunk she was. She had no hope of getting to sleep in the next hour. She put the bunny aside and wrote a text. Her phone had turned up at last, which was something; the stupid thing had been in the side pocket of her bag all along.

Are you awake?

The answer came straight back.

I'm always awake, sweetie.

Norah touched Coco's name on her screen; her friend picked up immediately.

'Can't you sleep either?' Coco asked.

'No.'

'What's keeping you awake?'

Norah shrugged.

'Nothing. Everything. The human condition. And you?'

'The usual.'

Norah bit her lip.

'I went out today,' Coco said. 'Some kids stared at me.'

'Kids stare at everyone,' Norah replied. 'The other day I was on the underground and this little boy started staring at me—he was about three? So I stared back. And then suddenly he turns to his mum and says, all serious, Mum, is that a man or a lady?'

Coco laughed, as Norah had been hoping she would, but she was soon serious again.

'I saw him today,' she said, 'in the paper. He's got a new girlfriend.'

Norah froze. No matter what she said, Coco always came back to the same topic.

'Poor woman,' said Norah drily.

'Yeah,' said Coco, 'I should warn her.'

'No, sweetheart, you must keep away. Promise me?'

There was silence at the other end of the line.

'Promise?' Norah repeated.

'Promise.'

Neither of them spoke. Then Norah heard a soft sniffing sound.

'Coco, are you crying?'

'No,' said Coco with a sob.

Norah fought back a sigh. She never knew what to say when people cried on the phone.

'I was so stupid,' Coco said softly.

Yes, Norah thought, you were. But that doesn't mean you deserved what he did to you.

'What film did you watch today?' she asked, to change the topic.

She knew that Coco only ever left the house to go to the cinema—partly because she loved films; partly because it was dark in the cinema and no one could stare at her.

'*Beauty and the Beast*,' Coco said.

'You're not serious.'

'No, really,' Coco said, and Norah pictured her smiling through her tears. 'Fitting, eh?'

'I'm speechless.'

'That,' said Coco, 'is an expression I've never understood. I'm never speechless.'

Norah smiled to herself. She loved Coco's wry humour.

'I googled him,' Coco said suddenly, like a sinner in a confessional, keen to come clean before losing courage.

Norah groaned.

'Oh my God, Coco.'

'I know, I know. But I did it. I found an article about him, a new one, from last week. I thought I was going to freak out completely. All those clichés of his. I'm a simple man. A leopard can't change its spots. Bla, bla, bla, bla, bla. But do you know what made me really angry?'

'What?' Norah asked resignedly.

'There's this story he tells the interviewer about how he learnt what fear is. He was playing in the garden one day as a child, and a stranger came along with a knife and attacked him, apparently leaving him slightly injured.'

'And?'

'It's not his story. It's mine. It's something I told him on our first date.'

Wow, Norah thought, but said nothing.

'I've no idea how I let him take me in. That pretentious piano-playing. And the way he's always tossing out Shakespeare quotes. He's such a conceited bastard. I can't tell you how revolting I find him.'

Norah said nothing.

'I could kill him,' Coco said.

'Don't say that,' said Norah. 'You're no more capable of killing than I am.'

'You have no idea.'

Norah laughed, anxious to take some of the tension out of the situation.

'You laugh,' said Coco—she had stopped crying. 'But everyone is capable of killing, if they have good reason. Even you.'

14

Norah couldn't sleep after talking to Coco; her guilty conscience got the better of her. There was her poor friend, stuck in a tiny flat in that dump of a small town where her parents lived, hardly daring to leave the house—and it was all Norah's fault.

Well, not quite all. But she'd done her bit.

She lit a cigarette, went to the window and looked out onto the street.

It had all begun when her boss had sent her to interview that art professor. The first interview had been held in the restaurant of a hotel—the second in the professor's house. He'd got Norah's hackles up right from the start. While at his house, she had briefly met his beautiful and considerably younger girlfriend Nicolette, who called herself Coco, and whom he referred to as *my muse*. He had sat in an armchair with his legs wide apart, while his muse sat in a corner of the sofa, her arms and legs entwined in an acrobatic pose that seemed designed to ensure that she took up as little space as possible.

The professor's mouth was set in the rictus of a great white shark.

During the interview, Coco kept getting up and darting out of the room. She moved almost soundlessly, but everything about her was screaming.

Norah knew that cowering posture, that look of fear. The first time she'd seen it had been at a party in her early student days, when she'd burst into the bathroom to find a girl staring at her with the wild eyes of a deer caught in headlights, crying and trembling. It turned out that their host, a boy Norah hardly knew, had spiked the girl's drink, then taken her up to the bathroom, got her down on the tiles and done pretty much everything a boy *can* do to a girl who is just about conscious but completely defenceless. Norah persuaded the girl to go to the police and she went on to press charges, but the boy, not yet twenty, got off more or less scot-free—who wanted to mess up the future of a promising young man from a good family just because he'd made a silly mistake? The girl grew as thin and translucent as a ghost and ended up moving away. The boy stayed on and graduated.

Years later, Norah saw him again, at a reception given by the publishing house she was working for at the time. She recognised him immediately. He looked confident, successful. To her horror, he made a beeline for her. He said he knew her from somewhere—he never forgot a pretty woman—but he couldn't think where. They hadn't gone to the same school, had they? No? Ah, they'd been students together—wonderful. Might he introduce her to his wife Johanna?

A beautiful, fragile-looking woman in a short black dress appeared at his side. 'Pleased to meet you,' she said. 'How do you two know each other?'

'Oh, your husband raped a friend of mine when we were students,' Norah replied.

Then she turned away and went home, images of the trembling, frightened girl flashing across her mind, and a sick feeling in her stomach because the world was so fucking unjust and she was powerless to do anything about it.

•

Norah stood at the window, thinking of the first time she'd met Coco. It wasn't long afterwards that the professor made such a mess of her that her own mother probably wouldn't have recognised her. Norah did her best to help. For the second time in her life, she talked a woman into putting her faith in the law, and once again it backfired. She soon discovered that the professor was extremely astute and legally almost untouchable—especially given Coco's history of mental illness. He ended up suing the two women for libel and Coco was left a quivering wreck.

Then Nora did something that was to cost her her job and eventually her relationship: she wrote about him. As a student she had learnt that a good journalist must never resort to malice, however good the cause, but she abandoned this principle for Coco. She wrote the article that the professor deserved, and by the end it was less an article than an indictment—an indictment in which not only Coco was given a voice, but all the other women whose lives the professor had destroyed. Because that was what he did; he destroyed women.

When the article was published, all hell broke loose—for Coco *and* Norah. Norah's boss was furious about the libel charges. That didn't surprise Norah, but what did surprise her was the way everyone rushed to defend the bastard, dismissing the women Norah had quoted in the article as greedy and limelight-seeking. She still felt sick just thinking about it.

When it was clear that Norah's initiative had completely failed, the professor turned up on her doorstep one day. She let him in, her belly full of disgust and hate; she was too curious to turn him away. They stood facing each other in Norah's study and she asked how it felt to destroy someone's life. He only smiled smugly, swinging himself onto her desk as if he owned it. Everything about him revolted her—his violence, his greed, the way he smelt, the way he grinned and the suit he was wearing that must have cost as much as Norah's car.

'Malice, egoism, vindictiveness—all these things are in our nature, my dear Miss Richter,' he said. 'There's no getting away from that.'

'Spare me that bullshit. I'm not one of your students. You're a sadistic bastard, that's all. And one of these days, I'm going to get you, I swear I will.'

He laughed in her face.

'I like your sense of humour,' he said, looking about him attentively, as if he were trying to memorise the contents of the room.

'We're not so very different, you and I,' he said at length, his eyes piercing her, as she stood there with her arms folded. 'I have seldom seen such anger. I bet that if I were to take a scalpel and cut open your chest I'd find a heart that's every bit as black as mine. The only difference is that I accept my dark side.'

He flashed his teeth.

'What do you say to burying the hatchet?'

She felt like punching him in the face.

Is that what he's come for? she wondered. Does he want to provoke me until I hit him? This thought alone held her back.

'We have nothing in common,' Norah said coolly. 'Nothing at all. And now please leave.'

The professor smiled again.

'That,' he said, 'is the trouble with women like you. You think you're superior to everyone else. But you're not.'

'At least I'm not a sadistic old bastard who gets his kicks out of destroying young women,' she said. 'And now get out.'

The smug grin he gave her as he left haunted her for days.

'Why can't you just drop it?' Alex had asked one evening.

She looked at him as if he were off his head and gave him the only answer she could think of.

'Because what he's doing is unfair.'

Alex wasn't convinced.

'Norah, wake up. The whole world's unfair.'

'What are you saying?' she asked. 'That I should give up? That I should just accept everything?'

Alex had smiled condescendingly, as if she were a child refusing to accept that she couldn't adopt every dog in the dogs' home. She saw him differently after that.

It was soon afterwards that she found the ring, hidden away in a drawer, under his clothes. For a few seconds she stared at it, as if it were something gruesome, but fascinating—an open wound showing white bone.

When Alex came home that evening, she told him it was over. Coco's life was ruined; Norah's reputation, her job, her relationship—all gone to pieces. *A total disaster.* The professor's triumph was complete.

Norah stubbed out her cigarette. She mustn't think of all that now, or she'd never get to sleep. She lit up again and blew smoke into the night.

15

Wrapped in a once-fluffy dressing gown that was now rough and scratchy, Norah stepped onto the balcony, sipping her coffee. The sky was wide and grey; there was no way of knowing what kind of day it would be. She went back into the flat and googled the article that Coco had mentioned. It didn't take her long to trace the contact details of the professor's latest 'muse'. She wrote the young woman an anonymous email from a disposable address—a brief, but unequivocal warning about her new boyfriend—and began to feel better.

An hour or so later, Norah was sitting at her desk in the office, translating her interview with the Hollywood star. When the letters began to blur on the screen, she headed for the kitchen.

Luisa and Eva were standing by the coffee machine, chatting over steaming mugs. Norah said hello, opened the window and lit a cigarette.

'Are you doing the Abramović?' Luisa asked, and Norah pricked her ears. She was a big fan of Abramović and would have loved to talk to her.

'I wish,' Eva said. 'The boss bagged that one.'

Norah knew that she would have to wait her turn to be offered that kind of work. She'd only got the interview with Michael because she knew someone from the studio that had produced his latest film. Even so, she felt a small pang of envy. She consoled herself by planning to go and see a museum sometime—the Kunsthistorisches Museum or the Albertina.

'What's the boss bagged?' asked David, who had come into the kitchen soon after Norah.

'The interview with Marina Abramović.'

'Who's that?'

Blowing smoke rings out of the window with her back to the others, Norah pulled a face. It didn't matter that she wasn't best friends with her new colleagues, but she had a feeling she was going to run into real trouble with David at some point.

'Er, let's see,' Eva said sarcastically, 'maybe the most famous performance artist on the planet?'

'Never heard of her.'

'God, you really are a philistine.'

'I prefer to think of myself as an *outdoorsman*,' said David, and Norah didn't have to look at him to know that he was grinning complacently.

'Action art?' Eva said. 'Marina Abramović? Hermann Nitsch? Wolfgang Balder? Ring any bells?'

David shrugged.

'I've heard of Balder. Isn't that the guy with the gutted animals?'

Norah's stomach turned over.

'No, that's Hermann Nitsch. Balder's the one with the electric shocks.'

Norah dragged on her cigarette, closed her eyes and tried to think nice thoughts. She'd been to the Kunsthistorisches Museum twice, but she'd never visited the Albertina.

'The what?' David asked.

Yes, Norah thought, she'd go to the Albertina as soon as she had a moment to herself; she could see Dürer's *Young Hare* and Degas' *Two Dancers*.

'He did this performance once where he had three women sitting in a room, a blond, a brunette and a redhead. The public could look at them through glass and give them electric shocks.'

Any second now, he'll ask which woman was given the most shocks, Norah thought. As if that were the point. She looked out at the milling pedestrians.

'And another time he poured pig's blood all over a man waiting at a station.'

'God!' David said. 'What gives him the right to do that?'

'It's art, you uncultivated morons,' said Eva. 'The guy's a genius!'

'You're not serious,' Luisa cried. 'That's perverse!'

'No, it's not. The electric-shock thing was a fascinating combination of action art and social experiment.' Eva sounded teacherly.

Norah only just stopped herself from groaning out loud. She was interested in art and hated it when people spouted specious half-knowledge. She bit back the caustic remark on the tip of her tongue. What did Max say: *No one likes a smartarse, darling.*

'Oh, okay,' Luisa said sarcastically. 'And the thing where he cut up that woman's face? Was *that* a social experiment?'

'He *what?*' David asked.

'Ah! Now you're interested!' Eva cried.

'How can you cut a woman's face without breaking the law?'

'He calls it performance,' Luisa said, pulling a face.

'God!' David said again. 'How does he find people willing to let him do that to them?'

Eva shrugged.

'That's sick,' David said. 'That's not art, it's grievous bodily harm.'

'Oh, come on,' Eva said. 'What if the girls agree to it? How can it be grievous bodily harm if it's voluntary?'

'Didn't one woman sue for damages?' Luisa asked.

Norah turned round; things were getting interesting.

'That's out of order,' Eva said. 'She could have decided not to get involved. But coming along afterwards and saying, *Oh, by the way, I've decided that wasn't what I wanted after all; I'd like a hundred thousand euros, please*—that's not on.'

'In the end, all you girls are interested in is money,' David said.

Norah imagined taking a fork out of the drawer and ramming it into his neck.

'Ha ha,' Eva said, feigning annoyance.

'Well, I don't know who I find worse,' Luisa said, 'the old perv or the girls who go along with it.'

Norah bit back another caustic remark. She was bad at keeping her mouth shut. It had got her into a lot of trouble at the last place she'd worked and, in her more honest moments, she knew it was an annoying habit.

'He's a genius,' Eva said, refusing to give up.

'You're bonkers.'

'But he's got us talking, hasn't he? Even David, who doesn't usually join in unless we're talking cars or mountaineering.'

'Go on, take the piss,' said David, 'but as far as I'm concerned, all this conversation's done is reinforce my belief that modern art is not for me. Nothing but a load of nutcases.'

'Philistine!' Eva shouted.

'Silly bitch!' David said with a grin.

Norah looked away. Typical David—always testing his limit.

'Watch it!' Eva said, with mock menace. 'I won't stand for sexist names. If I hear anything like that again, I'll go straight to the equal opportunities officer.'

'*You're* the equal opportunities officer,' David said.

All three laughed.

'I can't imagine the women knew what they were letting themselves in for,' Norah said.

She could hear how harsh her voice sounded. A sudden quiet fell over the room, as if her colleagues hadn't realised that the shadowy figure smoking silently at the window could talk. Norah regretted having spoken.

Luisa nodded politely, as if she thought it a point worth considering, but she said nothing. The other two raised their eyebrows at each other.

Thirty seconds later, the kitchen was deserted except for Norah. She stubbed out her cigarette.

'Hey, which of the three women got the most electric shocks?' she heard David ask, and thought to herself how much simpler her life would be if everyone were as predictable as he was.

In the late afternoon, as Norah was getting ready to leave the office, she got an email from Werner.

It turned out, he wrote, that there were several people in Vienna called Arthur Grimm: a two-year-old boy, a man who was getting on for ninety, and another man in his forties. Which would she like him to focus on?

The man in his forties, Norah replied, and after adding a few words of thanks, she hurried out. She had to be in the seventh district at 5 p.m. to meet a young woman who ran a 'cold bus'—a converted minibus to help the homeless make it through the winter. But first, she wanted to have another look on the pedestrian precinct for 'her' homeless woman. The idea that her colleagues might be playing a prank on her now seemed ridiculous. She considered herself a good judge of character and could see that although certain of the editorial staff might not be entirely happy that the supposed new talent was a standoffish German, they were, as far as she could tell, hard-working and professional people with no time for such childish nonsense. Luisa and Tom had seemed honest, when she'd asked them about the woman with the begging bowl. And Anita? Norah wondered as she left the office building. Yes, Anita, too, she thought. In fact, it was only David who might be capable of funny games, but he didn't seem particularly interested in her—why would he want to freak her out? Norah could make no sense of any of it.

She stopped, wondering how to proceed. If she didn't get anywhere with the homeless people, she could always ask the people who worked in the local shops; maybe one of them knew the woman or had spoken to her at some point.

'Excuse me,' said a hoarse voice behind her.

She turned round and saw a man in jeans, worn shoes and a stained black anorak. Dark, intelligent eyes gleamed in a large-pored skin shot through with red veins. Nora looked at him, wondering whether he was going to ask for change or a cigarette.

'You look for woman.'

She raised her eyebrows.

'Yes, that's right,' she said cautiously.

Had talking to the girl paid off after all?

'I can show where woman live,' he said, grabbing Norah's arm as if he wanted to take her to the woman then and there.

'Hang on,' Norah said, pulling free and taking a step back. 'First of all, I'd like to know if we're talking about the same woman.'

The man smiled a practised, obsequious little smile that didn't reach his eyes and made him look suddenly dangerous.

'Tall woman. Dark hair. Not young.'

He puckered his forehead dramatically and pointed at his face, as if to say: *wrinkles*.

Yes, Norah thought. But you could have got all that from the girl with the Alsatian. The man registered her suspicion.

'Woman stand there,' he said, pointing to the spot where Norah had seen the woman—a monolith in the flood of people. 'Gold bowl in hand.'

Norah nodded and the man's smile deepened.

'Dorotea,' he said.

'Is that her name?'

'Come,' he urged.

'First I'd like to know what the information costs.'

'Only hundred euro.'

Norah shook her head. She almost laughed out loud at the man's cheek.

'That's too expensive,' she said. 'I'll give you twenty euros, if you take me to her.'

The man's eyes twinkled.

'Not enough,' he said. 'Is long way.'

Norah thought for a moment. All she needed was the address; she had no desire to tramp the streets with a man who looked like a small-time crook, even if he wasn't planning to lure her into a quiet alleyway and steal her wallet. But how did she know that he wouldn't give her any old address, pocket the twenty euros and do a runner? The answer was: she didn't. But it was worth a try.

'Fifty euro,' the man said.

'Twenty.'

'Forty euro.'

'Twenty.'

The man clicked his tongue and gave Norah a disparaging look.

'You change your mind, you find me in Walcher's Bar,' he said. His smile had seeped away into his pores.

He walked off, without looking back. Probably for the best, Norah thought. And then: *Dorotea*. Interesting. If it was true.

16

The weekend was an empty canvas and Norah had neither paints nor brushes. Coming home from a leisurely visit to the Albertina, she was alarmed at how much of the day was left. What was she going to do with so much time? Although she'd been gone for hours, it was only early afternoon. For a desperate moment, she thought of going in search of the man who'd told her about Dorotea and throwing fifty euros of her hard-earned money at him.

How had she filled her weekends in Berlin? She and Alex had lingered over breakfast or had brunch with friends, and in the evenings they'd gone to the cinema or theatre or had dinner out. Or they'd stayed in and ordered pizza and watched a Netflix series, sprawled on the sofa. But what on earth had they done in those hours in between—that wilderness between breakfast and afternoon, that bleak steppe between afternoon and evening? She had no idea. Couldn't begin to remember. It was as if such empty moments hadn't existed in her old life.

She wondered whether to go and look up Theresa, but decided to ring Sandra instead. No answer. Norah hung up and tried again—still no answer. She rang Max; he didn't pick up either. But Tanja did.

'Hello, sweetheart!' Her cheerful voice rang out across the ether almost before the dialling tone had sounded. Tanja was so infectiously bubbly that just hearing her speak made Norah feel better.

'Hey,' Norah said. 'Lovely to hear your voice. How are you?'

'I'm great,' said Tanja. 'I'm so sorry I haven't been in touch since you moved. We must catch up when I get back. I'm in Hamburg until Monday, then I'll take you out to dinner, yeah?'

Norah grinned. She didn't know anyone who spoke as fast as Tanja.

'Okay,' she said. 'Cool. Have fun in Hamburg.'

'Thanks, sweetie. Let's be in touch on Monday, shall we?'

'Sounds good.'

'Great! Speak to you then. Bye.'

Norah fought back her disappointment. That was Monday evening taken care of, but what about today? She put her phone down and switched on the TV. Red *Breaking News* banner, people running from an invisible threat—a terrorist attack in the UK. For a few minutes, Norah sat and watched the horror, zapping back and forth between news channels and occasionally checking Twitter. Then she turned off the TV and put her phone aside.

There was a gentle roaring in her ears. Out on the street, somebody slammed a car door; otherwise all was silent. But Norah could feel something swelling. She took a deep breath and tried Sandra again, then Max, then Paul. No answer. Norah went over to the window and looked out at the people hurrying across the square, then turned away again. The silence was buzzing.

She had to get out. It was no good sitting around in her flat, breathing spores of loneliness. They were clogging her lungs, making every breath heavier.

In the newsagent's a few streets away, there was a strong smell of lily of the valley which Norah soon traced to the young woman at the till. She was sitting hunched over a book, but greeted Norah quietly when she entered the shop, and Norah recognised the woman the three old ladies had been discussing in the bistro the other day. What was her name again? Marie? Norah turned to the magazines and newspapers—it wouldn't be a bad idea to have something to distract her when she got back to the empty flat. Just the thought of it made her heart sink. She let her gaze wander over the covers and front pages, and Trump's face stared out at her from almost every one—he'd been sworn in only a few days before. A mixture of anger, despair and helplessness rose in her throat; she turned away and asked for a packet of Gauloises at the counter. From close up, Norah saw that the young woman's face was slightly puffy as if she'd been crying, but she surprised Norah by giving her a big dimply smile as she handed her the cigarettes. Norah was about to leave, when the woman called out after her.

'Wait!'

Norah turned and saw her get down off her stool and come round the counter.

'Like one?'

She was holding out a bag of caramels. Norah looked at her in surprise.

'No, thanks,' she said, without thinking.

'Sure? You look as if you could do with something sweet.'

She had a point. Norah smiled and reached into the bag, then popped a caramel out of its crackly gold wrapper and put it in her mouth. It tasted of childhood. 'Thank you,' she said.

The young woman flashed her dimples again and Norah went out into the cold, feeling properly warm for the first time in ages.

17

The tattoo needle buzzed. The tattooist was a tall woman of few words with big hands and a strangely fierce look that was at odds with her round, pale-blue eyes. Something about her had inspired immediate trust in Norah who now lay stretched on the couch, her blouse and bra on a stool beside her. She was glad the woman didn't feel the need to speak, but most of the tattooists she'd come across worked in silence. Maybe it was hard work talking over the constant whirr of the needle, or maybe they understood that they were performing a ritual too sacred to be disturbed by small talk.

Norah felt the inky needle prick the soft skin under her left shoulder blade. Sometimes the tattooist paused and she felt her wipe away a couple of drops of blood with the thumb of her gloved hand and then reinsert the needle. Norah had come into the studio on a whim, but although she hadn't made an appointment, she'd known exactly what tattoo she wanted. The room was tiny and clean-looking, divided from the rest of the studio by a curtain. Norah closed her eyes.

Only a few days before, she'd been speeding through the night in her battered Volvo, leaving her old life behind her. It already seemed so far away.

'Okay,' said the tattooist, 'you're done.'

Norah let out a deep breath and realised she'd been clenching her jaw. She sat up carefully and looked over her shoulder to examine the tattoo in the mirror.

'What do you think?' the woman asked.

Norah stared at the black lines sticking up out of her swollen skin and said nothing.

Then she said, 'It's wonderful,' and saw how pretty—almost child-like—the tattooist looked when she smiled.

Norah was glad when Monday morning came. She leant back in her office chair and felt a twinge of pain in her new tattoo.

She'd started having tattoos done when she was twenty—whenever she felt she'd reached the end of a chapter in her life. Her beautiful scars. One on her left hipbone for the carefree student years, a time of letting go and skin-shedding, hanging out in the laundrette, skiving lectures and drinking plonk in communal kitchens. One on the inside of her upper right arm for the dismal years in Frankfurt and London, when the dark thoughts had returned, nastier and more insistent than before, and she'd tried to keep them at bay with drugs. One on her right ankle for the tough years spent getting clean—dropping her druggy friends, escaping to Hamburg, plunging into work with sudden ambition— her job at the magazine like a new addiction. Late nights at the office, endless coffees and cigarettes, a perpetual sour taste in her mouth. And now this last tattoo on her shoulder for the Berlin years with Alex—but she was still too close to them to know what they meant to her.

Max's words popped into Norah's mind. *I always thought Alex was the one.* Then she thought of the conversation she'd had with Sandra after leaving Alex. Sandra had been appalled at the news.

'We just don't have the same values,' Norah had said. 'Sometimes it feels as if he doesn't give a fuck about the things that really matter to me.'

'He spends hours every day saving people's lives,' Sandra replied. 'Maybe he's just too tired.'

'He should have stood by me.'

'You're always so severe,' Sandra said. 'Okay, so he didn't react the way you wanted him to, but that's no reason to get up on your high horse. You can't leave a man like Alex for something as petty as that.'

'Petty?'

'Yes, petty.'

For a moment neither of them spoke. Then Sandra said, 'I'm on your side, Norah. You know I am. But I don't always understand you. I thought Alex was good for you. I thought he was Mr Right.'

Should she have listened to her friends? Had she made a mistake?

Whatever, she thought, trying to concentrate on her work. It made no difference now anyway; that door was closed.

It was good to be back at the office. While her colleagues moaned about having to start work again and were probably secretly longing for Friday, Norah was glad not to be left alone with herself any more.

She rang Tanja to arrange something for the evening, but Tanja hung up on her. Maybe she was in a meeting.

Just before leaving the office Norah glanced at her phone for the hundredth time that day. There was a text from Tanja. She smiled and opened it.

Dear Norah, things are pretty hectic at work just now, as you know. I don't have the energy for anything else at the moment. T.

Norah read the message twice and her smile faded. It didn't sound anything like Tanja, whose texts were always full of endearments and superlatives and typos. Norah wrote back.

Are you OK? Has anything happened? You'll let me know if there's something I can do, won't you?

No answer. Oh well. Looked as if someone was having a bad week—she knew all about that.

18

In the past, Norah had often longed to be alone. In her teenage years, when her mother bombarded her with annoying questions. At work, when stress levels soared and she thought how wonderful it would be to have a remote control that put the world on mute. Or when Alex had wanted more intimacy than she could give and she'd caught herself thinking wistfully how nice and quiet it had been when she'd had a flat to herself.

Be careful what you wish for.

Norah stood at the window, smoking, and the silence clenched into a fist behind her.

She'd asked for leave to work from home because she was having furniture delivered.

The evening before, she'd sent Max an email when she hadn't got through on the phone: *Feel like doing something tomorrow evening? All work and no play makes Norah a dull girl.*

Max had replied: *Don't know yet. Got a lot on. If we go out, we'll let you know. xx*

Then Norah had rung Tanja, but Tanja had hung up on her again. Norah thought maybe it was a mistake and redialled. This time Tanja did pick up, but the conversation—if you could call it that—didn't go at all well. Tanja briskly informed Norah that she'd rather spend what little time she had with people who really appreciated her, asked her not to call again and hung up.

What was going on? It was weird; Norah had never known her like that. She stifled the impulse to call back and heard a ring at the door. A few moments later, two delivery men were outside her flat with six enormous cardboard boxes on their backs.

Now, as well as a bed, a sofa and a desk, Norah had a wardrobe, a table and four chairs. It was a start. She slit open the ridiculously large boxes with the little Swiss Army knife on her key ring—a present from Werner—and pulled out vast quantities of corrugated cardboard, polystyrene and bubble wrap. She screwed legs onto seats and stacked the still-unpacked removal boxes against one of the living-room walls to make space for the table and chairs. Then she began to assemble the wardrobe. This turned out to be quite a challenge—at least for someone tackling the job alone—but it was something to do and kept her mind off Tanja's atrocious behaviour. Eventually the last shelf was in place and the hundredth tack hammered into the back panel.

That evening, when everything was finished, Norah sat down on one of her new chairs. As soon as she'd unpacked them, she decided she didn't like them anymore. She liked the chairs in Berlin, fuck it—in the flat that was no longer fucking hers.

And now the noise was back. An electric buzz—a painful, drawn-out sound, like a double bass being bowed agonisingly slowly; a dark, sonorous note that swelled into an ancient-sounding tune. If icebergs had voices, Norah thought, they'd sing like that when they calved and floated out to sea.

Her gaze fell on the tarot card from the Imperial that was lying on the table. Norah turned it over so that she didn't have to look at the scythe-wielding skeleton beneath a Roman thirteen.

She would have liked to drop in on Max and Paul, but Max had sent an email to say that Paul had a filthy cold and a high temperature, so he was staying in to look after him. No escape—she was on her own.

Loneliness was creeping up on Norah like the incoming tide.

PREMONITION

My grandmother lived to be a hundred and two. She outlived two husbands, two of her four children and countless friends, and whenever anyone in her village died, she knew in advance. (Or so she said.) I thought of her the other day when I was reading about Soviet military research into paranormal events such as telekinesis and extrasensory perception. One experiment in particular stuck in my mind.

The scientists took a mother rabbit and her litter. The mother had electrodes inserted in her brain to measure the brainwaves. The young rabbits, meanwhile, were placed in a submarine and put to sea, presumably to keep them as far from their mother as possible. Then the scientists killed the young, one by one, and each time a clear reaction could be observed in the doe's brain.

A fascinating experiment, not only because the thought of those bunnies on a Soviet submarine is so bizarre, but also because it proves something that many people have been claiming for centuries—that some living beings can *sense* the presence of death. I find it a beautiful and poetic notion, and since I have started observing *her*, I wonder whether *she* too possesses this gift.

Can she sense the presence of death? Can she feel it growing closer? Does she know how close it already is?

19

Being alone in the cinema was nothing like what she'd expected. Norah had decided to watch a French comedy, but sitting there, surrounded by couples and groups of friends, she realised that jokes were funnier if you had someone to laugh with, and when she heard that dull, menacing sound again, over the actors' chatter and the film music, she understood that the noise hadn't been coming from her empty, lonely flat, but from her.

Leaving the cinema between clusters of happy people, she looked about her. The men and women around her—holding hands, discussing their favourite scenes, imitating the lead actor's accent—all seemed to glow with a warm light, as if their shared laughter had charged them with energy.

Norah felt like a black hole. She was glad to leave the cinema and the glowing people behind her and plunge into the darkness of a dismal, rain-scented night. On her way to catch a tram, she saw a beggar kneeling on the ground in a pose of humility, head lowered, hands raised. Like a statue, Norah thought, rifling through her bag for coins for him. The man mumbled something without looking up. A handful of people were waiting at the tram stop, dark and mute and cold. Across the road, a bright-pink poster was printed with large black letters.

DEATH SMILES AT US ALL.
ALL WE CAN DO IS SMILE BACK!

Norah didn't smile; she put a cigarette in her mouth and glanced at her phone. There was a text from an unknown number.

The Goldfinch, now.

She shook her head in annoyance. Some idiot must have made a mistake—like the time she'd got all those texts for someone called Mesut.

Think you've got the wrong number, she replied, and slid the phone back into her bag. She felt surrounded by strangers.

Her tram came, the windows fogged from the passengers' breath. The doors opened and the strangers who had been waiting with Norah got on. She looked about her. Weird—she had suddenly been hit by the same feeling that had overcome her the first time she'd noticed that sickly sweet smell—on her way home in the small hours the other day, up by that wall that she now knew to be the wall of Belvedere Park. But why?

She could smell nothing but exhaust fumes and the perfume of an elderly lady who had just walked past with a small white fluffy dog. She could see no one she knew. And yet. Norah had always trusted her instinct, and her instinct told her that something wasn't right. Someone was watching her. Norah scanned the pavement. The bustle caused by people getting on and off the tram made it hard to get a clear picture, but a quick glance revealed nothing out of the ordinary. No weird beggarwomen—nothing at all to arouse her interest. She turned back to the tram, which had closed its doors and was about to move off, and her eye was caught by a figure who turned away just as she looked at him. Was it coincidence or had he deliberately avoided her gaze? Norah had no time to find out because at that moment the tram started off.

She watched it go, thinking hard. The figure she'd seen had been a man—she was pretty sure of that. But it was as much as she could say with any certainty. Norah decided to walk the few hundred metres to her flat. She saw the rear lights of the tram as it approached the next stop, and as it retreated, her sense of alarm faded. She walked briskly to get warm, but then realised that she hadn't come out on the square as she'd meant to. Taking her phone out of her bag to look at Google Maps, she saw another text from the unfamiliar number.

They don't deserve you.

Norah frowned. Her fingers hovered over the touchpad of her phone for a second. Then she clicked on the green telephone symbol and waited. She had to know who'd written. The dial tone sounded, then she was informed that the person she was calling was unavailable. No voicemail, nothing. Norah hung up and wrote:

Who are you?

No answer.

Coward, Norah wrote.

She entered her address into Google Maps, then changed her mind and searched for *The Goldfinch*. She knew it was a new, trendy restaurant with a bar, and when she saw that it was only a fifteen-minute walk away, she set off into the night.

The windows of the restaurant lay before her like an illuminated painting. Dark floorboards, petrol-coloured walls. Dozens of little brass-coloured lamps cast a warm light on the faces of the people at the window table who sat deep in conversation, goblets of golden liquid in front of them. One woman whose blonde hair fell in waves over her shoulders was so close that Norah could see her cherry-red nail varnish. The woman said something, tossing back her head with a laugh, and the man next to her—evidently her partner—shook his head, grinning; it looked as if the joke was on him. He raised his glass and toasted her. Another woman at their table, a beautiful redhead with short hair and elfin features, smiled and took a sip from her glass. More glowing people.

Norah felt as if she were in a museum looking at a brightly coloured picture painted especially for her.

She couldn't see the faces of the two men with their backs to the window, but that didn't stop her from recognising Max and Paul— Paul who was supposedly in bed with a high temperature. She was surprised by the intensity of the pain she felt and for a moment she simply stood there, letting it wash over her. Then her phone buzzed and after ignoring it for a little while, she took it out.

I'm sorry, it said. Norah looked about her, but there was nobody watching her.

She stood and stared at the painting for a moment longer, then turned and let the cold and darkness swallow her up.

20

On the way home, Norah bombarded the owner of the unknown number with texts. *What was all that about? How did you know? Who are you?* But she got no reply.

For once she was glad to be back in her flat; the city was beginning to spook her out. Soon she'd have things nice and cosy and could start to fill the rooms with life—buy some plants, ask her friends to dinner, maybe even get herself a pet.

What friends? something whispered in her head, and she bit her lip hard.

Norah had never known her father and was a teenager by the time she found out that he'd been dead for some years. Since her twenty-seventh birthday she had been motherless too, and she had no brothers or sisters, no close family. Now that Alex was gone, her small circle of friends was all she had.

She had just closed the flat door behind her when another text from the unknown number came in on her phone.

Are you okay?

Norah jabbed at the screen.

Where did you get this number?

The answer came immediately.

All your friends have your number.

Someone was playing with her. Norah decided not to answer anymore. One day she'd find out who was writing the texts—maybe Werner could help. Until then she didn't want to encourage this stranger, whoever he—or she—was. She'd been stalked once and that was enough for her. It was one reason she was so careful about giving people her mobile number.

She was about to go and sit in the kitchen when she heard someone on the stairs and recognised Theresa's voice.

'No, sorry,' she was saying. 'I don't mind seeing to the rest, but you'll have to take care of the birds.'

A male voice said something Norah didn't catch, then both were out of earshot.

Norah stood there, her hand on the door handle. She'd hoped to bump into Theresa on the stairs some time, because she felt bad about turning down her invitation so brusquely and would have liked to apologise. She heard the footsteps growing fainter and eventually a key being pushed into a lock, a door opened and closed. Soon afterwards, music came through the ceiling, fast and rhythmic. Usually it would have annoyed Norah, but today she was glad of any sign of life.

She had a shower, dried off and slowly rubbed cream into her skin, simply to give herself something to do. Then she rummaged around in one of the boxes marked *BOOKS*. She had just got into bed with a book of poetry—the one with that incredible Stephen Crane poem—when the music upstairs fell silent. Seconds later, a door slammed.

'You won't do that again,' an angry male voice shouted and Norah sat up, book in hand.

A female voice, presumably Theresa's, said something she couldn't make out. Then another door was slammed. Norah sat in bed, her ears pricked.

A clatter, the man's voice, incomprehensible this time, followed by a shrill cry, short and clipped. In seconds, Norah—who had only slipped on a sweatshirt before getting into bed—was back in her jeans and trainers. She grabbed her key and dashed upstairs. Outside Theresa's door, a shrivelled pot plant was dying a slow death. Norah rang the bell saying *Winkler* and the voices in the flat fell silent. She could almost feel the hesitation on the other side of the door and rang again.

'It's Norah,' she called. 'Your neighbour.'

No reply.

'Everything okay in there?'

Silence.

Norah was about to leave when the door opened a crack. A pale face, brown eyes, recalcitrant curls tied in an untidy bun. Norah had a good look at Theresa. She looked all right.

'Norah,' she said awkwardly, opening the door all the way to reveal a young man dressed in black, lurking at the end of the passage.

'Sorry about the noise,' she said. And then, jerking her head towards the man, 'Rico was just going.'

He stood there without moving, poised somewhere between humiliation, aggression and indifference. Eventually a jolt went through his body and he turned and vanished into a room, reappearing with an army parka over his arm and a black rucksack over one shoulder. He pulled on the jacket, bending to whisper something into Theresa's ear. Then he was at the door. Norah let him pass without looking at him. She waited until she heard his footsteps reach the ground floor and the front door open and then close again. She leant over the banisters, looking, listening.

'He's gone,' she said and it was only now that she felt the rush of adrenaline.

'Thank God,' said Theresa. 'Want to come in a moment?'

Norah thought of the emptiness waiting for her at home.

'Love to,' she said and followed Theresa down the bare passage into the living room.

'Wine?' Theresa asked, vanishing into the kitchen without waiting for an answer.

Norah looked about her. Unlike her living room, this one was crammed full of stuff. Cushions and blankets were piled up on a chocolate-brown sofa and on the wall above it hung a peculiar composition involving a photo collage, a pair of dainty antlers and a calligraphic print. Norah had to peer at it to decipher the curly letters. *Reality is just an illusion.*

A tattered chequered rug, pot plants, a small bookcase—and next to the bookcase, a record player standing on an old-fashioned cupboard. In one corner of the room was an empty birdcage, its little door wide open. Flea market finds, Norah thought, stepping closer—and bit back a shriek of delight when she saw the cat she'd met on the stairs, lying asleep on the rug, half under the sofa. Norah could hear Theresa moving about in the kitchen.

'Who was the guy?' she called out. 'Your boyfriend?'

She could hear her voice oozing disdain. Norah hated men who treated women badly.

'No, God forbid,' Theresa called from the kitchen. 'Not anymore, anyway. He just hasn't quite got it yet.'

'Are you sure you're all right?'

'I'm fine. He didn't do anything. Shouted at me and knocked over a few chairs, but he's basically harmless.'

'If you say so.'

Norah went over to the bookcase and crouched down so she could read the spines better. The books seemed to have been sorted by colour. She soon found a whole bunch of her favourite authors: Donna Tartt, Zadie Smith, Meg Wolitzer, Jonathan Safran Foer, Siri Hustvedt, Maya Angelou, Robert Seethaler, Haruki Murakami. She also spotted Shakespeare's *Complete Works*, everything by Kafka and all seven Harry Potters. The rest of the shelves were filled with a dozen or so Stephen Kings and on top of the bookcase lay a well-thumbed copy of Astrid Lindgren's *Ronia the Robber's Daughter*. Norah felt a smile spread across her face. Her childhood favourite. She took the thick book in her hands, opened it and leafed through. Something fell out onto the floor and she started and picked it up—a little plastic sachet of weed. She slipped it back between the pages and had just replaced the book on the bookcase when Theresa came in from the kitchen carrying two brimming glasses of red wine.

'Sorry to keep you waiting,' she said. 'I had to wash a couple of glasses.'

'No worries.'

'Why don't you sit down.'

Theresa put the wine on the floor in front of the sofa and sat down herself. Norah joined her, taking a sip from her glass. The sofa was so soft that she sank deep into the cushions and so small that the two women had to sit closer than Norah would usually have been comfortable with. For once, though, it didn't bother her; something about this flat was making her feel relaxed.

'I still haven't thanked you for getting rid of Maurice,' Theresa said.

'I thought he was called Rico.'

Theresa rolled her eyes.

'He calls himself that, but actually he's called Maurice. Ridiculous. I don't know what I ever saw in that moron. But anyway: thanks.'

'I didn't do anything. I just wanted to make sure you were okay.'

'Yeah, but not everyone would have bothered.'

For the first time, Norah allowed herself to have a good look at Theresa. She was slender, almost fragile-looking, and although she spoke incredibly fast and always gave a hectic, chaotic impression, she moved with great elegance, like someone who has been forced to take ballet lessons at an early age. Her extraordinarily pale skin was covered in freckles although it was the middle of winter—and she drank red wine as if it were water.

'Norah with an H or without?' she suddenly asked.

'With,' said Norah. 'And you?'

'Hm?'

'Your name. With or without?'

'Oh, I see,' she said, laughing. 'I'm with an H, too.'

Norah never failed to be astonished at how perfectly people's names seemed to suit them. Did parents know through some form of clairvoyance what kind of person their newborn would turn out to be? Or was the secret that all children gradually adapted to their names, in the same way that liquid precious metals hardened and set in the shape of whatever mould they were poured into?

'It's a nice name,' said Norah. 'With or without an H.'

'Thanks.'

Theresa got up.

'Feel like some music?' she asked, releasing her curls from the untidy bun with a flick of her wrist. She flung her hair band into a corner and went over to the record player. Then she turned back to Norah, staring at her through narrowed eyes as if she could read her music taste in her face, opened the cupboard door and pulled out a record.

'Oh my God,' said Norah, as the first notes rang out. 'I love Arcade Fire.'

'Thought you might,' Theresa said, smiling. 'One of my talents.'

'I'm impressed!'

Theresa took a stage bow. When she threw back her hair, something flared up in Norah's hippocampus again and her heart tightened.

'More music, more wine!' Theresa cried, as if a whole troop of liveried footmen were waiting in the wings, ready to rush into the room and serve them with the best burgundy. She turned up the volume and topped up their glasses.

An hour or so later the bottle was empty and Katinka had left the rug for Norah's lap. Norah now knew that Theresa came from Innsbruck, was a few years younger than her and still studying. She'd met Maurice at uni. Exciting sex with him had helped her get over a messy break-up, but as time went on, he'd become increasingly clingy and jealous.

'Vienna's full of weirdos,' said Theresa, and Norah told her the story of the woman with the begging bowl who had prophesied that she would kill a man called Arthur Grimm.

'Whoa,' said Theresa. 'Creepy.'

That made Norah laugh. 'D'you think?'

'Completely. Who is this Arthur Grimm?'

'No idea. But he kind of keeps popping up.'

'How do you mean?'

And in a few words Norah told her.

'Oh my God,' said Theresa, when Norah had finished.

She chewed her lower lip.

'Maybe you should talk to him.'

'To be honest, I'm more interested in the weird fortune teller.'

'Why?'

'Hard to say. There's something about her. She kind of fascinates me.'

Theresa screwed up her nose.

'I think you should let this Grimm have it.'

She pulled a fierce face and clapped her fist against the flat of her hand. Norah laughed again.

'Really? Why?'

Theresa shrugged.

'No idea. But maybe the old fortune teller knows more than you.'

'You're drunk,' said Norah, smiling.

The cat rearranged itself on her lap, then decided it was time to move on. Norah stroked its soft black fur one last time and set it carefully on the floor. She immediately missed the creature's warmth—and, at the same moment, realised that she was no longer entirely sober herself. Then—who knows why—a thought came to her.

'Theresa?'

'Hm?'

Theresa was trying to coax a last drop of wine out of the empty bottle.

'What do you associate with pipe smoke?'

Theresa looked confused.

'Pipe smoke?' she said, with a thick tongue.

Norah nodded.

'Grandads,' said Theresa. 'And cosiness.'

She lit a cigarette and passed it to Norah.

'How about you?'

Norah took a drag and slowly pushed out the smoke, searching for the right words.

'Something evil,' she said.

21

It took a certain amount of concentration to get the key in the lock.
Norah had drunk more wine than was good for her.

The flat lay dark before her, with its creaking floorboards and
humming television. Somewhere in there, too, loneliness was
lurking—probably rolled up in a corner like a sleeping snake just
now, but sure to re-emerge soon enough. Norah put on the lights and
went into the kitchen for a glass of water. She wondered what time it
was. She hadn't looked at her phone all evening—a clear sign of how
comfortable she had felt with Theresa.

She had, though, found herself thinking repeatedly of Valerie. At
a second glance, the resemblance was less striking, but seeing Theresa
had been enough to wash up all the old questions. Would Norah's life
have been different without Valerie? Would she have been less full of
anger, more cheerful? Would she find it easier to let others get close
to her? There had been a time when she could, but that was years ago.

Valerie had been so vulnerable and yet so forceful—lightness and
weight and sweetness and destruction. Yes, Norah thought, my life

would have been different without Valerie because I would have been somebody else. If a butterfly beating its wings in Brazil could trigger a tornado in Texas, then a single event could throw a person's life off course.

But it was no good thinking about it. It was what it was.

Fitful sleep, dreams of Theresa and Valerie—and of a dark figure with disturbingly pale eyes who stood by her bed, looking down at her, unmoving.

When Norah woke, her mouth and throat were so dry they felt sore, and the sheets so rumpled and damp with sweat that she sat up in disgust, despite her throbbing headache. Her second hangover in a fortnight. She got up and staggered to the bathroom, let the water run and drank a few gulps straight from the tap. The face that stared out at her from the mirror—a relic from the previous tenant—looked bleak and grim, like the wanted posters of the Baader-Meinhof gang that had hung in the post office when she was little and spooked the hell out of her. Norah pushed the hair out of her face and reached for her toothbrush—but her fingers closed over thin air. Confused, she stared at the empty tooth mug. She looked on the shelf. Toothpaste, dental floss, heaps of perfumes and cosmetics—but no toothbrush.

Norah ran her hand over her face. She was still tired, that was all. She closed her eyes and looked again. Nothing.

'I can't believe it,' she said softly.

What had she done with the thing? Norah knew that she'd been living in permanent chaos since moving to Vienna, but even she hadn't yet managed to lose her toothbrush. Had she walked around the flat when she brushed her teeth last night, like Alex used to—a habit that had always amused Norah? No, she was being silly. Even if she had been drunk enough to wander around with her toothbrush, she'd have ended up coming back to the basin to spit out and rinse her mouth. Norah looked in all the rooms. The damned thing was nowhere to be found.

The pink pen she'd been looking for the other day still hadn't turned up either. She really needed to be more organised. Norah cleaned her teeth with a spare toothbrush and went into the kitchen to get some breakfast. As she bent down to peer into the fridge her head began to throb even more. She groaned, then screwed up her nose when she saw what was in the fridge: a mango, yoghurt, butter and a green smoothie. There wasn't even any coffee left.

Smoothies, fruit and muesli were the last things she felt like. She wanted coffee, bacon and eggs. A quick shower, then she'd go out. Once she'd got some caffeine and food in her, the world would look different.

She'd got as far as getting undressed when she caught sight of her phone next to the bed. Somewhere in the back of her muzzy brain, a vague memory stirred and came into focus.

Oh no.

She picked it up and checked her outgoing calls.

4:01 Alex

4:03 Alex

4:05 Alex

Oh dear. She'd made drunken calls to her ex in the middle of the night. Thank God he hadn't picked up—who knew what rubbish she'd have spouted. Good thing he always put his phone on silent when he went to bed. He'd probably been fast asleep with Oskar snoring at his feet.

Just then, a text came in and Norah saw with dismay that it was from him. She was annoyed to see that her fingers trembled as she opened it.

No, fuck it. It's not mine. (And couldn't it have waited till tomorrow?)

What had she written? Norah scrolled frantically up to the text she'd sent.

4:07 *Found a little white cuddly bunny here. Did I pack it by mistake? Is it yours?*

That's right, she'd found that rabbit and been meaning to post it to Alex, but instead—

Norah frowned. It had taken her a moment to process the information The cuddly toy didn't belong to Alex. Was that true? It must

98

be. Why would Alex lie? Could she remember unpacking the rabbit? No, she couldn't. It had just suddenly been there. In the same way that her pink pen and her toothbrush had suddenly disappeared. A thought flashed into her mind and she broke out in a cold sweat. *Had somebody been in the flat?*

Naked, but not caring about being seen through the windows, she hurried back to the kitchen. Her flat might be a complete tip, but she knew exactly where the book was. She hadn't entrusted it to the removal men, but had kept it next to her on the passenger seat on her night drive through the woods to Vienna. And since she'd got here, it had been lying on the top shelf of one of the kitchen cupboards, waiting to be put somewhere safer, invisible to anyone who didn't know what they were looking for.

Norah went up on tiptoes, reached into the cupboard and felt for it. Nothing. Frantically, she ran to the living room to fetch one of the new chairs. Put it in front of the cupboard. Climbed onto it.

There it was, of course. How could it have been anywhere else when nobody knew about it? A thief might take her laptop or her designer watch, but not a thing like that. Still. For a few minutes Norah stood there with tears in her eyes, her hand clapped to her mouth. Then she collected herself and put the book back in its place. She closed the cupboard door, staggered to the bathroom on trembling legs, got into the shower cubicle and turned the water on so hot that it burnt.

When she'd had a shower and got dressed, she felt a bit more clear-headed and rang Sandra. Surprisingly, Sandra picked up almost immediately.

'Hi,' she said.

'Hello.'

Norah could hear Greta in the background.

'Just a minute, darling, Mama's on the phone.'

'Is this a bad time to call?' Norah asked.

'It's about as good as it gets,' Sandra said, and Norah couldn't work out whether she sounded amused, annoyed or resigned. 'So what's up?'

Something told Norah that Sandra didn't have the patience for a long phone call and she decided to cut to the chase.

'I have a feeling someone's been in my flat,' she said.

'What do you mean?' Sandra asked, her voice strained, as if she were lifting something heavy. A full shopping bag, a kicking toddler. 'A burglar or what?'

'Yes. No. I don't really know.'

Norah could almost see Sandra frown.

'I'm missing things. Stuff keeps disappearing from my flat.'

'How do you know you haven't just lost it?'

Sandra was right, of course. She'd shared a flat with Norah ten years ago and knew how disorganised she was.

'This morning my toothbrush wasn't there,' said Norah. 'Do you think I could lose my toothbrush?'

Sandra said nothing.

'It's more than that,' Norah went on. 'It's not just that stuff vanishes. Things suddenly appear in my flat too. Things that don't belong to me.'

'Like what?'

'The other day I found a little cuddly toy.'

'Maybe things you packed by mistake when you moved out?' Sandra asked.

'That's what I thought at first. But it's not that.'

'Do you have anything valuable in the flat?' Sandra asked. 'Are you missing anything expensive?'

'No,' said Norah. 'Nothing. And there's no trace of burglars. But...'

'But you're worried.' Sandra finished her sentence for her.

'You know me. Do you think I'm the paranoid type?'

'I don't actually, no,' Sandra replied pensively. 'Tell me, do you know your landlord?'

'I met him once, briefly. Elderly man, early sixties maybe.'

'Does he have a key to your flat?'

'That's the stupid thing,' Norah said. 'I don't know. I haven't managed to get hold of any of the property managers. Is he allowed in my flat if I'm not there and haven't given my permission?'

'God, no,' Sandra said. 'Of course not. But I don't quite know how I can help you when I'm so far away.'

'You've helped me already,' said Norah, and in a way it was true.

'But there's something else,' said Sandra, 'isn't there?'

Norah hesitated.

She decided it was almost certainly a very bad idea to tell someone as cool-headed and down-to-earth as Sandra about the events of the last few days—and then told her everything. Sandra asked her a question now and then in the course of the story—she was a lawyer, after all—but when Norah had finished, she was silent. Greta had gone quiet too; Sandra must have escaped to another room to talk to Norah in peace.

'And you think there's some connection between these things?' she asked eventually.

Norah said nothing.

'Yes,' she said after a while. 'I have a funny feeling there is.'

Sandra made a strange little noise, sympathetic and condescending at the same time.

'The woman who spoke this…' Sandra hesitated, '…this prophecy. You say she was begging.'

Norah nodded, though she knew quite well that Sandra couldn't see her.

'That was a trick, Norah,' Sandra said. 'People will come up with anything to get money off you, you know. Seriously. Fortune telling's the oldest trick there is. I shouldn't have to explain that to someone like you.'

'Someone like me?'

'A journalist. Come on, Norah. You know how these things work.'

'And the other stuff? Things vanishing from my flat? The smell of pipe smoke? A colleague of mine randomly mentioning Arthur Grimm? His office happening to be one floor up from my dentist?'

'Selective perception,' Sandra replied. 'You see everything through a filter and think that perfectly normal, chance occurrences are tied in with your story.'

Norah could feel an angry knot forming in her belly.

'You think I'm completely bonkers, don't you?'

There was a short pause.

'You really are worried, aren't you?' Sandra said eventually.

She sounded pensive again.

'*On February 11 you'll kill a man called Arthur Grimm*,' said Sandra. 'It's a trick to make you scared. The first prophecy's free, after that you pay through the nose. That's how it works.'

'I know it sounds silly, but it didn't seem to me like a trick. I haven't seen the woman since. And she didn't want money either—she just vanished.'

'I think you should forget the whole thing,' said Sandra. 'She was just trying it on. Don't worry about it.'

'And the tarot card? In the hotel? Can you explain that?' Norah asked.

'You're getting upset because someone dropped a tarot card?'

Norah didn't reply. The line went quiet; she could hear Sandra thinking.

'I'm going to ask you something,' Sandra said after what felt like forever. 'Promise me you won't be angry.'

'Promise. And now get on with it.'

'Are you back on drugs?' Sandra asked.

For a moment Norah sat there, open-mouthed.

Then she hung up.

22

Anthracite and asphalt greys and an icy rain as fine as needle points—only a couple of degrees colder and it would have been snow. The pale houses rising skywards on either side of Norah were the colour of dirty polar bear fur.

Returning home from a long day at the office, she didn't even try to fight the shivering. She'd have a proper meal and an early night tonight. Her reflection in the shop windows showed a slim figure, hurrying along in a dark coat. She decided to walk home rather than take the train; the cold air would do her good.

When she looked up, she saw that dusk had given way to night. The entire city was surging home from work. Norah studied the people coming towards her, but couldn't catch their eyes; they were wrapped up in their own thoughts, intent on their cigarettes and phones—waking somnambulists, homing in on an invisible goal.

She turned into a street where there was a small theatre, and was about to cross the road when the pedestrian lights turned red. Norah watched a jogger who had set off as the lights were changing and just made it to the other side before the dense rush-hour traffic started up again. It was a long wait; more and more people gathered next to her, their impatience almost palpable. *Tired, hungry, thirsty. Get me out of this cold! Get me home!*

She watched the people on the other side of the road, also waiting to go on their way. A mum in a pink bobble hat pushing a twin buggy. A cyclist so well wrapped-up you could barely see his face. A couple of about fifty, dressed for the opera. A good-looking man in a suit who made eyes at her over the tops of the cars, which she pointedly ignored. A small group of business people, talking animatedly, all wearing the same dark coats and black shoes and carrying the same leather bags.

The traffic stopped, the lights changed, the throng spilled out onto the road. Norah had almost reached the other side when she saw her.

Appearing behind one of the business people just as the lights turned red again, she hurried past Norah without so much as a glance and was soon on the other side.

There.

Norah could see her only from behind, moving swiftly away from the crossing, but there was no doubt in her mind. The tall physique, the dark hair, the upright posture, the gait. It was her—the mysterious fortune teller. Norah was about to run after her when the traffic started up again. She cast frantic glances left and right—the cars weren't moving fast, but they were practically bumper to bumper and none of them wanted to be the one who didn't make it across in time. Norah cursed as the dark figure turned a corner and disappeared from sight and, raising her left arm, she stepped determinedly onto the road. A woman in an old red BMW who was forced to stop threw her a look of disgust and leant on the horn. Norah paused in the middle of the road, then went on her way, holding up another, smaller car, whose driver clearly took her for some kind of lunatic. Once on the other side, Norah set off at a run and didn't stop until she came to the corner where the woman had disappeared.

She looked left. No sign of her. She looked down the street. Teeming masses. But it was only football or ice-hockey fans on their way to a match. The woman had less than a minute's head start; she couldn't simply have vanished. Had she disappeared into one of the houses in the alleyway on her left? Or was the crowd hiding her from view?

Fifty-fifty. Norah plunged into the crowd, fought her way through, dodged and elbowed, stood on tiptoes, wheeled round—nobody there. If she'd gone this way, Norah would have found her by now. She turned on her heel and headed back to the little alleyway, moving faster now that she was going with the flow. She saw a cyclist, a young couple walking hand in hand, an empty taxi with its hazard lights on. That was all. Norah looked left and right, hoping for a clue, but found nothing.

She ran a desperate hand over her face, then pulled herself together, got out her phone, took a photo of the alleyway and another of the street sign—just in case—and headed home.

Back in the flat, Norah found an email from Werner in her inbox headed *Arthur Grimm*. She opened it and skimmed through the information Werner had tracked down, but there was nothing that leapt out at her. He sounded like a perfectly normal guy. Her mind was on other things anyway. She thanked Werner and clapped shut her laptop.

Later, in bed, staring at the ceiling and waiting for her thoughts to come to rest, Norah replayed the moment at the crossing in her mind and realised there was something strange about it. Something surprising and disconcerting—and not just the shock of seeing the woman again. She closed her eyes, trying to conjure a precise picture.

She had only seen her very briefly and in the middle of a crowd of people, but something about her appearance had bothered Norah.

And suddenly she knew what. *Her clothes.* She hadn't been dressed as a beggar.

23

It seemed to Norah that she had only to reach out a hand to feel the rough, porous surface of the meteorites; the pen-and-wash drawings were so lifelike that she was awed. Another series showed a starry sky and there was a third of woods at night whose almost abstract shapes began to reveal face-like images if you stared at them for long enough. Norah tore herself away from the mesmerising images and sauntered on, weaving her way between the other private-view guests who were making small talk over champagne and canapés. The gallery was agreeably crowded with middle-aged couples, hip twenty-somethings and well-dressed thirty-somethings who all looked as if they were shopping for the perfect painting for the lobby of their creative agencies. Since Norah's review wasn't due for a few days, she had no reason not to linger a little.

She'd had a hectic day, which was a good thing, because it had given her less time to think about the painful question she had been trying to push to the back of her mind for days: why had Max and Paul lied to her? Max had rung twice since, but Norah had ignored his calls.

Instead she had spent every free moment ringing round, trying to find someone to change the lock on her front door—not tomorrow or sometime in the next few days, but right away. She was still spooked out by the way things had gone missing from her flat lately, or appeared out of the blue. Who had a key to her flat? The landlord? The previous tenant?

As soon as she'd found a locksmith, she sped home in a taxi and waited as he replaced the lock. Then she went back to Kärntner Strasse and looked for Walcher's Bar, the place mentioned by the man who'd said he could get hold of Dorotea's address for her. He grinned when he saw her. She thrust thirty euros at him and he took the money without a word, noting down in exchange the name *Dorotea Lechner* and an address. She would have liked to set off immediately, but it would have to wait; she had work to do. Back at the office, she put the finishing touches to her interview with Michael, ignoring repeated calls from Max. Why was he bothering? He'd clearly been so keen to avoid having her at the dinner that he'd lied so as not to have to invite her. Luckily, Norah had no time to get upset; Berger had asked her to cover for Luisa who was off sick, so she had to leave for the private viewing as soon as she was done with the interview. She ran all the way to the first district in high heels so as not to miss her appointment with the gallerist.

The original plan had been to talk to the artist before looking at the exhibition, but the artist had let Norah know in no uncertain terms that she saw no point in furnishing her with explanations of her work. The gallerist was more amenable—a tall, slim woman with unnaturally firm waxen skin, almost colourless hair, bright-red lipstick and two realistic-looking snakes twisted into a heavy chain around her neck. Her cool manner gave her a Nordic air, but she spoke with a delicious Viennese accent and turned out to be something of a pro, with a good stock of anecdotes that made the artist's work instantly intriguing. A bare fifteen-minute interview gave Norah all the material she needed and at last she could turn her attention to the exhibition.

•

The drawings were followed by oil paintings and Norah was surprised to see that the artist worked even more brilliantly in oils than in pen and wash. She stopped at a painting alongside a couple in their mid-sixties, drinking champagne: he in jeans and a jacket, with a full head of white hair; she blonde and heavily made-up, wearing low-denier black tights under a turquoise dress.

It was a hyperrealistic painting of the ocean at night. The waves—so dark and viscous that they resembled oil more than water—looked as if they might slosh out of the picture at any moment.

'Nice,' the man said.

'It's good,' said the woman, 'but it's not great.'

She went on her way and the man followed her, so Norah was able to have a better look at the painting. She had to get very close indeed to see that this piece of reality, plucked out of the world like a ripe fruit, was made up of paint on canvas and not waves and spray and night air. If the other visitors hadn't kept distracting her with their conversations, she felt that it might have soaked her to the skin and tumbled her ashore with seaweed in her hair.

'Did you know that Valeska boycotts her own private viewings on principle?' said a young man behind her. She pricked up her ears; Valeska was the name of the artist.

'I know,' a woman replied. 'Incredibly pretentious. Really, of course, she's the biggest attention whore of them all. Jerome says she's impossible to work with.'

They spoke like actors, as if they weren't talking to each other, but in order to display their knowledge of the artworld to as many people as possible.

'Oh my God,' the man said. 'I can believe it. Although Jerome isn't in my good books just now. He took me to see a performance of that ridiculous Belgian woman last week.'

'Bride de Jong? Isn't she Dutch?'

'Who gives a fuck? The point is, she does performance art that was out of date in the seventies.'

Norah moved away from the picture to get a better look at the pair of them.

He was tall and rangy in skinny jeans, an apricot-coloured T-shirt, a striped blazer and horn-rimmed glasses, while she wore slacks with braces over a shirt and had hair dyed a matt pale grey.

They drifted away from the picture towards the waiter with the champagne glasses.

'Are you going to Big B's private view?' Horn-rims asked.

'Oh my God,' the woman shrieked. 'Are you kidding? Of course!'

'I thought maybe action art wasn't really your thing...'

'That's hardly relevant. Compared with him, Nitsch is a nobody.'

Norah suddenly didn't feel like looking at paintings any more. Where was the cloakroom? She scanned the room, looking for the gallerist who had taken her coat and then stopped in stunned shock when she saw the last picture of the exhibition. It was another oil—white and every shade of blue beneath a strip of black. Norah shuddered.

A frozen lake under a starry night sky.

24

After the private viewing, Norah knew she wouldn't be able to sleep, so she set off towards the thirty-euro address which was supposedly Dorotea Lechner's, wondering whether the money wouldn't have been better invested in cigarettes or a few drinks.

The city was surprisingly quiet. There was no one in Norah's carriage except a stubbornly silent couple of about sixty and a group of young men talking to each other in a language Norah couldn't understand. The train stopped and spat her out and she paused to get her bearings. No one had got out with her; she was alone in an area where—apart from the station—there didn't seem to be a great deal. A high-rise block was visible in the distance and the water of the canal glistened beneath the steps leading down from the station. Norah had never been to this part of Vienna before. She opened Google Maps, entered the address she'd been given and followed the instructions on her phone. Asphalt, darkness, dirt and emptiness—only the fluorescent light of the station flickering behind her. Ahead, the extinguished neon sign of a discount store and, in the distance, houses strung out along the water.

Norah walked along the deserted canal. Not a soul about, not even a couple snogging or an old man walking his dog. Only the biting cold and the shallow water, as black as the oily ocean in the gallery. Norah shivered with cold as she hurried along the canal, dodging frozen puddles and potholes to avoid slipping. As soon as she could, she took a flight of steps up from the canal to the street and when her phone told her she was almost at her destination, she looked up to see that there was a bar on the ground floor of the house she was heading for.

It really was a quiet neighbourhood; Norah still hadn't seen a soul. But there were lights on in a lot of the windows—a comforting sight.

Norah stepped up to the front door of the nondescript house whose colour she couldn't make out in the dark—maybe cream, maybe white or grey—and studied the names on the doorbells. There *were* names, which there weren't always in Vienna, but not the one she was looking for. Krstic, Müller, Celi, Talhouni/Nägele, Wagner. And there was one bell without a name. As Norah saw it, that meant three possibilities. Number one, the woman lived in that flat. Number two, the woman didn't live here at all and Norah's reticent informer had simply piloted her to the bar where she was a regular. Number three, her informer wasn't an informer at all, but a con man. Norah glanced at her phone. Half-past nine. Too late to ring a stranger's doorbell. If Dorotea Lechner did live here, Norah would have to come back another time. Nobody liked being surprised late at night; you didn't need to be a journalist to know that. She'd try in the bar and if that didn't get her anywhere, she'd come back in the daytime. She was also going to have to come up with some way of getting these people to talk if she wanted to write a feature about them. Who liked talking about living on the streets and begging?

Norah went into the bar. It reminded her of Werner's favourite drinking hole: a long dark counter, a football match on a small TV high up in a corner, walls hung with various pennants and an Austria Vienna scarf, a no-nonsense landlady who looked as if she'd turn you out if you tried to order an alcopop, and in front of her, at the bar, a row of men—and they really *were* all men—who evidently took their drinking seriously. The underbelly of Vienna's nightlife.

Refreshingly, a few heads turned to look at Norah as she went in, but none of them showed any real interest in her, so she took a seat at the far end of the counter and ordered a beer, which the landlady set down before her with a mute nod.

Norah thanked her and decided to lay her cards on the table, guessing that careful questioning wouldn't get her anywhere with this formidable woman. Mid-fifties, Norah reckoned. She had bright eyes and a fierce updo and looked as if she had a healthy dose of common sense.

'I'm looking for someone,' Norah said. 'Dorotea Lechner.'

The woman frowned.

'Friend of yours?' she asked.

'Not exactly.'

'Colleague?'

Norah decided to take pot luck and nodded—it couldn't hurt. The landlady's face instantly brightened.

'From the theatre,' she said. 'Thought so, as soon as I saw you.'

Norah managed to conceal her surprise by downing half her beer—which got her a satisfied smile.

'Dorotea will be pleased. You've only just missed her, by the way.'

'She was here this evening?'

The woman nodded.

'You don't happen to know where I might find her, do you? Or where she lives?'

'Well, I don't know that she'd want that.'

Norah said nothing and tried to look harmless.

'I can give you her mobile number,' said the landlady.

'Really? That would be great.'

The woman leant over the counter towards Norah.

'Is it about a part?' she asked.

'Have to see about that,' Norah said and smiled.

The landlady wrote the number on a beermat and Norah thanked her, finished her beer and paid, leaving a generous tip. As soon as she was out of the bar, she dialled the number. She let it ring for a long time while the cold took hold of her again, attacking her earlobes, the tips of her fingers, her feet through the thin leather of her shoes. Nobody picked up and there was no voicemail, so Norah couldn't leave a message. She walked along the canal, thinking hard. Dorotea Lechner worked at a theatre. This new piece of information needed processing. She tried the number again. A cyclist whizzed past her; between the houses, bare trees stretched their limbs imploringly to the sky. All was quiet. And then suddenly Norah heard something. A little way down the embankment, not far from where she was walking, she thought she heard a phone ring. She stopped and listened. She heard a train in the distance and a car a few streets away, but that was all. Norah tried Dorotea's number a third time, and almost as soon as a connection had been established, the ringing sounded again, only a few metres away. Norah felt as if she'd been plunged into the icy canal; she was suddenly wide awake. She wished she was at home in her flat. Why had she come here? Couldn't she have waited until the next day to search out the creepy fortune teller? Norah's heart hammered in her chest and she knew she was afraid. But she got a grip on herself and followed the sound.

Looking down at the water from the embankment, she saw it. A dark shape. Norah stopped and blinked, as if to force her eyes to get used to the dark, but whatever it was remained elusive. Norah stood and stared, trying to get a grasp on the situation and when at last she realised what she was looking at, everything seemed to stall and slow, as if the flow of time were suddenly as thick and sticky as tar. There, black against the darkness, was a human figure. It was floating face-down at the shallow bank of the canal, and if it hadn't snagged on a big, bare branch, it would have drifted away. The ringing stopped and Norah realised that it had come from a dark bundle that was just visible on the grass at the water's edge. A bag, perhaps, or a rucksack, she thought, running towards it, slipping on the frosty grass in the thin high-heeled shoes she had put on for the private viewing, not for a night walk. She arrived at the bank out of breath and, kneeling down, stretched out an arm to the figure floating on the water, but she couldn't reach it. She dropped her bag on the grass, lay on her belly and pulled herself as close to the water's edge and the motionless figure as possible without getting completely drenched herself. She could almost touch the soaked cloth of the woman's coat, but as soon as she got it between her fingers, the lifeless form drifted away a little, as if trying to escape her grasp. Norah reached out a bit further, panting— she wasn't shivering anymore, but sweating—and managed to grasp a piece of coat between her fingers. Straining, she pulled the figure over to her, a centimetre at a time to begin with, and then, with a last heave, all the way to the bank, where she grabbed the body in both arms, turned it over and pulled it out of the canal, puffing and cursing, feeling the icy water seep out of the clothes. Then she laid it on the grass and looked down at it. The dark hair was no longer in a thick plait, but loose. The face pale and serious. An aging Ophelia. Norah saw at once that Dorotea Lechner, if that was her name, was dead. She felt her pulse, just in case, but all was still; the woman was cold as ice. As so often in situations of stress, Norah was suddenly calm. She dried her wet hands on her damp jeans and took out her phone. Then she sat down on the grass a few metres away from the corpse, wrapped her arms around her trembling body, and waited for the ambulance and police to arrive.

25

The journey home seemed to go on forever. The fluorescent light in the train, the laughter of late-night revellers, the smell of grease wafting over to her from the seat opposite where a teenage boy was impassively eating chips—it was all suddenly unbearable to Norah. The doctor on call had confirmed that the woman was dead. It seemed that she really was called Dorotea Lechner. The policemen, two men of Norah's age with lean, muscular bodies, had taken her statement and contact details. She had decided to tell them the more plausible part of the truth—that she was working on a feature about beggars and homeless people in Vienna and had been hoping to speak to the woman about her experience. The officers had implied that they were treating the case as an accident. Ms Lechner had been walking by the canal in an advanced state of inebriation and had, for whatever reason, strayed from the path to the edge of the water. There, presumably, she had slipped and fallen, banging her head on a stone so that she had landed in the water unconscious and drowned.

But Norah had a funny feeling in the pit of her stomach. Yes, it was true, the policemen's explanation sounded plausible, and Norah ought really to be glad that nobody suspected her of being involved in the incident. And yet. A few days ago, the woman had appeared out of the blue and told her she brought death.

And now death had caught up with *her*.

Rarely had Norah so badly needed a drink. The little bistro on the corner of her street seemed just the place to warm up and escape for a moment longer the silence and loneliness waiting for her in her flat. It occurred to her what a mess she must look in her muddy jeans and tattered shoes, but no one seemed to take any notice. Norah sat down at the bar and ordered a vodka. After downing it, she ordered another—and another—and then, in a last, desperate attempt to kill time, she asked for a beer.

When she finally climbed the stairs to her flat an hour or so later, she had trouble getting the key in the lock. Inside, the floorboards seemed more uneven than usual, the kitchen lamp swung from the ceiling like a pendulum, and getting out of her dirty things and into clean, dry clothes was something of a struggle. But although it hadn't been Norah's first dead body—she'd once done a stint reporting on crimes for a local daily in Hanover—she wasn't done drinking yet. There was still white wine in the fridge. She filled a glass and went and stood at the window.

A man was standing in the light of the streetlight, staring up at her. Confused, she moved away from the window, pulled herself up onto the kitchen benchtop (another relic from the previous tenant) and drank her wine, watching the swaying ceiling light.

She suddenly found herself thinking of the photo of Arthur Grimm she had found on the internet. The short dark hair, the square chin, the steely blue eyes.

Norah slid down from the benchtop and went back to the window.

The man was still there, standing motionless. A slim man, neither tall nor short, with close-cropped dark hair. That was as much as she could make out in the darkness, but something told her he had deep-set blue eyes. Then—as if he'd been waiting for Norah to reappear at the window—he began to move.

He turned and stepped out of the light of the streetlight and had soon vanished into the dark night. Norah couldn't have said what made her so sure, but she knew she had just seen Arthur Grimm for the first time.

26

Chocolate and weed, soft light and guitar music, the early dark of winter. Katinka lay curled up on Norah's lap, her eyes half-closed, while Theresa alternately stuffed chocolate into her mouth and sucked on a joint. It did Norah good to talk to Theresa. She never made her feel she was bonkers, the way Sandra sometimes did. And she clearly liked being with her—unlike Max and Paul. Norah had told Theresa about Max's lie—and about the calls he'd made since. So far she'd continued to ignore him.

'Do you think I'm overreacting?'

'Oh, *please*—your supposedly best friend lied to you! I wouldn't want to talk to him either if I were you.'

'Maybe he wants to apologise.'

Theresa gave a derisive snort.

'Do you really want to know what I think?'

'Go on.'

'I think you can do without friends like that.'

Norah felt gloom descend on her and drowned it in another glass of the red wine she'd brought with her. She knew she'd have to have it out with Max sometime. But right now she was still too hurt.

The bastard, as Theresa had taken to calling her ex, hadn't reappeared. Theresa was sitting on the sofa next to Norah, barefoot in jeans and a woolly jumper, prattling on about her seminars, her dishy professor, a novel she was reading, a hip new bar that had opened in Margareten. Norah's mind wandered.

After finding Dorotea Lechner's body in the canal, she had thrown herself into her work more than ever, but the strain of the last few days was making itself felt. The police officers in charge of the case were still convinced that the woman's death was an accident and Norah accepted that. But what about the man who had appeared outside her house that evening and stared up at her flat? And who had written those strange texts? There was something else, too. Somewhere at the back of Norah's mind, some dark, murky knowledge was stirring, struggling to reach the surface and connect with the recent goings-on. A shred of memory? A hunch? Norah was plagued by the feeling that she'd seen something important, but ignored it or misread the signs. It was like having an eyelash in her eye that refused to be dislodged.

'Crocodile tears, schadenfreude, whitewash, iceberg,' Theresa was saying and Norah resurfaced from her thoughts.

'Sorry, what?' she said, halfway between confusion and amusement.

'Oh, nothing,' Theresa replied. 'You didn't seem to be listening to me, that's all.'

Norah laughed.

'I'm sorry.'

Theresa grinned, then grew serious again.

'What's up with you?'

'Do you remember the weird fortune teller I told you about the other day?'

'Of course.'

'She's dead.'

Theresa, who had just sucked on her joint again, choked on the smoke.

'My God! What happened?'

'Accident,' said Norah.

That was what they'd told her at the police station anyway: *a tragic accident*.

She thought about the results of her internet research on Dorotea Lechner. Born in 1948 to a Serbian mother and an Austrian father, she'd been an actor and had lots of parts in small theatres, even landing a few film roles in the eighties. As she grew older, though, it had become harder to find work, and at some point she must have fallen on hard times. Google had yielded nothing, of course, but Norah could imagine.

'Oh my God, how awful,' Theresa said gravely.

Norah had expected her to ask hundreds of questions, but she didn't. Silence spread. Only Katinka minced nervously back and forth.

'Have I ever told you about my theory of attraction?' Norah asked.

Theresa shook her head.

'Okay then,' Norah said, putting a piece of chocolate in her mouth. 'Have you ever wondered why some people attract good luck and others bad?'

Theresa frowned, as if to say: *not really*.

'We all know someone who seems to have all the luck,' Norah said. 'And we all know some poor person who seems to attract accidents and disasters. I would say there are also people who attract love or loneliness or money or envy or sickness or pity or adventure or danger or bizarre situations.'

Theresa listened attentively; only her glazed eyes betrayed that she had consumed a certain amount of alcohol and THC.

'In my kindergarten,' Norah went on, 'there was a boy called Eddy, a little red-headed bruiser. Every year, on Shrove Tuesday, we had doughnuts—always jam doughnuts, except for one, which was filled with mustard. It was supposed to be lucky to get that one, and although we kids were scared of biting into the mustard, we all hoped we'd be the lucky one. Especially as whoever bit into the mustard doughnut was always given one of the ordinary ones too. Eddy got that doughnut three years in a row. He didn't examine them or anything; he hadn't found a way of working out which was which. He was just the kind of person that sort of thing happened to. A few years later—we were in primary school by then—there was a nasty accident in the area. A huge tanker skidded on a bridge, broke through the crash barrier and plunged into the valley. Eddy saw the truck fall. He lived within sight of the bridge and his mum had sent him out into the garden to pick a lettuce for dinner. Eddy saw a flaming tanker fall from the sky.'

'Wow,' said Theresa. Norah nodded.

'Amazing, isn't it?' she said. 'A few years later, when we were in year five or six, the circus came to town and one of their monkeys escaped. Guess who found it?'

'Sounds like a great guy, this Eddy,' Theresa said.

Norah shrugged.

'Actually he was just normal. But he attracted unusual situations.'

Theresa looked pensive.

'I'm sure we're all magnets for something,' Norah said. 'What I want to know is: can we change? Can we reverse our polarity? Can someone who has always been plagued by bad luck learn to attract good luck?'

'What do you attract?' Theresa asked.

'Not sure. It's easier to see patterns in other people. For a long time I thought I attracted nutcases. Nutcases and cats. Where we lived there was a black tom called Professor Snape. I don't know where he got the name. He was so timid, he wouldn't let anyone stroke him—most of the kids couldn't get him to go anywhere near them. Whereas me, I wasn't really interested in him, but he followed me everywhere. It's the same today. If there's a cat in the house, it'll find me. I don't know why. Same with nutcases.'

Theresa smiled.

'Like me,' she said.

Norah laughed.

'No, seriously,' she said, 'if I'm on a train and some psycho gets on, you can be sure he'll come and sit next to me, even if the carriage is half empty. In Berlin I was once followed for I don't know how long by a young woman who thought I was the High Priestess of Evil.'

'Christ,' Theresa said.

'No kidding,' said Norah. 'Those were her words: *You are the High Priestess of Evil*. She followed me everywhere, shouting at me. The scary thing was, she looked completely normal. Jeans, Converse, designer top, messy hair in a bun, hipster glasses. Pushed her bike along next to me and yelled at me.'

'Creepy,' said Theresa, stubbing out her joint.

Norah nodded.

'I felt sorry for her,' she said.

Theresa was silent for a moment.

'And what do you think now?' she asked.

'What do you mean?'

'You said that for a long time you thought you attracted nutcases. It sounded as if you didn't think that anymore. So what do you think now? What *do* you attract?'

Women I can do nothing to save, Norah thought.

Leonie, the girl I found on the bathroom floor at that party. Coco. Dorotea Lechner. And...

'No idea,' Norah said with a laugh, hoping it sounded natural. 'I'm just rambling on.'

'You're lying,' Theresa said gravely. 'Something's bugging you and you don't want to tell me about it.'

Norah said nothing.

'Do you know what I do when something's bugging me or scaring me?'

'No,' said Norah. 'What?'

'I confront it head-on—straight away, before I can think better of it.'

Silence.

'What's the latest with this Anton Grimm, by the way?' Theresa suddenly said.

'*Arthur* Grimm,' said Norah. 'What made you think of him?'

'No idea,' Theresa said, starting to roll another joint. 'But the old fortune teller mentions him to you and a few days later she's dead. I call that freaky.'

Yes, thought Norah, *so do I.*

The red wine hadn't done its job; Norah's mind was still buzzing when she got back to her flat. If she went straight to bed, she'd toss and turn for hours. So she sat at her desk and did what she always did when she wanted to put her thoughts in order: she wrote. Dorotea Lechner was dead. Arthur Grimm kept popping up in her life unexpectedly and seemed in some creepy way to be getting closer to her. She didn't think she knew anyone by that name, but she couldn't get him out of her head; it was like a snatch of tune that kept eluding her. And for some reason—though she couldn't have said what—she associated him with Valerie.

She opened her laptop and found the email from Werner containing all the information about this mysterious man. On the first page, right at the top, was his private address. Norah called a taxi. It was time to get a closer look at Arthur Grimm.

27

Rilkeplatz was deserted—no trams, no passers-by. The taxi hadn't arrived yet. While she waited for it at the front door, Norah took her phone out of her coat pocket and peeled off her leather gloves to enter Grimm's address in Google Maps, cursing herself for not having done it earlier.

The cold knew no mercy; her fingertips immediately began to ache. Norah waited impatiently for the website to load, then almost jumped when she saw the location. Arthur Grimm lived very close indeed.

Hearing the taxi approach, she looked up and raised her arm to get the driver's attention. He stopped and she got in.

'Good evening.'

The driver, a walrus-like man in his late fifties with a droopy moustache and a leather jacket, didn't return her greeting and Norah almost smiled. Unfriendly taxi drivers always reminded her of Berlin. She gave him the address, adding that she didn't want to get out there, but one street further on.

'You do know it's basically round the corner,' the driver said in a thick Viennese accent.

Norah didn't bother to reply and waited for him to drive off. She looked out the window, thinking she might see Theresa at the brightly lit window of her living room, but the flat lay in darkness. And the taxi driver showed no sign of going anywhere. He seemed to be waiting for an answer.

'Is anything wrong?' Norah asked.

'All you need to do,' he said, 'is walk to the end of the road and take two lefts. I'm not driving you three fucking metres.'

'You're not serious,' Norah said.

The man muttered something incomprehensible.

'Arsehole,' Norah mumbled, getting out of the cab.

'What did you say?' he asked.

'I said: *Have a nice one*,' said Norah, slamming the door.

She'd just have to walk. There were still a few cars on the road and the occasional cyclist, hooded and swaddled as if for urban combat, but no one else on foot. It was too cold. When she got to the street where Grimm lived, she stopped. That would be it—the big building with the lovely pale facade and the crane towering behind. And the chances were, she was being silly; Arthur Grimm was probably a perfectly ordinary man, a harmless and respectable engineer who lived a peaceful life, got up in the mornings, went to bed at night, and in between times worked and ate and drank, met friends and minded his own business. But, call it a journalist's hunch or call it paranoia—Norah had to see him; she had to *know*. Slowly and calmly, she walked towards number eighteen, the building where Dr Arthur Grimm lived.

Not far from the cream stucco house, she stopped and lit a cigarette without taking her eyes off the street in front of her or the door of number eighteen. As soon as the smoke reached her lungs, she began to relax. A car drove past. Norah watched it go—only another taxi.

Maybe the passing car distracted her for a split second, or maybe the soothing feeling produced by the nicotine in her bloodstream caused her attention to slacken for a moment. Either way, she didn't realise there was anything wrong until it was too late.

Behind you.

Norah turned and froze. Backed away. Because of course she rec-ognised him instantly, the man standing before her, staring at her out of the darkness.

Arthur Grimm didn't have the kind of face you forgot in a hurry.

28

He stood directly in front of her on the dark pavement, only his posture betraying his tension. Norah's head was suddenly clear. They'd never met. He couldn't know she was here because of him. She would simply carry on walking, a mere passer-by.

She stepped aside to pass him, but he stood in her way.

'What are you doing here?' he asked.

He spoke softly, but with a distinctly aggressive undertone.

Norah was taken aback. The man couldn't know that she'd found out about him, got hold of his address and come here to have a good look at him. Did he think she was someone else?

She set her chin and slipped her left hand into her coat pocket where she kept her phone.

'Do I know you?' she asked.

The man didn't reply.

'Let me past, please,' Norah said, 'or I'll call the police.'

His eyes narrowed.

She took her phone from her pocket. She only had to press the

Home button twice and the *Emergency Call* option would appear in the bottom left-hand corner of the screen...

'Piss off,' the man said and let her past.

Norah kept going until there were a few metres between them. Just go home, she thought. He's not right in the head. Keep walking and don't look back.

'I don't want to see you here again,' Arthur Grimm called out to her. 'That's a warning.'

Norah paused mid-step and turned to face him—she couldn't stop herself.

'Who the fuck do you think you are?' she said. 'This is a public street. As far as I'm aware, there's no law against walking down the road. So either tell me what your problem is or I would suggest you leave me in peace.'

The man said nothing—only stared at her with his deep-set eyes. He had a strange face; Norah had noticed when she saw his photo on the internet that there was something funny about it. But she couldn't work out what.

Arthur Grimm looked at her as if he were weighing things up.

He's going to attack me, Norah thought. He's going to drag me between the parked cars, wrestle me to the ground and bash my head against the road till I stop breathing.

No, that was irrational; he wouldn't dare—not here in public, in full view of a whole street of lighted windows. Norah fought the impulse to back away from him. Whatever she did, she mustn't show him she was scared. He was still staring at her. Then a jolt went through his body.

'I don't know why I'm even talking to you.'

And he turned and walked slowly away.

Norah watched him go, uncertain what to think. He blurred and merged into the darkness and it was only when he reached the light of his doorway that she saw him more clearly again. He turned to face her once more and there was no mistaking the menace in the look he gave her.

I don't want to see you here again. That's a warning.

Norah stood there for a moment, astonished by the turn her little evening walk had taken. Then she set off. Her heart didn't begin to steady until she'd rounded the corner.

Back in the flat, Norah collapsed on a kitchen chair and as she sat there, warming up, she tried to put her thoughts in order. Thanks to the cold air and the shock, she was feeling surprisingly clear-headed, but she couldn't get her head round what had just happened. What was the man's problem? Who did he think he was?

A beep from her phone announced a new text and she made a little noise of surprise when she saw that it was from the same unknown number the other texts had come from. Was all that starting up again after days of radio silence? Bewildered, she opened her inbox.

That was stupid of you. Dangerous too.

For a moment, she could only stare at her phone. The blood rushed in her ears and she felt her fingers tremble and had to put her phone on the table. When she'd calmed down a little, she read the text again—not that there was much to read. It was like a slap in the face; there could be little doubt that the text referred to her meeting with Grimm. Norah closed her eyes. Had somebody followed her? She went through the last hour in her head. The taxi driver who had turned her away. The short walk to Grimm's house. Had she seen anyone on the way there? Or outside his house? She couldn't say for certain. She'd been far too wrapped up in herself—and in Grimm.

Norah opened her eyes again. Reply or ignore? She made a spur-of-the-moment decision and picked up her phone.

Are you following me? she wrote.

The reply came so quickly that she wondered whether her virtual contact had been expecting the question.

I'm protecting you.

Who the hell could it be?

What do you know about Arthur Grimm? she asked, but received no reply.

She put the phone back on the table. It was impossible to find out who the number belonged to. Even Werner, the best investigative journalist she knew, hadn't managed.

But Werner knew a great deal about Grimm. The printout with the file he had put together for Norah was still on her desk. Was there anything she'd overlooked?

Arthur Grimm had been born in Frankfurt in 1974. He'd studied mechanical engineering in Aachen, then switched course. Werner had tracked down all the firms where Grimm had worked as an intern during and immediately after his studies. Norah skimmed the almost endless list and saw that Grimm had been living in Austria for some time. He'd started off in Salzburg—evidently moving there to join his then-wife—and ended up in Vienna where he had been living for the last four years, alone.

Norah compared the main points of her own life with those of Grimm. When she was born, he was eight years old and attending primary school in Hanover. By the time she started school, he'd moved on to secondary school. When she started secondary school, he was taking his final exams. The year of Valerie's suicide, he was studying engineering and working on his dissertation. At around the time Norah took her final exams—passing by the skin of her teeth, which was, everyone agreed, only natural, when you thought of what she'd been through—he graduated and moved to Munich. And so it went on. Norah leant back resignedly. No overlap in their biographies; they hadn't ever lived in the same place or known the same people or done the same things.

She heard his voice.

What are you doing here?

Piss off.

I don't want to see you here again.

That's a warning.

Who did Arthur Grimm think he was? Where had he seen her face before? How could he know that she was after him? She didn't know him and had assumed that when they met he would take her for a simple passer-by. Norah shook her head, perplexed. Even if Werner had been careless in his research—which Norah knew he never was—how could Grimm have made the connection to her? It was impossible. Norah closed the file, put it in her bag and folded her arms behind her head.

Grimm might know *her*. But *she* had never met *him* until this evening.

29

When Norah returned home the following evening after a hectic day at the office, her thoughts were still focused on Arthur Grimm. It was time to get to the bottom of things; she needed clarity. She had his number from Werner and wasn't going to think too hard about whether it was a good idea to make use of it. She prepared for the phone call as if it were an important interview, going through various openings, questions and even possible answers in her head. Then she switched off caller ID on her phone. Just because she had Grimm's number, it didn't mean he had to have hers. Norah entered the digits. She heard the dialling tone. It rang once, twice. *Pick up*, she thought. *Please*. Three times, four times. Then there was a ring at the door.

'Shit,' she muttered. She was tempted to go and see who it was, but stayed put. She had to sort this out now. If she couldn't reach Grimm this evening, she wouldn't be able to sleep all night. She had to get to the bottom of this without delay. Whoever it was at the door could come back another time. But the doorbell rang again. And again.

Fuck. Norah crept to the door as quietly as she could and was about to look through the spyhole when she heard a voice.

'I know you're there.'

Theresa.

Norah shut her eyes for a second, not sure whether to be amused or annoyed, and opened the door.

'Yo,' said Theresa, holding out her fist to Norah.

Norah bumped fists with her. Theresa grinned.

'Is it a bad time? I'm going out for a drink with some friends and thought you might like to join us.'

'I'd love to. But I have to work. I'm sorry.'

'Oh, come on, you can work later.'

'No, really, I can't, I'm afraid. Another time, but not today.'

'Party pooper,' Theresa said.

Norah took a deep breath, trying not to show how tense she was. That would only lead to a whole spate of questions.

'If I finish early I'll come and find you,' she said. 'Promise. But I really must get back to my desk now.'

Theresa snorted.

'You don't even know where we're going.'

'Where are you going?'

'Starcode Red.'

'I know where that is. I'll come and join you, okay?'

'Promise?'

'Cross my heart. Give me half an hour.'

'All right. See you.'

Norah stood in the doorway for a moment, watching Theresa bounce down the stairs. Then she closed the door and locked it behind her.

Back to square one. She sat down, went through the phone call in her head again and took a deep breath.

This time he picked up immediately.

'Grimm.'

'Good evening, Dr Grimm. This is Norah Richter speaking. I—'

That was as far as she got. Grimm had hung up. Norah tried again. She let it ring for a long time, but there was no answer. She tried a third time, but got no further. She reactivated caller ID and redialled. It rang once, twice, three times—then he picked up.

'Grimm.'

'Dr Grimm, please don't hang up. I only want to—'

The engaged tone, then nothing. Norah shook her head in annoyance.

She tried yet again. Let it ring for a long time. Hung up. Dialled again.

'Where did you find my number?'

Norah drew breath, but didn't get a chance to reply.

'Leave me in peace,' he said.

'Dr Grimm, I don't understand why you're being so aggressive. Can't we talk to each other like adults?'

There was a moment's silence at the other end of the line.

'Don't you mess with me,' he said. 'I'll finish you off. I mean it.'

A click, the engaged tone, then silence. Norah stood there with her mouth open and slowly lowered her phone. The fear that until now had been curled up like an animal in its nest, hidden in the shadows of the flat, suddenly pulled itself up to its full height, tall and scraggy and dark.

Although she had almost no idea what was going on, one thing was clear: it had been a terrible mistake to get in touch with Grimm.

Norah's nagging headache was worse, the light suddenly too bright for her eyes. She switched off the lamp and sat down on the sofa for a moment, Grimm's voice in her ear, his words going round and round in her head. It had been no empty threat; the man meant what he said. Norah made up her mind to go to the police first thing the next day. She didn't like the idea at all; she was used to sorting out her affairs herself. But she didn't have much choice. Immediately she felt calmer. Around her, too, all was quiet; the house was asleep and Theresa was getting drunk in some bar. Norah could have done with a drink herself, but she was too upset to go out.

She lit the last cigarette of the day and night took hold of her, creeping into all her crevices. She looked at the dark shapes of the furniture looming before her in the blues and blacks of the darkness. Norah put out her cigarette and was about to get undressed and go to bed when she heard something at the door. A scratching. A scraping. She froze when she recognised the sound: it was a key being fumbled into a lock. Wasn't it? Then all was silent again, only the rush of blood in her ears and the thump of her heart. Had she imagined it? She'd changed the lock and locked the door. No one could get in. But someone was trying. Weren't they? Norah tiptoed down the passage to the front door and peered through the spyhole. It was dark on the stairs. There was only one way of being sure. Unlock the door. Open it. Have a look. Norah was debating the matter with herself when she heard sounds on the stairs again. This time, they were easier to place. Somebody had opened the door to the building and let it fall shut. Probably the mute neighbour from downstairs, because soon afterwards Norah heard another door being opened. Had he turned on the light on the stairs? Again Norah went to the door and peered through the spyhole, grimacing when the floorboards creaked underfoot.

Someone was there. But she only glimpsed a pair of dark eyes and a pale face before whoever it was vanished out of sight and down the stairs. Norah heard footsteps.

He—or she—was running away. That triggered something in Norah. She turned the key frantically in the lock and opened the door. The footsteps were downstairs now and Norah flew after them. She heard the front door being flung open, reached the ground floor before it fell shut again, flung it wide again and was out on the street. A truck roared past, drowning out any sounds. Norah looked left. Nothing. She looked right. Nothing. Left again. This time she saw something. Almost at the other end of the square. A narrow figure. But it wasn't running; it was walking away at a comfortable, leisurely pace. Norah could see it only from behind. Was it the figure from the stairs? Or just a passer-by? Norah looked about her again. A young couple were coming along on the right and a cyclist was emerging from the street opposite—but apart from them and the retreating figure, there was no one in sight.

When she looked again, the figure had vanished.

30

Norah woke to a beautiful, clear day, bright and vivid.

She'd felt better since deciding to report things. Whatever else happened, she'd head for the nearest police station as soon as she got off work.

On the stairs she met her mute neighbour on his way to the dustbins with a bunch of wilted flowers. He glared disparagingly when she said good morning and, as usual, didn't return her greeting. Who'd buy flowers for that old boot face?

Norah lit a cigarette and set off. Old ladies walking their fluffy little dogs, locals drinking their first espresso of the day at the coffee stall by the church, schoolchildren, students, ordinary life, unconcern, routine.

She left the church behind her and as she took a right, her eye was caught by a fluorescent pink poster, not much bigger than A4, pasted onto the wall of a house. Thick, black letters.

A PREOCCUPATION WITH DEATH
IS THE ROOT OF CULTURE

Death was everywhere in this fucking city, Norah thought—this beautiful, strangely unbearable city. She wondered whether the posters would turn out to be guerrilla advertising for a play or a film or some product or other; they were all over Vienna.

As she turned into the pedestrian precinct with a takeaway cappuccino in her hand, she thought for a moment of Dorotea Lechner.

That afternoon, when she left the office, the weather had turned. The crisp frost had given way to a chill damp. Norah walked briskly towards a police station she had found on Google, not far from her flat.

Hurrying along the street with other cold-looking people, she went over the conversation she'd had that afternoon with the property management office. The woman who'd taken Norah's call had told her that the landlord was away with his family in Florida. No, of course he didn't go in the flats without the tenants' permission. No, nobody else had keys to the flats. And no, she couldn't tell Norah where he kept his keys—what a question; no one had ever complained before. And why did she want to know all this? If something had gone missing, that was a matter for the police. Nothing missing? Well, then. It would be best if she rang again when the landlord was back from his holiday. Goodbye.

Norah saw the sign from a distance as soon as she rounded the corner: *POLICE*.

After a long wait, she was called into the office of a middle-aged female police officer who introduced herself as Kern. There was a hint of cold cigarette smoke in the small, sparsely furnished room. Norah sat down in the chair that was offered to her, wondering how much of her story she should tell.

The policewoman looked at her. She had a nice frank face.

'Would you like a glass of water? Cup of coffee?'

Norah shook her head.

'So, what can I do for you, Ms…Richter, isn't it?'

'Yes, Norah Richter,' Norah said, her voice firm. 'I'd like to report something.'

She gave Constable Kern the bare bones of what had happened: the woman in the pedestrian precinct and her subsequent death, her suspicion that someone had been in the flat, her encounter with Arthur Grimm and his threats to her. She also mentioned the figure she had seen at her door the previous evening. The longer Norah spoke, the less coherent the whole thing sounded, and when she came to the end, there was a long silence. Constable Kern looked at her pensively.

'Were there signs of a break-in?' she asked eventually.

'No,' said Norah, 'there weren't. I think whoever was in my flat must have had a key.'

Kern made a note.

'Can you give me a list of the things that have gone missing from your flat? Slowly, so I can write it down.'

Norah suppressed a sigh; she knew it would sound funny.

'A toothbrush and a pen.'

'Any items of value?'

Norah shook her head.

'No.'

'How long have you been living on Rilkeplatz?'

'Three weeks. I've just moved here from Berlin.'

The woman looked at her and jotted something down.

'Do you know your landlord?'

'Not personally. I found the flat through an agent.'

'Do you have your landlord's name?'

Norah gave it to her and told her about the phone call with his office. The woman made another note. Then there was silence.

'And the man you say threatened you. What was his name?'

'Arthur Grimm.'

'How do you know this Arthur Grimm?'

Norah frowned.

'As I said, I don't know him. I'd never heard the name until this strange woman mentioned him.'

'So why did you go looking for him?'

Norah reflected.

'Curiosity, I guess.'

Kern laid her head on one side.

'Interesting,' she said, drawing out the word.

'You make it sound as if you don't believe me.'

Kern gave Norah a narrow-lipped smile.

'I just find it interesting that you claim not to know Arthur Grimm.'

'I don't,' said Norah coldly.

'But you told me that you were recently in the building where he works and yesterday went to his home.'

'Yes, and I told you why. Listen, why don't you just take down my report?'

'Right,' Kern said, pulling a form out of a drawer. 'By the way, we'd have been in touch with you in the next few days anyway, Ms Richter.'

'Really?' Norah said in surprise. 'Why?'

Kern looked up from the form and fixed her intently.

'An Arthur Grimm was here yesterday to report you for harassment.'

31

She stared at her plate. The veal schnitzel was in the shape of North America; the vivid green broccoli florets looked like little trees. Even the boiled potatoes were artistically arranged, as if for an Instagram picture. Norah would have liked to make a cutting remark, but as there was no one to make it to, she swallowed it with her first mouthful of schnitzel. As usual, since the move to Vienna, she was eating alone, and it was beginning to get to her.

Mechanically spearing a broccoli floret and putting it in her mouth, she looked about her. She had asked for a table by the window so that she could see everything that was going on outside. At the table next to hers, two men of about sixty were drinking beer. One of them had his back to her; the other, a convivial-looking bloke with a bushy moustache, looked like a Herbert or an Erwin. Beneath his open leather jacket, a black T-shirt strained over a formidable belly. After a glance at Norah he said something she couldn't hear to the other man.

Was it sad to be eating out alone? Did people find her sad? Norah sniffed scornfully and went back to cutting her schnitzel into little pieces.

Since when have you cared what other people think about you?

Coming out of the police station in a fury, she had put her differences aside and immediately rung Sandra who, apart from being her friend, was also her lawyer. But Sandra hadn't answered the phone, so Norah had left a short message on her voicemail. No, she wasn't taking drugs again. Yes, she had forgiven her the outrageous insinuation. And she needed her help. Could she ring her back when she had a moment?

Later that day, Sandra had finally got in touch, but the call was unsatisfactory. Sandra was in a hurry—one of the kids was ill—so Norah had to be brief. Sandra advised her to keep calm and on no account have anything else to do with the man who had reported her. It would sort itself out. She promised to ring again soon when she had more time.

Norah sighed. She stared at the day's specials that were chalked up on a blackboard, wondering whether to order pudding. She was already full, but it would be nice to stay a bit longer in the coffeehouse. The earlier she got the bill and left, the sooner she'd have to return to the flat, and right now—even with the new lock—there was almost nowhere Norah felt less at ease. Glancing at her phone, she saw that she had a missed call from Coco and felt a pang of guilt, but when she tried to call her back, Coco didn't pick up. Maybe she'd gone to the cinema. No bad thing, Norah thought. She wasn't in the mood for a painful conversation just now. Especially as Coco was always harping on about her ex—a topic Norah was anxious to put behind her.

As she left the cafe through the small revolving door, cold wind lashed out at her. She turned up the collar of her coat and wrapped her arms around her body. Norah knew all about cold weather from Berlin but that didn't stop it from getting her down every year. She thought about taking a taxi, but it wasn't far to her flat and she could do with some fresh air and exercise. A tram passed her—one of the old, pretty ones.

Then, just as she was overtaking a group of tourists on their way to the theatre or opera, she saw a dark-haired man of about her age coming towards her. She was about to step out onto a zebra crossing when the lights began to flash—the signal that they would soon turn red. In flat shoes, she'd have run, but it wasn't a good idea in high-heeled boots. She plunged her hands into her pockets and waited. The first cars were starting up.

'My God,' someone said beside her. 'Valerie?'

Norah's head spun round and she saw the dark-haired man staring at her out of green eyes. She blinked in confusion, then realised that he was talking to her.

'What did you call me?'

The man raised his eyebrows in surprise; his smile vanished.

'Sorry,' he said. 'I thought you were someone else.'

He was gone before Norah had time to react. The lights turned green. People surged past her across the road—the tourists, a cyclist, a bald old man with a walking stick, a girl on an electric skateboard which glowed eerily as it vanished into the darkness. By the time Norah had recovered, the lights had changed again.

32

With its red velvet seats and white-and-gold stucco ceiling, the auditorium was like that of a nice old cinema, only much larger and with a big stage where the screen would have been. Dust danced in the beam from the spotlight. The man at the front of the stage looked exactly the way you'd imagine a magician. He wore a tailcoat and a top hat that almost covered his dark hair, and he had unnaturally pale skin and big dramatic eyes under deep-black eyebrows. The overall effect was something like a silent movie star in one of the films her mother was fond of watching. Especially the eyes. His voice was loud and booming, almost frighteningly so. Norah swallowed. She was ten years old, her favourite colour was blue, and she liked things that were almost frightening.

The other children were excited too. They were, of course, familiar with rabbits being conjured out of hats and gold coins being produced from behind ears; they'd seen magic shows on the telly. But to see it all up close—and in a proper grown-up theatre—was different. Norah's fingers were sticky with candyfloss, even after she'd wiped them on her trousers. *Edible clouds*, Valerie had said. *Beautifully sweet and sticky.*

Norah loved conjuring shows and had been pleased to get an invitation when they were handed round in the lunchbreak on Monday. Valerie's birthday parties were always special. Fair booths in the garden, bouncy castles, go-karts.

'For my next trick,' the magician said in a booming voice, 'I need a volunteer.'

Norah was still dithering when Valerie's arm shot up beside her.

The magician called Valerie onto the stage and she set off confidently. A warm feeling flooded Norah as she watched her best friend walk up the shallow steps—the same feeling she had when she got an A at school. She was as proud of Valerie's courage as if it were her own.

'What's your name?' the magician asked her with the hint of a bow.

The girls in the audience giggled.

'Norah,' said Valerie.

The children laughed. Valerie was so cheeky she even dared lie to a grown-up.

'Hello, Norah,' the magician said and turned to face the audience again.

The real Norah bit her lip.

'Is there anyone in the audience who would miss this young lady if she went away?' the magician asked.

Arms strained in the air. Valerie grinned.

'All right then,' said the magician. 'I am going to make Norah disappear.'

He looked at his volunteer and she returned his gaze.

'But to all those who put up their hands just now—there's no need to worry; I will bring the young lady back safe and sound from the realm of shadows.'

He raised his arms with a flourish and a cage appeared. Norah hadn't been quick enough to see where it came from—then she realised there was some kind of hoist under the stage.

'My dear,' the magician said, turning to Valerie, 'this is for you.'

He had conjured a torch from somewhere and pressed it into her hand.

'This will guide you into the realm of shadows.'

Norah watched, rapt.

'But whatever happens,' he added—and there was a sudden tone of urgency in his voice, which Norah hadn't noticed before—'do not let go of the torch. Switch it on when I tell you to and be very, very careful not to turn it off. Do you understand?'

Norah saw her best friend nod.

'May I?' the magician asked, and he took Valerie's hand and led her to the cage.

When she was inside, he closed the door with a bolt and padlock and took a step back.

Valerie stood in the middle of the cage, quite calm, her little figure silhouetted against the light. Norah's heart was pounding as if it were trying to leap right out of her chest. She didn't know why. She knew it wasn't real magic; she was old enough to understand that magicians work with tricks and trapdoors and sleights of hand. And yet.

'My dear,' the magician said. 'Do you think you are strong enough to break out of that cage?'

Valerie shrugged.

'Give it a try,' said the magician.

Valerie stepped up to the edge of the cage and tried to squeeze her dainty body through the bars, but they were too close together. She shook at the door which the magician had secured with a padlock, but the cage remained locked.

'I ask you again,' the magician said. 'Do you think you are strong enough to break out of that cage?'

'No,' said Valerie.

'All right then.'

He turned to the audience.

'I am going to make Norah disappear. For that, ladies and gentlemen, I need darkness and *absolute silence and concentration*. Without those things, there is a possibility that I won't be able to bring back our little friend.'

In front of Norah, in the next-to-last row, Ruth gasped audibly.

'And you, my dear, I would now ask you to switch on your torch and point it at the audience. Please remember not to turn it off.'

Valerie nodded and switched on the torch.

'Now then,' said the magician.

He closed his eyes as if he were going into a kind of trance. Then, without opening them, he took a few steps away from the cage and raised his arms. The lights went out. Some of the children made sounds of surprise, then giggled loudly to show they weren't afraid. Then there was silence again, as they remembered the magician's instructions. Valerie traced circles in the air with the torch—big circles and small ones. Norah saw her friend's eyes sparkling in the darkness; she was clearly enjoying herself. Norah even thought she saw her smile and, instinctively, she smiled back.

The moment dragged on. Valerie started to trace figures of eight with the torch in the dark—and then suddenly, the torch went out. Norah heard sharp in-drawings of breath all around her. Darkness. Complete darkness. Norah's heart beat faster and faster and she blinked frantically as if to force her eyes to accustom themselves to the dark. She sensed the other children's excitement, close to flipping over into fear. Valerie—where was Valerie?

'Behind you,' said Valerie and Norah felt her breath warm on her neck.

Norah started awake.

She blinked into the blackness. Shapes in the dark. Removal boxes, Vienna, her new flat, her new life—of course. A glance at her watch. Just gone two. She got up with a sigh, went into the kitchen and drank a few mouthfuls of water straight from the tap. She was cold, barefoot, dressed in only a baggy sweatshirt. The heating was on, but it wasn't properly warm. Norah went back to the bedroom, sat down on the bed and wrapped the quilt over her shoulders.

Her thoughts wandered to Valerie. She had never told Norah how the trick had worked. *Because I promised*, she said. *Because you like tormenting me,* Norah had always replied, only half-jokingly. And it was true that for a long time she couldn't stop wondering how the magician had done it. She'd always loved any kind of puzzle or mystery, going at them obsessively until she cracked them—and it drove her crazy that Valerie knew the solution and she didn't. Had there been a tunnel? A secret door? But how could Valerie have moved so quickly?

The memory was still fresh. After Valerie's sudden reappearance behind Norah, everything had happened quickly. The lights went up again on the empty cage; there were cries of surprise from the other children. And before Norah could say anything, Valerie was walking down the central aisle and onto the stage where the magician welcomed her back with a little speech about teleporting and asked her how she'd got on in the realm of shadows.

Norah hadn't thought about that afternoon for a long time. Years later she discovered not only that the magician was a fairly famous conjuror who usually did adult shows, but also that he was Valerie's uncle. When Valerie refused, even as a teenager, to tell Norah how he'd done it, Norah began to realise that she probably didn't know herself. But all her life, Valerie had remained obsessed with disappearing and was forever saying that she'd vanish into thin air some day. *You can't leave me*, Norah would say. *What would I do without you? I'd be lost.*

It was true. Valerie had been her best friend since kindergarten and she'd never again had anyone who had made her feel understood in quite that way. Yes, all right, Sandra was a good friend. But it wasn't the same. Typical Valerie phrases popped into Norah's mind. *If you run away, I'll come with you*—after a bad fight between Norah and her mum. *I'll kill him for you if you like*—after Norah had caught her first boyfriend Nico snogging that bitch from another class. And, over and over again: *Promise we'll be friends forever. Swear to me.*

And Norah had sworn.

Was it the age they were? Could unconditional friendship exist only between children and teenagers who were still free from the demands of everyday life, not yet worn down by the constant struggle for compromise?

Norah went into the kitchen and climbed onto a chair to get down the book she'd hidden in the cupboard. She ran her fingers over the cover of this book that had once been Valerie's and the image of a frozen lake at night flashed into her mind. The scene of all Norah's nightmares. Her throat tightened. Her eyes slid over the big black letters of the title.

How to Disappear Completely.

33

Norah stood at the kitchen window smoking. At least there was no one to complain about the cigarette smoke on her breath—that was something. She breathed a smoke ring into the evening sky, and then a second to slide through the first. She could still do it. Down below, walking past, she saw Marie, the young woman with the sad eyes who worked in the newsagent's. Shoulders drooping, eyes on the ground. Norah choked up when she saw her. Then Marie disappeared from view and Norah's thoughts drifted to the previous day. Why had she been so disturbed by the man at the zebra crossing? She kept seeing his face, hearing his voice. *My God, Valerie!*

Norah and Valerie hadn't looked anything like one another, but that hadn't stopped them from being like sisters. Even today, after all that had happened, Norah still felt it fair to say that no one had loved her as unconditionally as Valerie.

She recalled the conversation she'd had with Theresa the other day. It's true, she thought, I attract women I can't help. And it all began with Valerie; she was the first. The pain was so sudden and so keen that Norah found herself gasping for breath.

She must stop thinking about the past. The man at the crossing had made a mistake, that was all. Such things happened. How many Valeries must there be in Vienna? Hundreds? Thousands? One of them looked like Norah. So what? She must calm down. She must stop dwelling on it.

And she needed a drink.

When she woke the next morning, Norah was cuddled up to Alex, her belly against his back. It was lovely, feeling his warmth in the chilly bedroom.

But like a silk dress that is shrugged to the floor, the dream slid off her and she realised that something was wrong. Startled, she moved away with a jolt from the warm body in her bed and opened her eyes. A shock of dark hair, a bare back, pale skin, a scattering of moles. It all came back to her. She'd gone to the fridge the evening before for a bottle of wine and found it empty—then stormed out of the house and into the first bar she'd come to. She remembered the barman with the lovely dark eyes, apparently from his Japanese mum, and the gorgeous Viennese accent (from his dad).

What was the matter with her? Why was she suddenly acting like a ditsy student?

You're trying to get Alex out of your system. And you're failing miserably.

Norah rolled onto her back, trying not to think of Alex, and faked sleep until the man had gone.

Then she went into the bathroom to have a shower. In the mirror she looked at the new tattoo, which was now almost completely healed and only slightly itchy. She suddenly remembered the guy asking her about it in bed. *Is it a swallow?* She had only shaken her head.

Over a cappuccino and croissant in the corner bistro, Norah skimmed the newspaper. In the culture section she found a brief obituary of the actor Dorotea Lechner. A photo showed her—presumably some time ago—on the stage of a small independent theatre. An actor who fell on hard times and took to drinking, then ended up having to beg to make ends meet. The story Norah had been chasing was so much sadder than she had expected. And so much shorter.

Somehow she got through the day, doing her best not to think of anything but work. In the late afternoon, she had an appointment with a local politician who had set himself the task of getting as many homeless people off the streets as possible. Norah interviewed him in his office, then headed for the nearest tram stop. It was growing dark and she had to pause for a moment to get her bearings. She was in a part of Vienna where she'd never been before. To her left was a busy road and to her right a park, which now, in February, was more grey than green. Behind the trees a big wheel rose up into the sky. The Prater!

Curious, Norah set off across the grass and was soon standing at the foot of the big wheel. She stared up at the vast construction, imagining the cars full of shrieking teenagers and soppy couples. Then her eyes strayed over the surrounding area. Stretched out before her with its booths and rides was the fairground—the *Wurstlprater* to those in the know, although it was what most tourists meant when they talked about 'the Prater'. Norah wandered off down the twisty lanes between the booths. Rides, food stalls, Test-Your-Strength, souvenirs.

A bit of a walk would do her good, help her to unwind. For days she'd been able to think of nothing but Grimm. When she'd heard that he had made it to the police station before her, she'd been desperate; even Sandra couldn't calm her down.

I'll finish you off. I mean it.

Arthur Grimm was not the kind of man to play games, Norah was sure of that. He was deadly serious. The only question was *why*? Why was he so aggressive towards her? What did he think he knew about her? And what about Dorotea Lechner? Had she and Grimm known each other? Had he maybe…? No, Norah told herself sharply. Lechner's death was an accident. The police had said so. It was a fact. And Norah was a journalist, not a conspiracy theorist. She stuck to facts.

Perhaps none of it had anything to do with her. Perhaps Grimm was mentally disturbed, paranoid. But she didn't believe it. She was sure he had some reason for behaving towards her the way he had. What really got to her, though, was the feeling that she was staring at the solution without seeing it—unable to see the wood for the trees.

To her left was the first roller coaster, its red rails bright against the blue winter sky. To her right was the ghost train. Norah smiled—she'd always loved ghost trains as a child. Next to a sign saying *Tickets* was a picture of the grim reaper and Norah was reminded of the tarot card she had found in the Imperial. She went on her way.

Shooting gallery, bumper cars, swings. *Postcards with your photo.*

Norah turned around. So this was the Prater. She headed slowly for the exit. Back on the street, she hailed a taxi. The Prater, with its big wheel and all the booths and ghosts and shadows disappeared behind her, but she didn't look back.

Twenty minutes later, she was home.

Norah unlocked the front door and set off up the stairs. Halfway up, though, she stopped and turned back—she'd forgotten to check the post.

In her letterbox was a photo of Valerie.

34

She woke knowing it was the middle of the night; some primitive instinct told her that she was at the darkest point in the day's cycle.

She didn't open her eyes, didn't move. Pretending was something she had learnt at an early age. If you held yourself in the right way and acted confident, you really did feel better in the end. If you were caring and friendly towards someone, you sooner or later felt genuinely fond of them. And if you pretended to sleep—lay calm and relaxed, and concentrated on breathing slowly—you often really did fall asleep.

Norah lay there, thinking of Valerie. She tried not to think of anything, but the events of the last few days pushed their way to the surface, and scenes and faces flashed into her mind—a series of rapidly cut shots, like footage of a fairground ride spinning faster and faster, slinging its passengers out of its orbit, their arms and legs flying.

She vaguely remembered dreaming. Something about Valerie, she thought. Wasn't it? She tried to focus on the cosy warmth under the covers, on the reassuring knowledge that she'd had the lock changed— that she was safe in her own flat again. She strained her senses for some sign of Theresa, asleep in the flat above. But was she even at home? All evening, Norah had missed the familiar creak of the old floorboards overhead as Theresa moved from room to room. She was probably out again. Norah wondered what she was doing.

And by then she knew she wasn't going to get back to sleep. Not this time.

She turned on the light and screwed up her eyes. The photo lay on the floor by her bed, blurred, faded and yellowing. A smiling teenager. Summer. Shorts and a singlet. Norah had forgotten all about the photo. Who had sent it to her? Why was Valerie suddenly all over the place? Theresa, who looked so startlingly similar. The stranger at the crossing who had called Norah by her name. The old dreams. And now the photo.

Barefoot and dressed in only briefs and a sweatshirt, Norah went into the kitchen for a glass of water and began to shiver almost immediately; she'd switched the heating off when she went to bed. She fetched her dressing gown, which had turned up the day before in one of the removal boxes, put it on, and opened the kitchen window. Breathing in the fresh night air, she had a kind of inspiration.

She grabbed her phone and began to write.

Was that you?

She raised her eyes to the window and looked out. Someone had put junk out on the pavement for collection: a bike, a bed frame, an old armchair, a guitar. Norah found herself thinking of Valerie again, but the dream that had woken her remained elusive, just out of reach.

Norah returned to her phone and was surprised to see three bouncing dots on the screen telling her she had a reply.

Was what me? she read.

Was it you sent me that?

This time she had to wait longer for a response, but soon the bouncing dots told her that at the other end—wherever that might be—someone was typing.

The photo? Yes.

Interesting. The fact itself, for one thing—that this someone had sent her the photo of Valerie. But also the disarming frankness of the confession.

Why? she asked.

Because I wanted you to remember.

Resisting the urge to reach for her cigarettes, Norah closed the window.

Who are you? Where did you get the photo? she typed.

And then, because she could bear it no longer:

What do you know about Valerie?

At first there was no response. Then the dots bounced up and down on the screen again.

May I ask you a question?

Norah thought for a moment. Then she typed:

Go ahead.

She waited, tensely curious. Nothing. After staring at her phone for several minutes, she put it down—and at that moment, the next text arrived.

Are you sure it was suicide?

She almost dropped her phone. She closed her eyes and waited until she felt a little calmer. Then she opened them again.

What do you mean? she asked.

But staring at her phone brought no reply. Thinking hard, she sat down at her desk and got out the file with the printouts of all the information that Werner had compiled on Arthur Grimm. The moment she held it in her hand, she knew that it was the contents of this file that had given her subconscious no peace; over and over, even in her sleep, her brain had opened this file and read it through and pondered it, until at last it had found what it was looking for.

Norah studied everything again, making an effort to read with an open mind—not to skim the names and dates and places or the bits she knew by heart, but to focus on every word.

Arthur Grimm. Born in Frankfurt on 19 December 1974, the only child of Christa and Jochen Grimm. Primary school. Secondary school. Leaving examinations. Applied to various acting schools but was rejected. Military service. Began a degree in mechanical engineering. Switched to pure engineering. Graduation. A series of internships during and after university and eventually a first permanent position in Munich.

Hang on. There was something there. Like a little barb that she snagged on. What had she just read? The list of some of the essays Grimm had written at university…the names of the firms where he'd worked as an intern…his dissertation at Wilkau Engineering…

That was it. Grimm had written his dissertation in cooperation with Wilkau Engineering. Where had she heard that name before? Norah sat quite still, as if afraid that a sudden movement might frighten off the thought that was taking shape in her mind.

Yes, something was stirring. The name rang a bell. Had she read it in the papers? Had the firm been involved in a scandal? Or had she known someone who worked there? No, she'd remember that. Norah closed her eyes and decided to call up her own thoughts on the subject before resorting to Google and drowning all the information in her head with a flood of search results. But she got nowhere and eventually gave up.

Wilkau Engineering. The only Google entry of any relevance was the company's homepage. No scandal, no flotation, no mass layoff. Nothing like that.

Norah clicked on the link to the website. Wilkau. *Your Engineering Service Provider.* Tedium in blue, grey and white. Competent-looking men and women bending over plans, pencils in hand, or smiling inanely into the camera. Dozens of clickable keywords, providing information about the services offered by the company, about completed and ongoing projects. Not knowing where to start, Norah clicked on *Contact*, leant back in her chair and ran her hand over her face. As she lowered it onto the desk, she felt it tremble.

Wilkau Engineering. Of course. Angélique Wilkau. Little Angie from their year, who always got travelsick on school trips and was once too slow with the sick bag, earning herself an unflattering nickname and the privilege of being excused from all further outings. Angélique Wilkau who played golf as a child, but later developed into a teenager so rebellious that she would have been kicked out of school if her father's company hadn't donated a large sum of money for a new sports hall. (Or so rumour had it.) Angie Wilkau, whose mum had hair like a shampoo model and whose dad sometimes embarrassed her by picking her up from school in a station wagon emblazoned with the company logo.

Norah opened the file again. She found the page she needed in Grimm's biography and ran her finger down it until she came to the entry she was looking for.

Bullseye.

Arthur Grimm had worked at Wilkau Engineering while he was writing his dissertation. Less than a quarter of an hour from the town where Norah and Angie and Valerie had gone to school.

It took a few seconds for that to sink in. Grimm had been very close by. For an entire year. Norah squeezed her lips together when she compared the dates. It had been an awful year, perhaps the very worst. It was the year Valerie died. On February 11.

REVENGE

I was eleven when I first understood what it means to thirst for revenge, a sensation so physical that it really does resemble thirst. I was a plump child with arms and legs as pale and soft as white blancmange and I was often bullied at school—certainly until the summer I had a growth spurt.

One day, for reasons I have forgotten, my elder brother flushed my goldfish down the toilet. (It was called Silver after Long John Silver in *Treasure Island*, which at the time I thought a very clever name for a goldfish.) I was devastated and cried for two days. On the third day, I pilfered the snail poison from the shed and killed my brother's cat. My parents suspected the neighbours. My brother and I knew better.

There is, to my mind, only one way of dealing with injustice. If someone pushes you, you push them back twice as hard. That's something we learn in kindergarten—or not at all.

I am disappointed, then, that she went to the police. Is it all over before it has even begun? Did I misjudge her?

People have robbed me, insulted me, spat at me. When I was nineteen, someone broke my nose and two of my ribs. I never went running to the police. Diogenes the Cynic said that the best way of avenging yourself on your enemies is to make yourself better than them. God, how dull. I'd have expected something more thrilling from a man who scandalised the ancient Greek establishment by living on the streets and wanking in public.

I have always been in favour of revenge. I think it a mistake to demonise something so deeply human. When we avenge ourselves, we cast off the role of passive victim and take action. That feels good, of course. Revenge is a fine and splendid thing; not for nothing is it one of the oldest dramatic motifs. It is universal; we understand it instinctively.

And yet we rarely give in to it. The Americans are better at that than we are; they took to the streets to celebrate bin Laden's assassination—and quite right too.

I refuse to believe she is giving up. I must be patient, I must have trust. I am so tense I haven't slept for two nights. Don't disappoint me, I keep thinking. Don't disappoint me.

35

Norah sat at her desk for a long time, trying to put her thoughts in order; she was still sitting there when the sun rose. As soon as it was late enough for her to get hold of someone at the office, she rang her boss and told him she had the flu and thought she'd better work from home, so as not to pass it onto anyone. Then—presumably some form of displacement activity—she really did get on with some work, typing up and going through the previous day's interview with the local politician. It was only when she stopped for a break that the thought hit her and she saw clearly the shape of the suspicion that had wormed its way under her skin and into her organs.

A woman, whom Norah now knew to be an actor, had told her that she would kill a man named Arthur Grimm on the anniversary of Valerie's death. Soon afterwards, that woman had died. And now Norah had discovered a link between herself and Arthur Grimm.

Valerie.

Always Valerie.

Norah shivered and reached automatically for her cigarettes, amazed at how quickly she'd fallen back into old habits since leaving Alex. Even after all those years of not smoking, every bad feeling had her groping for the fags. But the packet was empty.

She leant back in her chair. Don't jump to conclusions. Don't let your emotions get the better of you. Try to think rationally.

Was it possible?

Norah's hand jerked towards the cigarette packet again, as if it might have miraculously refilled itself in the intervening seconds. As she pulled her hand back, she felt the new knowledge take possession of her like a virus.

She got up and had a shower. Then she scrubbed the bitter taste from her teeth, tied up her hair and slipped into jeans and a jumper. That was better. She made the bed and flung open all the windows in the flat, leaving them open until she began to feel the cold. Much better. She sat back down at her desk, found an online delivery service and ordered some Vietnamese food. She smoked too much and ate too little, she knew she did. But she mustn't let herself go just because Alex and Sandra were no longer there to stop her. She must keep her strength up.

A ring at the door made her jump. She looked through the spyhole, almost expecting to see Theresa, but there was nobody there. She picked up the intercom receiver and pressed it to her ear.

'Hello?'

'Delivery for Norah Richter,' said a young male voice.

It couldn't be the food; they weren't *that* fast. More furniture? But that wasn't supposed to come until next week.

'Hello?' the voice said again, sounding impatient.

'Hang on, please.'

Norah ran to the window and looked down onto the street. A UPS van was parked outside the building. Back in the hall, she buzzed open the door. Footsteps clattered up the stairs and a shock of reddish-brown hair appeared behind a huge gift basket wrapped in rustling cellophane.

'Good morning.'

'Morning,' said Norah, watching the postman set the basket at her feet.

'If you'd sign here, please,' he said, thrusting a small digital gadget at her. He looked so young that Norah felt like asking whether he shouldn't be at school, but she bit back the question and signed. She always felt sorry for the parcel postmen she saw scooting around all over the place—paid a pittance and forever in a rush.

'Bit like you,' Sandra had once said, when Norah mentioned this to her, and Norah had laughed.

The man had already dashed off to his next job. Norah heard the downstairs door close behind him and eyed the delivery with suspicion. She couldn't see a card anywhere—perhaps it had slipped into the cellophane under the basket. Cautiously, she began to take off the rustling wrappings. What an eco-sin, Alex would have said—he was stricter about such things than she was. She looked more closely. It was a huge basket of fruit. Apples, pears, green and red grapes... Had Tanja sent it to apologise for her behaviour the other day? There didn't seem to be anything weird or dangerous about it, so Norah picked it up, carried it into the flat and put it on the living-room table. Then she stuffed the cellophane into a bin liner in the kitchen and was on her way back to the living room when the doorbell shrilled again.

This time it was the food, and as Norah unpacked it, she suddenly realised how hungry she was. She ate the two summer rolls straight out of the polystyrene box without even sitting down. Then she tipped the noodles into a dish and got out a fork. Today she would eat at the dining table like a civilised person, not at her laptop again—she'd got into bad habits these last weeks.

In the doorway she stopped.

The sun shining in at the window threw a broad strip of light across the living room onto the table, making the basket of fruit look like a Dutch still life. But it wasn't the painterly beauty that captured Norah's attention; something had been hiding in among the apples and pears and grapes. Scuttling across the table, heavily antlered, their black bodies almost surreally large, were three stag beetles.

36

'm on the moon. That was her first thought when she opened her eyes and blinked in the sunlight.

Or Mars.

She couldn't speak, could only stare as she took first tentative steps on the slippery ground, conscious that there was usually nothing here but water. Gallons and gallons of water.

'I know,' said Valerie, as if Norah *had* said something, or as if she'd read her thoughts. 'Amazing, isn't it?'

Norah nodded.

All her life, the reservoir had been a vast lake. She had picnicked on its shores as a child, camped by it with her friends when she was old enough, swum in its clear waters more often than she could remember. Now, since being drained for repair works a few weeks before, it was transformed. The reservoir bed was dry—an apparently endless waste of pebbles and mud in every shade of brown and grey. Norah turned and looked up at the dam, dizzy at the sheer height of the wall and the thought of the unimaginable quantities of water that usually filled the lake.

They walked along the lakebed, as if it were the most normal thing in the world.

'I kind of imagined it cooler than this,' said Bastian, and Norah didn't have to look at Valerie to know that she was glaring at him with a mixture of scorn and pity. Everyone knew that Valerie only put up with Bastian because he was three years older than her and willing to ferry her around in his old VW Polo. He wasn't her boyfriend; he was her chauffeur. Today, as usual, he'd done her bidding, falling in with her idea of blindfolding Norah and driving her to a place that she would—*I swear to you, Norah*—absolutely love.

They wandered around the drained reservoir for most of that hot spring afternoon, completely undisturbed after abandoning Bastian at the dam with his cigarettes and his stupid remarks. They ran off in different directions, then came together again, screeching and giggling; they spun wildly round and round and collapsed on the dry mud. They told each other they were on the bottom of a vast lake beneath a huge mass of water, but could still breathe and talk because they were mermaids—though not the kind who sacrificed their tails just because they'd seen a young man they liked the look of. No way.

'No way,' said Norah. 'Not that kind.'

Later that day, they lay in Valerie's back garden on the bumble bees' approach path, surrounded by buttercups and daisies, and Norah watched a ladybird crawl over her fingers as if over hilly countryside.

Suddenly Valerie said, 'I think I'm in love with Milo.'

Norah peered at the ladybird—the shiny red shell, the neat black dots that looked as if they'd been painted with a tiny brush.

'Give me your hand,' she said.

'Did you hear what I said?' Valerie asked. She stretched out her hand and the ladybird climbed onto it.

'Of course,' Norah replied. 'You fancy Milo. Who doesn't?'

The ladybird crossed the back of Valerie's hand with astonishing speed. She turned her hand and let it move over her palm, back and forth over her lifeline.

'I didn't say I fancy him; I said I'm in love with him.'

The ladybird had reached the tip of Valerie's index finger and took off, maybe to find more girls lying on the grass, drinking warm iced tea and talking about boys, despite their vows to stay mermaids forever. They watched it go. It looked as if it were wearing a red cape, slit in the middle.

'No,' said Norah, 'that's not what you said.'

'What?'

'You said: "I *think* I'm in love with Milo."'

Valerie rolled her eyes.

'I *am* in love with him.'

Norah laughed.

'What's so funny?'

'I was just thinking of Bastian,' she said. 'He'll be devastated.'

And now Valerie laughed too and the warm spring day was so light and carefree, so beautifully insubstantial that Norah couldn't later remember how it ended. Had Valerie's dad got the barbecue going? Had they gone back to Norah's and watched TV with her mum while Valerie painted Norah's nails? Had they gone out on their bikes?

Norah hadn't thought of that afternoon for ages; she and Valerie had shared so many happy moments. If some people attracted good luck and others bad, some strange situations and others cats and weirdos, Valerie—so it had seemed to Norah—attracted these almost magical moments.

Now, though, it came back to her as she hovered by the phone, trying to muster the courage to ring Valerie's mother Monika. She had always liked Monika, often finding her easier to get on with than her own mother. She was a real mumsy type who cooked and baked and loved and scolded, always worrying when Valerie didn't get home on time, while Norah's young mum, with her wacky hairdo and laid-back nature, was more like a big sister—something that Norah didn't find nearly as cool as she pretended to her admiring friends. Now her mum had been dead for years and she hadn't seen Monika for half an eternity. *Monika.* It was at Valerie's funeral that she'd told Norah to call her that. Norah had suddenly felt very grown up—and immediately realised that it wasn't a good feeling.

Her gaze fell on the dining table and she couldn't keep from shuddering at the thought of those big brown-black beetles scuttling over the wood on their sturdy legs. No mere insects, those beetles; they'd been living warnings. Norah thought of Baroque vanitas, still lifes where the fine things of life—fruit and bread, wealth and pomp—are displayed in all their glory, but invariably subverted by symbols of death, decay and transience: moths, rats, snails, hourglasses, skulls. And—a particularly popular motif—stag beetles.

She had caught the beetles and set them free on a patch of grass outside the house. Then she'd thrown away the fruit. But the feeling of menace had remained.

Norah took a deep breath and reached for the phone. She had to know. Had to hear it from someone who was around at the time. Was it absolutely certain that Valerie had taken her life? Absolutely, indisputably, definitively certain? *Because if not,* she thought, *maybe I know what's going on here.* Maybe someone's trying to tell me something. Trying to tell me that Valerie didn't commit suicide, but was murdered. Maybe someone out there knows the murderer and is trying to put me on his trail, hoping I'll find him and punish him. Maybe they don't have the courage to do it themselves. Maybe they know that I'm one of the people who loved Valerie the most.

Maybe they know that I'm the only person who loved Valerie who is capable of killing her murderer.

37

Norah couldn't have said how she'd expected Monika to react, but she hadn't reckoned with such a frenzy of joy.

'How are you?' Monika asked, when she'd calmed down a little.

Norah smiled. Her mother had always annoyed her by speaking rather contemptuously of Monika as *the hen*, but now, listening to Monika's clucking laughter, it struck Norah that there really was something henlike about her.

'Tell me what you're up to.'

'I'm doing all right,' Norah said, because she had to say something.

'Where are you living? Still in Berlin?'

'Vienna.'

'Wow.'

'Yes, it's a great city.'

'And?' Monika asked.

'And what?'

'Seeing anyone?'

Norah hesitated. *She* was the one who'd left Alex, not the other way round. So why was it still so painful?

'Not right now,' she said.

'Nothing to say you have to. It'll happen when it's meant to.'

Norah usually rolled her eyes when someone felt obliged to offer her comfort like this, as if singledom were a terminal illness. But she couldn't bring herself to be angry with Monika.

'Any other news?' Monika asked.

Norah searched frantically for a satisfactory answer, but she was too slow and Monika sighed.

'You girls,' she said. 'You always were closed books, the pair of you.'

Norah suddenly felt cold, as if a cloud had passed over the sun. Guilt rose in her gorge like heartburn. Even if she'd tried, she wouldn't have been able to get a word out. She hadn't expected Monika to mention her daughter unprompted. Not now—not today, after years of talking to Norah on the phone without a word about Valerie.

'Do you know what Valerie's dad used to call her?'

Norah shook her head. She tried to make a negative noise in her throat, but it came out as a croak.

'The black box,' Monika said.

Norah said nothing.

'Do you get it? A black box. All kinds of stuff goes into it. You know there's an awful lot in there—probably more than you can imagine. But nothing ever comes out.'

Norah didn't know what to say.

'You were both like that,' Monika went on. 'Maybe it's normal, maybe all teenagers are like that and I've just forgotten that I was the same.'

She was silent, then gave a short laugh, as if to take some of the gravity from her words.

'Not with each other,' Norah said softly.

'What?'

'We weren't like that with each other.'

'I know,' Monika said. 'I know.'

Norah heard the static in the line as the silence spread.

'Do you have someone you can talk to?' Monika asked suddenly.

'What do you mean?'

'What I just said.'

'Of course I talk to people.'

'Really? Properly?'

Norah said nothing.

'We need people,' Monika said. 'I know it sounds banal, but it's true. We can't live only for ourselves. We have to—'

She broke off and Norah wondered whether this was something she'd learnt during the therapy she underwent after Valerie's death.

'We have to learn to open up to others,' Monika went on. 'We have to learn to accept help. Do you understand?'

Norah croaked agreement. The turn of conversation was making her feel physically unwell and she seized the first opportunity to end the call without being impolite. Monika was well and Norah wanted things to stay that way. She'd get the information she needed somewhere else.

The call to Valerie's brother was rather different. Norah hadn't been in touch with him for years and knew only that he lived in Leipzig and ran his own IT company. But a quick Google search found his office number and, amazingly enough, she was put straight through to him. He sounded awkward when he took the call, but that was hardly surprising; there he was at work, expected to be serious, and suddenly his kid sister's best friend was at the other end of the line—a girl he used to smoke weed with, a girl who once slapped him round the face when he misread the signs and tried to kiss her.

'Hi,' said Sven. 'Hello. Good afternoon.'

Sven was a nice guy and Norah blushed when she remembered what a dance she and his sister had led him when they were fifteen and he only a year and a half older. She would have liked to have a bit of a natter with him—but her reason for calling was too serious for that. She forced herself to ask him the question she'd failed to ask Monika and soon realised that Sven was by far the better person to talk to.

He thought about his sister a lot, he said, of course he did, especially when the anniversary of her death came round. But Norah must stop reproaching herself. No one was to blame. His little sister had killed herself. They had to live with that.

Afterwards, they talked about this and that. Sven told Norah he was married and had two kids at primary school. They chatted for ten minutes or so and ended the call with warm goodbyes.

Norah put on the kettle and waited for the water to come to the boil. Then she made tea and left it to brew. Then she poured the tea down the sink. She took a tumbler from the cupboard—the wine glasses were still lying dormant in one of the removal boxes—filled it to the brim, and began to drink. Another memory was washed to the surface, a big memory, as spongy and misshapen as a drowned body.

She was at home, a few days after Valerie's death, at the glass dining table in the living room, under those ghastly Kandinsky prints. Next to her, her mum, with her wacky red hairdo, and opposite them, two police officers, well meaning but plainly bored. They'd heard that she was the deceased's best friend, they said, and Norah nodded.

Had she noticed anything?

She didn't answer. Not because she intended any disrespect, but because the question made no sense to her; she was so confused since hearing the news. Someone had given her a sedative, but that had only made things worse—added an extra layer of befuddlement.

Had Valerie seemed depressed?

Norah managed a nod.

Had anything happened? Could she imagine that Valerie was capable of harming herself?

She raised her eyes from the table—dry eyes, cried empty.

'Yes,' she said and felt her mother take her hand and squeeze it. 'I'm afraid I can.'

The police officers nodded as if they were sorry to hear it, but of course it was good news for them, because if it wasn't suicide, it was something worse and then they really would have their hands full.

'You're sure she killed herself? I can't believe she'd have done a thing like that.'

Norah glared at her mother, noticing with disgust that she was wearing blue mascara. It seemed all wrong to her. Valerie was dead and her mother's eyelashes were a lurid blue.

The officers nodded again and the older of them added in fatherly tones, 'Bar the absence of a suicide note, everything points to it.'

'She didn't leave a letter?' Norah's mother asked.

Nobody said anything.

'Oh, God, her poor parents.' Norah's mother clapped her hand to her mouth, smudging her lipstick—apparently without noticing.

Norah's heart was pounding so loudly that she thought everyone in the room must be able to hear it. Didn't it strike them as strange that bookish Valerie, with her dreams of being an author and her constant scribbling, hadn't left a note? Norah wanted to say something, but her mouth was too dry, her tongue too heavy; it felt as if someone had rammed a cobblestone into her mouth. The younger policeman threw his colleague a glance of annoyance.

'Even if there was a note,' he said, 'it wouldn't make a difference. All the evidence points to Valerie choosing to depart this life.'

Norah wondered how much thought he'd given his choice of words. Had he deliberately avoided saying *killing herself, taking her life, putting an end to it all, committing suicide,* and decided on *choosing to depart this life?* Her mind began to freewheel through increasingly absurd expressions for this act she couldn't get her head round, no matter what anyone called it. *Did herself in. Did away with herself. Ended it all. Topped herself. Committed felo de se.* And that night, when she lay in bed under the sky of glow-in-the-dark stars that had watched over her sleep all through her childhood, her mind drifted on—there was no stopping it—on and on, into the bleaker territory of fairytale. Norah tossed and turned. Got up, sat down, got up again, paced up and down her room, went into the kitchen, had a drink of water, sat at her desk, got up, went to the window, looked out, turned away, sat on her bed, lay down, closed her eyes, opened them, started over again. It wasn't the thought of Valerie's dead body that was so unbearable—though it was. Nor was it the thought of death. What drove her mad was imagining the moments before she did it. The pain, the fear, the loneliness.

Norah returned to the present and took a gulp of wine. Whoever was writing her these late-night texts wanted her to remember. And Norah remembered; it all came back to her. Those old-fashioned village policemen and their half-hearted investigations. And her teenage self—the victim's best friend—blithely confirming their conjecture.

When Norah fell asleep that night, she dreamt she saw a stag beetle creeping over Valerie's lifeless arm.

38

The next morning Norah woke shivering, worn out by the night, her bare legs cold and aching from desolate dreams. The noise was back. It had changed, from a whispering buzz, a gathering hum, to something deeper, more erratic. To a creaking and groaning, a bursting. It must sound like that in the Arctic, Norah thought, when a crack opened up in the ice.

Loneliness filled the rooms as if there were suddenly an iceberg in her Vienna flat, bluey white and hard as granite. She drank her coffee and left for work without washing up the cup, knowing she'd be annoyed at her own slovenliness when she got back in the evening. On her way past the bistro on the corner, she saw the three old ladies smoking at their usual table, and a small smile stole over her face. Some things, at least, didn't change. She went in and ordered an espresso and applied herself to the newspaper that someone had left on the table.

'Have you heard about Marie? About the court case?' the brunette was asking and Norah, who couldn't concentrate on the newspaper anyway, pricked up her ears.

The two other women shook their heads.

'She's been sentenced.'

'Go on with you. What for?' the blonde asked in disbelief.

'Grievous bodily harm. It was in the papers.'

'I can't believe it. Will she have to go to prison?' the redhead asked, puckering her thickly drawn eyebrows.

'No, but she'll have to pay a fine.'

'What with?' asked the blonde.

Shrugs and clueless faces.

Norah finished her espresso, put two euros on the table and left. On the train, she looked at her phone. Two new texts, both from Max, worried because Norah wasn't responding to his calls. Norah suddenly realised that she was no longer angry with him; so much had happened in the last few days that Max's white lie hardly seemed to matter anymore. She decided to call him as soon as she had a spare moment. She missed him. But she had other things to deal with first; he'd have to wait. Instead of replying to his text, Norah sent a message to the unknown number.

Who are you?

When Norah reached the office, there was still no reply.

Sitting down at her desk, she recalled the conversation she'd overheard in the bistro. She played around with various search terms until she found what she was looking for on the online pages of a local newspaper.

Last summer Marie T. was in a beauty salon in the Fourth District. Shirin W., who testified in favour of her customer at the trial, had just finished giving her a manicure when three men in their early twenties noticed Marie T. and began to knock on the window and make insulting comments about her appearance, especially her weight.

Marie T. stormed out of the beauty salon to confront the young men.

'I've put up with a lot in my life,' Marie T. told the court, 'but I'd had enough.'

'Stupid slag' and 'fat bitch' were among the more harmless insults spoken by the men.

It seems that one thing led to another until eventually Marie T. felt so threatened that she opened her handbag, took out a can of pepper spray which she carried for personal protection, and sprayed it at the young men.

The defence argued that Marie T. had acted in an urgent and stressful situation; she had, after all, been threatened by three men and had only defended herself. But the court rejected this argument, holding that the pepper spray had not been Marie T.'s only option; she could equally have taken refuge in the beauty salon. The court refrained from a prison sentence, but ordered the accused to pay a thousand-euro fine.

Marie burst into tears in the courtroom and had to be comforted by her defence lawyer. The victims of her attack appeared satisfied with the sentence.

Norah clicked the website away with a bitter taste in her mouth. A woman fought back and look where it got her. The old mantra popped into Norah's head: *life is so fucking unfair.*

She tried to work—to fit in with the busy rhythm of office life, the relentless ringing of phones, tapping of keyboards, clicking of mice, the constant coming and going. She tried to share in her colleagues' sense of urgency and enthusiasm, but couldn't get into her stride—couldn't concentrate on a job for more than a few seconds at a time. Her thoughts fluttered about like startled chickens.

She wrote Werner an email headed *Special Assignment*, asking him for his help—again.

And just as she clicked on *Send*, a text arrived on her phone.

You're asking the wrong questions.

Norah put down her glass of water.

Who are you? she wrote again.

The reply came immediately.

You're asking the wrong questions.

Norah groaned, ignoring Aylin's glance across the desk.

What do you want from me?

Whoever was at the other end answered instantly.

I'm helping you.

Norah sniffed.

What do you know about Arthur Grimm? she asked.

You know all you need to know. You just won't admit it.

Norah stared at the display. Soon afterwards—perhaps whoever it was had realised that she wasn't going to reply—another message appeared. Norah opened it.

On the night of February 11. At the big wheel in the Prater. You know all you need to know. What you do with that knowledge is up to you.

Norah gulped. There they were again. Dorotea Lechner's words. Not exactly the same, but clearly recognisable.

Who are you? Norah asked yet again.

No answer.

Feeling numb, Norah read the texts over and over. Her hunch had been right. It wasn't a joke; it was serious. Someone was expecting her to kill Arthur Grimm. On the very date and in the very place announced to her weeks ago by a woman who was now dead.

But this was crazy!

Norah sank back in her chair.

She remembered Valerie's funeral—the coffin, Valerie's parents (still together at that point), her brother Sven. Poor Sven had attracted horrified stares by bursting into laughter in the middle of the service, and Norah, who had always been terrified of laughing at a funeral, but had, until then, somehow managed to persuade herself that it couldn't actually happen, was gripped by panic.

She remembered the girls at school who had surprised her with their sudden kindness. They wanted her to hang out with them all the time, kept asking her round to their houses, seemed to have developed a new, keen interest in her. At the time, Norah had wondered whether it wasn't her close friendship with a dead girl that made her, in some macabre way, more interesting to them. Only years later did it occur to her that it was possible they had been nice to her all along; she just hadn't noticed. As long as Valerie was alive she hadn't needed them—hadn't wanted to spend time with anyone except her best friend.

She remembered the policemen. She remembered hearing her mother's whispered phone calls to her friends and knowing that she was talking about her. And she remembered the moment when she found out how Valerie had done it.

Norah returned to the present. Opposite her, Aylin was on the phone, talking about her latest meditation retreat. When Norah got up and crossed the corridor to go to the toilet, she felt like a sailor staggering across a pitching deck wet with spray.

39

That evening she waited a long time for him, hidden in the shadows across the road from his flat. She had taken up her lookout post early so as not to miss him when he came home from work. Charges or no charges, she had to see him again; it was as if some inner compulsion were driving her. She recognised him from a long way off and everything about him aroused her disgust: his precise, measured, almost soldierly movements; his cold, pale eyes; his square chin; his fake, narrow-lipped smile. He greeted an old woman, perhaps a neighbour, and the smile flickered across his face only to drain away like water into sand as soon as she had passed. When another woman passed him a few metres further on—this one taller and younger with a blonde ponytail and an aloof expression—he strode on without so much as a glance at her.

Norah saw him vanish into the building and soon afterwards a light went on at a first-floor window. So that was where Arthur Grimm lived. Norah stared up at his flat, but he didn't appear at the window. Then, just as she was turning to leave, the light went out and a moment later Grimm reappeared at the door, a black sports bag over his shoulder. She watched him walk down the street, get into his car and drive away. There had been some mention of sport in Werner's dossier. Norah racked her brain. Did he play football? Work out? Then she remembered: he went boxing. That figured.

This time she had been more careful not to get too close, and from a distance she was so inconspicuous—jeans, a khaki parka, her hair hidden under a black beanie—that Grimm probably wouldn't have noticed her even if he had happened to see her.

Norah stood on the cold, dark street, trying to work out what her intuition was telling her. Her phone buzzed and she pulled it carefully out of her bag. The unknown number.

Get away from there!

Norah stared at the message. Then she raised her eyes and looked about her. A street on a winter's evening in a well-off residential area, light at most of the windows. A couple passed on the other side of the road; an underground train jingled in the distance. 'Where are you?' Norah whispered. A second text arrived.

He's dangerous!

Norah looked about her again, but couldn't see anyone watching her. Had she been followed? A moment later she wrote:

Why should I believe you?

As so often, there was no immediate answer. Norah set off towards the underground, her gloved hands over her cold, aching ears. She tried to put her thoughts in order. Then, at last, the answer came.

I'll prove it to you.

40

All next day, she only pretended to work. She was stuck in a cul-de-sac. Valerie's relatives were sure she had taken her life, and though Norah might have her doubts about that—and her suspicions about Grimm—she had no idea where to look for proof. It was all so long ago. Her only hope was the latest message from the anonymous texter, but he—or she—hadn't been in touch since.

Norah tried to distract herself. All morning she had typed and cut, taken calls and talked to people, made notes and read—but all she had really been doing was waiting for another text message. It wasn't that she was short of work; she had an interview with a famous conductor in Salzburg in a few days and hadn't even begun to prepare. She opened her browser and found trains that would allow her to spend all afternoon and evening in Salzburg and still be back in Vienna by midnight. When she'd bought the tickets, Norah leant back in her chair to think about the interview. But however hard she tried, she couldn't concentrate.

As she neared her flat that evening, she was exhausted from the relentless tension. She did a quick supermarket shop, got herself home, manoeuvred herself and the bags through the door, mechanically opened her letterbox—and found a letter that she stuffed into one of the shopping bags.

After putting the food away in the fridge, she had a closer look at the letter. There was no return address, no postmark. Carefully Norah opened the envelope. Inside was a single printed sheet. Nervously she unfolded it and read it through, then dropped onto a chair with a relieved sigh. The letter, addressed to all tenants, informed them that the drains would be cleaned between 9 a.m. and 2 p.m. on 14 March and asked them to leave a key with a neighbour if they weren't going to be in. God, she really was getting paranoid.

Norah was about to make a note of the date when a loud beep announced the arrival of a new text. Irritably, Norah put the letter down and reached for her phone. The text was from the unknown number and contained no answer—only an eleven-figure number. A mobile number.

It rang once, twice, three times, four times, five times. Norah was about to hang up, half disappointed, half relieved, when somebody answered.

'Reiter?'

A woman's voice. Norah's age, or maybe a little younger. Slightly unsure of herself. Was this the person who had sent Norah all the messages?

Norah cleared her throat.

'Hello,' she said, 'this is Norah.'

Silence.

Norah felt her heart thumping in her chest and was briefly reminded of the time she'd sat in on an autopsy as a very young journalist. She'd never forgotten the astonishingly garish colours, the shocking smells—or the moment when she'd seen her first human heart, scarlet and shiny and beautiful.

'Norah who?' the voice asked suspiciously.

Norah decided to put her cards on the table.

'Norah Richter,' she said. 'I think we've exchanged texts.'

'I'd know about that,' the woman said, suddenly sure of herself.

'Please don't hang up,' Norah said quickly, but it was too late. She sighed.

Then she checked the text message to make sure she hadn't entered the wrong number by mistake. She hadn't. Norah put her head in her hands and tried to think. She'd evidently been wrong to assume that it was the anonymous texter's number; the woman she'd spoken to hadn't been expecting her call. And why would she have given Norah her number only to hang up on her? Norah realised she was being stupid, because of course she already had the texter's number; this was a new number, belonging to somebody else. Norah studied the chain of messages she'd exchanged with the unknown contact.

Get away from there!

—

He's dangerous.

—

Why should I believe you?

—

I'll prove it to you.

Norah pressed her lips together and tried the new number again. She had to let it ring for a long time, but eventually the woman picked up.

'Hello?'

'I'm sorry to disturb you again, Ms Reiter,' said Norah, trying to sound respectable and a little formal. 'But I'm afraid it's very important.'

There was a moment's silence.

'Okay,' the woman said. 'What's it about?'

Norah thought of her friend Coco and how much she hated talking about what had happened to her.

'I'd like to talk to you about Arthur Grimm,' she said.

The woman made a strangled sound; Norah had hit the mark.

'Where did you get my number?' the woman asked.

Norah decided to be as honest as possible.

'Someone gave it to me,' she said, adding with a flash of inspiration, 'Ms Reiter, I'm on *your* side.'

Her gaze fell on the tarot card which she still hadn't got rid of. The grim reaper looked out at her; she turned the card over.

'How do you know Arthur?' the woman asked.

Good question, Norah thought. Should she reveal all without even knowing who she was talking to? And where would she begin if she did?

'He's been threatening me,' said Norah, following her gut instinct.

'Are you his new woman? If you are, I can only warn you.'

'No,' Norah said quickly. 'No, I'm not.'

'Count yourself lucky. So what do you want from him?'

How could she explain without sounding like a complete weirdo?

'I'm afraid it's rather complicated,' she said, to buy time. 'A friend of mine is seeing him. And I can't quite put my finger on it, but I've had a bad feeling about the guy right from the start. I don't usually do this kind of thing, you know, but I'm a journalist—curious by profession… So I asked around a bit. I just want to know who the man is—what my friend's letting herself in for.'

She stopped for a moment. Did it sound plausible?

'Well, and then I met someone who gave me your number and said if I wanted to find out what kind of a man Arthur Grimm is, I should ask you.'

Norah held her breath as she waited for an answer.

'Who was this someone who gave you my number?' the woman asked.

'Does it matter?'

The woman made a strange noise; it sounded to Norah like a little snorting laugh.

'I think I have a pretty good idea.'

Norah said nothing. The woman, too, was silent for a moment, giving Norah time to think. She'd been sent this number so that she could find out what kind of a man Arthur Grimm was—she was sure of that. What did this woman have to tell her? Norah resisted the temptation to light a cigarette; she didn't move a millimetre, anxious not to disturb the woman in any way as she made up her mind. She could sense the woman poised between speaking and remaining silent and knew how it felt—knew, too, that she mustn't push her now, mustn't try to pressure her into anything. All she could do was wait.

'Okay,' the woman said. And began her story.

41

Even using a lighter was suddenly too much for Norah; it took her several tries to light up. Vienna lay quiet in the dark, as if night had sucked up the sounds as well as the colours. People moved almost noiselessly, as though anxious not to mar the beauty of the city at night. Norah wandered here and there, with no particular aim, trying to think things over as she walked. When she came to the Karlskirche, she stopped to admire the glorious baroque dome and columns; it never ceased to amaze her that humans were capable of creating such beautiful things. Especially, she said to herself, when you think of all the ugly things we get up to as a species. She crossed the square in front of her flat, sending a can clattering over the asphalt with her foot. After coming off the phone to Angelika Reiter, she'd given the kitchen wall a good kick, but that had brought back bad memories and she'd gone out for a walk instead, to cool down and work off her anger. Norah pumped as much cold evening air into her lungs as she could. The woman's story had been awful.

Realising, though, that walking and fresh air were no help and that she was getting hotter rather than cooling down, Norah headed back and stopped outside the bistro on the corner of her street. It looked cosy and inviting; warm light shone out into the darkness like a promise of warmth and company and happiness. Seconds later, Norah was sitting at a little table in the far corner. The three old ladies weren't there at this hour—only a few lonely souls like her, staring into their drinks or out of the window. Norah ordered a glass of Veltliner.

Blows, threats, physical and psychological abuse, blackmail. If what the young woman had told Norah about her two-year relationship with Arthur Grimm was true, the man was a monster. Clever, manipulative and cold as ice. Norah had no trouble believing it. But what now? She took out her phone and yet again she typed: *Who are you?*

She toyed with the thought of adding another question or two, but decided against it and pressed *Send*. All at once she felt the same surge of cold anger she had felt sitting numbly in her flat after the phone call. This time, though, it was directed not only at Grimm but also at the person sending her these messages. Why all the fucking secrecy? Why the funny games? If this person really knew all about Grimm and wanted to call him to account, why had they involved Norah—and couldn't they at least be open with her?

Okay, she wrote. *I've spoken to the woman. If she's to be believed (and I think she is), AG is a bastard and I hope the woman goes to the police. But what the fuck has this got to do with me?*

When she looked up from her phone, her eyes met those of a greying blond man sitting at the bar, a smart coat draped over the stool beside him. He wore a suit and shirt without a tie and had a trendy mixed drink in front of him that made him look a little out of place in the old-fashioned bistro. Norah quickly averted her eyes. She had to think. No distractions now. She got the bill and left.

Back at home, she sat down at her desk, booted up her laptop and logged in to her email provider. One new message. From Werner. Had he already carried out the special assignment she'd set him? Norah clicked on the email, which had no subject heading—Werner seldom bothered.

It was short.

I'm afraid I haven't managed to carry out your 'special assignment' yet. But I have something else for you. Didn't want to ring so late. Give me a call in the morning. Werner

In the morning? How was she to get through the night after an announcement like that? She was dying of curiosity. Norah was about to close the email when she noticed the time. Werner, always a night owl, had sent the email only ten minutes ago. Norah leapt up, grabbed her phone and dialled his number. He picked up almost immediately.

'Still the old night owl,' he said, without even saying hello.

'Just what I was thinking about you,' Norah said smiling.

After they'd finished talking, she sat there for a long time. She stared out of the window and then at her hands, trying to process what she'd heard. But it was no good; her head was so full it felt ready to burst.

It was 5 February and she had a motive to kill Arthur Grimm.

42

There was blood everywhere. It was still sticking to her when she sat up with a start, clutching her chest—and when she dropped her hands and caught her breath, the rust-coloured goo spread all over the cream covers of the sofa.

What was the time? Norah looked about her for her watch and spotted it next to her phone on a cardboard box that served as an improvised coffee table. Half past two.

Norah got up and went over to the window. The street below was deserted. She opened the window, trying to shake off her tiredness. She had stretched out on the sofa to think—and because her back had ached after sitting at her desk for so long. She must have fallen asleep straight away. Shivering, she closed the window.

She went into the kitchen. In the fridge were apples, yoghurts, ready-made sandwiches, plastic containers of salad. Things that demanded no preparation or effort—things you could simply shovel into yourself. For a moment Norah stared at the food as if she'd forgotten what you did with it. Then she took out a yoghurt and a sandwich and began to eat mechanically.

As she was eating, she heard the floorboards creak overhead—so Theresa was still up too. Norah jumped to her feet. She had to talk to someone. Now. She hurried into her clothes, reached for her keys, unlocked the door, stepped out onto the landing and dashed up the stairs—but stopped abruptly when she saw a young man coming out of Theresa's flat. He locked the door behind him and turned to face Norah. It wasn't the little idiot who'd shouted at Theresa—the one Norah had got rid of a few days before. This man was older than Theresa, closer to Norah in age, short and stocky, with reddish blond hair, watery blue eyes and a cleft chin. And he had a key.

He was clearly startled to meet someone on the stairs in the middle of the night, but said nothing—only nodded at Norah and tried to squeeze past her in silence.

'Hi,' said Norah. 'Are you a friend of Theresa's?'

The man stopped and stared at her, uncomprehending.

'Theresa?'

Norah could feel her eyes narrowing to slits.

'Yes,' she said. 'Theresa. The young woman who lives here.'

Something in his face changed. Then he smiled briefly.

'Oh, I see,' he said. 'Theresa. Sorry, it's just that I never call her that. Anyway, I must be going. Three in the morning's hardly the time for a chat on the stairs.'

Again, he tried to push past Norah, smiling apologetically.

'What *do* you call her then? Theresa, I mean.'

The smile vanished.

'Is that any of your business?'

Touché, Norah thought. No, he was right, it wasn't. Theresa, or whatever this guy called her, was old enough to do as she pleased—and give her key to whoever she liked.

'I'm sorry,' said Norah. 'Is she in?'

'No,' said the man, finally managing to manoeuvre his way past Norah and setting off down the stairs at a leisurely pace. A moment later, she heard the front door slam shut.

Norah rang Theresa's bell, but, unsurprisingly, nobody came to the door and she had no choice but to return to her own flat where the rusty smell of blood still hung in the air.

She sat down and went over what Werner had told her. He'd found out every detail of what Grimm had been doing at the time of Valerie's death: what he'd been working on, what departments he'd been employed in, exactly where he'd lived. He'd been a lodger in an old lady's house and this lady hadn't forgotten the *upstanding young man*—a violinist like her youngest son, but also very handy about the house; a great help with repairs. Ever so quiet, apparently, and terribly hard-working and studious; he'd even found the time to give French and maths coaching on top of all his other work.

The memory had hit like a bolt from the blue. A golden autumn day. Norah had got a B in her French vocab test, but Valerie had fared less well. Norah was going to the cinema to see the new Leonardo DiCaprio film.

'Want to come?' she asked.

Valerie rolled her eyes.

'I can't. I've got French and maths coaching,' she groaned. 'Mum's found me a new tutor.' Was that the first time Norah had heard Grimm's name? She wasn't sure. But all the evidence suggested that Grimm had known Valerie—that he'd been her tutor. The thoughts went round and round in Norah's head: Valerie and Grimm knew each other and Grimm is a violent bastard. She heard his voice, over and over. *Don't you mess with me. I'll finish you off. I mean it.*

She saw Valerie before her as if it were yesterday. Still a child. Then she saw Grimm. His harsh eyes. His coldness, his measured movements, the soldierly precision.

What had he done to her?

Norah closed her eyes. She saw the images from her dream again— her bloody hands, the lifeless figure—and realised that she had known all along; Werner's call had merely confirmed the vague suspicion that had been floating above her, just out of reach. The name of Arthur Grimm had unnerved her right from the start; she had always associated it with Valerie. Now, if this awful hunch proved right, everything would suddenly make sense.

Arthur Grimm had killed Valerie and got away with it.

Somebody knew that.

And whoever that somebody was, they wanted Arthur Grimm to be punished.

She didn't know why they didn't do it themselves. Whether they couldn't or didn't dare or simply didn't think that it was up to them.

She knew only that this somebody wanted *her* to do it. She had no idea why that somebody was going about persuading her in such a strange way, but their goal was clear.

She was the one.

She was to bring death to Arthur Grimm.

And since last night she knew something else. Something that scared her more than any of the other goïngs-on of the last few weeks.

Again the dream images enveloped her and she not only saw, but *felt* everything: Arthur Grimm, wounded and frightened before her on the ground, his face twisted with pain, his voice. *Please don't.* And then the second shot. That sense of finality. And the mixture of shock and satisfaction that followed. Norah's mouth was suddenly very dry.

Somebody wanted her to kill Arthur Grimm.

And deep down inside, she wanted it too.

43

Norah sat in the office, staring at Grimm. Arthur Grimm stared back. And although he was only a mass of pixels, there was something frightening about the way he looked at her.

Being at work was like finding herself dropped down in a foreign country with unfamiliar customs. Now and then she overheard snatches of conversation. Her boss, saying that if the interview with the new Burg director fell through, he wouldn't have a cover story for the next issue. David, suggesting a topic. It all meant nothing to her and she was glad nobody asked her for an opinion, because she could think of only one thing: Valerie and Grimm.

Norah stood at the window, smoking, thinking. It would soon be time to knock off, but she couldn't stir herself to go back to the office she shared with Aylin. The things that Angelika Reiter had told on the phone were still ringing in her ears and she felt her jaws grind as she thought about it. A man who abused women and had always got away with it.

Yet another.

Now she knew what Grimm was capable of. He'd already proved how clever he was by getting to the police before she did. Eventually Norah could stand it no longer and wrote a text message.

Did Grimm know Valerie?

No reply. Norah made herself a cup of coffee and waited. Then a beep announced an incoming text.

You know the answer.

Norah's eyes narrowed.

Why didn't you tell me?

This time the reply came almost immediately.

You had to find out for yourself.

Why? Is he connected with Valerie's death?

Again, she didn't have to wait long for a reply. It was almost as if whoever it was had nothing better to do all day than sit around waiting for her texts.

You know the answer to that too. You just don't like it.

Too true, I don't, Norah thought, and wrote:

Answer my question!

Yes! the somebody wrote.

Norah stared at the screen, not knowing what to feel.

How do you know?

We're going round in circles.

Norah closed the chat and, on a whim, rang the number. She let it ring for a long time, but nobody picked up.

Norah hung up and wrote:

Why won't you speak to me?

Because it wouldn't make a difference. Because none of the information I'd give you would make a difference. He did it. He's guilty. You know that as well as I do. And not only do you know it; you feel it too. The only question now is what you're going to do with that knowledge.

When Norah didn't reply, another message arrived.

Do you still doubt his guilt?

I'm not sure, Norah lied.

For a time nothing happened. Then, just as she was thinking that the somebody had called it a day, three dancing dots appeared on her screen again.

Why don't you just ask him? Ask him about Valerie. Look him in the eyes.

Norah was still staring at this message when another arrived.

He's usually in Cafe Horvath at this time.

With its simple vintage furniture and stylish new ceiling lamps, the coffee house was a welcome distraction from Vienna's usual showy pomp. Norah hadn't hesitated for a second. She'd said goodbye to Aylin, thrown on her coat and set off.

Arthur Grimm was reading a newspaper in the far corner with a cup of coffee in front of him. She had forgotten how terrifying he was in the flesh. The coffee house was more or less empty: the afternoon customers had gone home and the evening customers were yet to arrive.

Grimm glanced up when Norah went over to his table. She still hadn't worked out what it was about his face that so terrified her. On the surface of it, he was good looking, but when you studied his face for a long time, it was impossible not to feel that something wasn't right. His eyes, Norah thought. They were set at a strange angle. Was that it?

'What do you want?' he asked tonelessly.

'Valerie Fischer,' Norah said.

The effect of the name on Grimm was remarkable. His eyes widened, his lips parted—for a split second, he looked genuinely stunned. Then he recovered himself.

'Who are you talking about?' he asked coldly.

'You know that as well as I do. It's written all over your face.'

Grimm stared at her, then looked around the cafe, but nobody had noticed them. He shook his head and Norah could see a thought taking shape in him; something in his face shifted almost imperceptibly.

'Listen,' he said, suddenly and unconvincingly well-meaning. 'I didn't do anything to your little friend. And now please leave me in peace or I'll call the police.'

Grimm rose, slapped a few euros on the table, took his coat and left the coffee house. Norah saw no point in running after him; he'd told her everything she needed to know.

The bang of the car door, the taxi driver's greeting, the traffic, the rain that had just set in—Norah heard everything as if through cotton wool and her hands were trembling so much that she had to press her palms against her thighs to still them. Grimm's words echoed in her head as if in an empty ballroom.

I didn't do anything to your little friend.

All Norah had done was say Valerie's name.

If he was innocent, why did he react the way he did?

If he was innocent, how did he know that Valerie was her friend? Or that anyone had done anything to her? Norah had told him nothing.

She had suspected it for some time, but knowing for sure was different; it did something to her. It was her call now.

She walked the last block to her flat. A few metres from her front door, she raised her eyes from the pavement and saw a poster pasted onto a wall—big black letters on a bright pink background.

THERE IS MORE THAN ONE DEATH.
THE ONE THAT CARRIES US OFF IS ONLY THE LAST.

Back in her flat, Norah looked about her, bewildered. She hadn't been gone an hour, but everything looked different, as if someone had taken her world and shifted all the things in it by a millimetre or two.

She sat down at her desk, looked at her notes and resumed the train of thoughts that she had previously forbidden herself to follow through to the end.

She put her slips of paper in order and went through all the facts, one by one.

Grimm lived alone. She was sure of that now. He was alone. No wife, no children.

Norah noticed how quiet it was in her flat. Only the hum of the fridge and the occasional creaking floorboard. She, too, was alone. Nobody rang at her door, nobody called her, she had no one. The only person who had ever understood her had been taken away from her by Grimm. She had nothing to lose. The thought gave her sudden strength. Norah took a piece of paper and began to write.

He works as an engineer.

He drives to the office.

He's a regular at Cafe Horvath.

He likes going to football matches (Rapid Vienna).

He often goes to the cinema (mostly on his own).

He's strong and looks as if he works out (amateur boxer!).

She considered. Just say I did it, she thought. How would I go about it?

The days were supposedly getting longer, but it still got dark early. In theory it wouldn't be hard to wait for Grimm. Maybe one evening when he came out of the cinema. In fact, it would probably be no trouble to get into the building where he lived. No. The risk of being seen was too high. She'd have to catch him on his own, far from neighbours or passers-by. She must find out where he went jogging. A wood would be perfect, or a remote park. Some deserted place. Just supposing.

But how was she going to get hold of a weapon in Vienna? In Berlin she knew people; she had once spoken to all kinds of gun freaks for a magazine feature and even got on quite well with one of them. Maybe he could put her in touch with someone in Vi—

Norah stopped. Her thoughts jarred to a halt. She felt the blood drain from her face and stared at the paper in front of her, her hand clapped to her mouth. She sat there like that for a long time, stunned at the thought of what she was doing.

She had begun to plan a murder.

The Aztecs had more than 1600 gods. Whenever they subjugated a people, they adopted its gods, and so the number grew and grew. Isn't that staggering? 1600 gods. We don't even have one.

Religion has never interested me, but I have always been intrigued by religiosity. It is a source of endless fascination to me to observe the many things people believe in—whether gods or horoscopes or simply fate.

Me, I believe in decisions. In free will, if you like. Each of us has the choice, but so few of us use it. Most people are trapped in routines and since these tend to be an unsophisticated mixture of habit, herd instinct and self-interest, human behaviour is almost disappointingly easy to predict.

The science of decision theory is highly complex and there are, of course, decisions that defy expectation. But they are exceptions. As a general rule, people do not make decisions on a rational level; they depend on their emotions. Even if they do manage to factor complex information into their considerations, most of them make the same mistakes over and over again. They make things more complicated than they are. They are alarmingly easy to distract and see only what they want to see.

In this respect she is no different. She didn't recognise me when our paths crossed the other day. She is inattentive. It isn't her fault; it's the way our brains function. Although we tend to know everything, we often understand nothing.

I am not saying that I am more intelligent. I just take more care. That is why I know exactly what she is going to do. She will toy with the thought of running away—maybe think of going travelling. But then she will tell herself that she is not the kind to run away and she will stay after all. She will tell herself she is too intelligent to go to the Prater. She will resolve to stay at home. But she will come—as inevitable as the tide.

44

The spirits of the night had crawled back into their hidey-holes, sighing and whispering. The pressure that had been weighing on Norah's chest hadn't exactly gone, but it had lifted a little. How different things looked by daylight. All right, so there was still something menacing about the situation. But even if she was right and someone was trying to get her to kill Arthur Grimm (and it was a pretty wild hunch), what did she have to be afraid of? She was not a murderer, and nothing and nobody could make her kill anyone.

She had dreamt of him again. She was lying on the ground beneath him, gasping for breath, his hands at her throat, and however much she thrashed around, she couldn't free herself. Then the gun appeared. She hadn't known she had a gun, but suddenly it was there, in her hand. Dream logic. Norah shot and Grimm's face exploded in hers. She could still feel the blood and gore on her skin, warm and sticky.

Norah took a deep breath. All right, so February 11 was fast approaching, she had a reason to wish Grimm dead, and it sure as hell wasn't going to be easy to bring him to justice through official channels. But that was no reason to kill him.

Still, it's what you want.

No. There was no reason to be scared. No one could thrust a gun into her hand and force her to shoot a man. And she wasn't going to do it of her own free will—she had enough trust in herself to know that.

Are you sure?

'Norah?'

She jumped like a schoolgirl caught sleeping in a lesson. Everyone looked at her. She hadn't expected to be addressed. Most editorial meetings simply went on until the boss had come to the end of his monologue.

She looked at him.

'If you could stay behind a moment,' Berger said.

Norah nodded, bewildered.

'I wish the rest of you a productive week,' Berger said and everyone went off, talking in low voices, until only he and Norah were left in the cold conference room.

He turned to her, an inscrutable look on his soft face.

'How are you liking it with us?'

'Fine,' she said dully. 'I'm happy here.'

'That's good to hear,' Berger replied. 'You're doing a great job. I liked your last interview. And I'm to send you warm regards from Mira.'

'That's nice,' said Norah. 'Thank you.'

And then, when Berger said nothing, 'I love interviews.'

'In that case, you're going to be pleased when you hear the news.'

Norah tried to look interested, but she could feel her thoughts wandering and was pretty sure that Berger sensed her abstraction.

'Our cover story for the next issue,' Berger said.

'The interview with the new Burg Theatre director?' Norah asked—even she had picked up that much.

Her boss nodded.

'A whole hour. Quite a coup—he usually refuses to give interviews because he believes, as he puts it, that *his work speaks for him*. He's making an exception for us. Or rather: for you.'

'I don't understand.'

'I'd like you to conduct the interview.'

'Please don't get me wrong,' said Norah. 'I'd be delighted to. But why me? Why not Eva?'

It was a fair question. Norah knew a lot about the theatre and had often written reviews of premieres in Berlin, but Eva was the magazine's official theatre expert. Norah didn't want her to think she was encroaching on her territory.

'Well,' he said. 'It wasn't my decision.'

'What do you mean?'

'Preller seems to be a fan of yours. He specifically asked to speak to *you*.'

'Are you serious?' Norah asked.

Berger shrugged.

'Okay,' Norah said. 'Good. I'd love to interview him. Maybe I could take Eva along with me?'

Berger shook his head.

'He wants you on your own. No idea why. Shouldn't think it has anything to do with you; probably just another of his little power games. He has a reputation for that kind of thing.'

Great, Norah thought.

Out loud, she asked, 'Is there a date?'

'There is,' said Berger, rifling through his papers. 'February 11, 10 p.m. At the entrance to the Prater.'

Out in the corridor, Norah almost crashed into David.

'You're white as a sheet,' he said. 'Is everything okay?'

Norah gave a brief nod and headed for her office.

'Why are you always so aloof?' David asked.

Norah wheeled round to him.

'I'm sorry?'

'I don't understand. We're all so nice to you, but you seem determined to keep yourself to yourself. Have we done something to offend you?'

'I don't keep myself to myself,' she said.

'Oh, come on, Norah. We all have lunch together every day. You're the only one who doesn't sit with us.'

Norah didn't reply.

'Oh well, suit yourself,' David said, looking at her again for a moment before turning to leave.

Norah felt as if she'd been slapped in the face. What did he mean, she kept herself to herself? Wasn't it them? Hadn't they shut her out right from the start? Then reality shifted. For a second she saw the world through their eyes and realised that he was right. Suddenly she heard Alex's voice in her ear. *People aren't as bad as you think. You'd know that if you gave them a chance now and then.*

45

Norah was sitting on her bed with her legs tucked under her, a pillow at her back. She'd been sitting there, staring at the wall, for a very long time. Reinhold Preller wanted to see her in the Prater on the evening of February 11. Could it be a coincidence? No, she decided, it could not. But how the hell did a prestigious theatre director fit into all this?

Again, she thought of Alex—of the way he used to listen to her when she was pondering a problem out loud, the way he would wrinkle his forehead and rub his cheek and then come out with something that was—generally speaking—very clever. Her longing to hear his voice was suddenly so intense it was almost unbearable.

She must have dropped off in the end, and when she woke up, she didn't know where she was. She had fallen asleep in a twisted position on the phone book, her head on the crook of her right arm, which was now so numb that she had to massage it for a few minutes to bring it back to life. Her notes lay scattered on the floor by her bed. So many questions and no answers. They had whirled around her head and worked their way into a strangely realistic dream in which Norah had run hopelessly from one place to another, knocking on doors that remained locked. A glance at her watch told her that she hadn't overslept. It wasn't yet seven; she'd had a bare three hours' sleep. Norah swung her legs out of bed, went into the kitchen and put on some coffee. When it was ready, she poured herself a cup and took it back to bed. With the coffee inside her, she felt vaguely able to face the day. She had a shower, dressed, poured muesli into a bowl, covered it with milk and ate without appetite.

When she'd finished, she still had a good hour before she had to leave for work. She went back into the bedroom and opened the window to give the room an airing and drive out the stale air and cold smoke. She made her bed, plumping up the pillows and quilts, then bent down to gather up the papers on the floor. As she did so, she glanced under the bed. And froze.

She was suddenly icy cold.

Slowly Norah straightened up. She left the room, as stiff as a poorly oiled robot, and sat down on a box in the hall. Everything was spinning. She closed her eyes, but that only made it worse.

It took her a moment to force herself to get up and go back into the bedroom. Norah crouched down, stretched out a purposeful arm and pulled the case out from under her bed.

She might be untidy. She might be suffering from sleep deprivation. It was also possible that she ate too little and drank and smoked too much. But one thing she was sure of: this black case, a little smaller than a shoebox, was not hers. She put out a hand to open the lid, then stopped, mid-movement, as if something was holding her back. Then she screwed up her courage and lifted the lid.

At first she only stared in disbelief, but a moment later she stood up and took a few steps back. She couldn't calm down, though; her mind was racing.

It was some time since she'd written the feature for a German news magazine; it had been one of her favourite projects. For weeks,

Norah had hung out with 'gun freaks', visited shooting clubs, spoken to huntsmen (there weren't many hunts*women*), and interviewed gun collectors. She'd been to the police shooting range and learnt how to shoot. Norah hadn't held a gun in her hand since, but in the course of her research she had learnt enough about firearms to know that the revolver in the small, black case under her bed was not a fake.

The thought that somebody had come into her flat and up to her bed while she was asleep made her feel sick. She turned and walked down the passage to her front door, and pushed down the handle. Locked. What was going on? She tried to put her thoughts in order. Yes, she'd locked up behind her the night before, the way she always did since suspecting she'd had an intruder in the flat. Whoever had put the gun under her bed must have unlocked the door, deposited the gun and then locked the door behind them. They must have a key. A new key!

Then she realised she wasn't thinking straight. Who said the case had only been there since last night? When had she last looked under the bed? For all she knew, the gun could have been there for weeks. Perhaps it had been deposited in her flat at the time when all those little things had gone missing.

Norah returned to the bedroom. The gun lay in the open case like a big black scorpion, shiny and lethal—the promise of an as-yet-unrealised, but inevitable, horror.

46

She knew what she had to do, but it was a huge struggle to make herself do it.

If her mother was to be believed, she had always been fiercely independent, even as a child, and hated asking for help. Norah remembered the time she had climbed the tall chestnut in her neighbours' garden when she was a little girl. It was only when she reached the top and looked down that she realised how high she was—and that it was far easier to climb a tree than to get down again. She was stuck there like a cat. Too embarrassed to call for help, she had sat out an entire hour alone in that tree, listening to the other children playing in the distance, until eventually the nice grandmotherly lady from next door had spotted her and got her rescued.

That was how she felt now: a long way from everyone, unable to solve her problem on her own, but equally incapable of asking for help.

In the end it was probably David's remarks that persuaded Norah to climb down from her tree. She sat at her desk, going through the options. There were three people on the planet whom she would describe as real friends: Sandra, Max and Paul. And she needed them now. Any differences they may have had in the past no longer mattered; the situation was too serious to bother about such niceties. It was 8 February, she had fantasies of killing Arthur Grimm—and she had a gun.

Norah reached for her phone before she could change her mind.

Only a few hours later she was sitting in Max and Paul's beautiful apartment, the morning light pouring in at the windows, a smell of coffee and fried eggs in the air. Norah squirmed on her chair. Her head ached, but more than anything, she felt embarrassed. It suddenly seemed stupid to have ignored Max's calls for so long. All right, so he hadn't behaved as well as he might, but she was old enough and had known him long enough to be able to speak frankly to him about such things and sort them out. Instead she had sulked. And now she'd sprung this on him. And what had he and Paul done? They'd immediately freed up their morning to listen to her and offer what help they could.

She had just finished telling her story for the second time that morning. First, she'd told Sandra everything on the phone, and now Max and Paul, too, knew all there was to know—about the woman in the pedestrian precinct who had prophesied that she would kill a certain Arthur Grimm and had soon afterwards died herself. About the tarot card Norah had found in the Hotel Imperial and the smell of pipe smoke that seemed to follow her around the city. About the mysterious text messages, the dark figure beneath her window and the things that had gone missing from her flat. About Valerie. About Grimm. About her futile visit to the police. About her suspicion. About her phone call to Grimm's ex. And finally, about the developments of the last few days: her boss's announcement that she was to go to the Prater on the night of the eleventh—and the discovery of a loaded gun in her flat. The reaction was the same both times: appalled silence. Sandra had eventually asked a few factual questions and advised Norah to keep calm and avoid Grimm at all costs. She said she'd ask around among her lawyer friends to find out whether it was even possible that Valerie had been murdered. Norah had felt incredibly relieved. No more disbelief, no more hints that she was imagining things. As soon as there was a gun involved, everyone knew it was serious.

'Wow,' said Paul when Norah had finished. 'That's some story.'

'Fucking spooky,' Max said.

Norah nodded.

'I know.'

'Have I got this right?' Max said. 'You want us to help you convict Arthur Grimm of murder?'

'No,' said Norah. 'I want you to stop me from killing him.'

After breakfast they decided to spend the day thinking over Norah's problem separately, and then reconvene at Max and Paul's in the evening to discuss what to do. Norah flew through her day on autopilot, unable to concentrate; it was only when she was back at Max and Paul's with a glass of Malbec that she finally began to relax a little. She and Max were sitting on the sofa; Paul was barefoot in his favourite armchair. Sandra's voice came over the loudspeaker on the telephone.

'Okay,' she said. 'I've asked around a bit. It meant begging for a few favours, so I'm going to be spending the next few months taking people I can't stand out to dinner—but hey, what don't I do for my friends?'

'We all have our little burdens to bear, sister,' said Max with a grin.

'A little less suspense, please,' said Norah. 'Finding a gun under my bed has strained my patience.'

'Dorotea Lechner's death was an accident,' Sandra said. 'Sure as can be. And your school friend committed suicide. There's absolutely no doubt about that. There wasn't the slightest sign of external influence or anything back then. Grimm is innocent.'

There was a moment of silence.

'How sure are you?' Norah asked.

'Almost a hundred per cent,' said Sandra.

'Why only *almost*?'

'Because nothing's ever a hundred per cent certain. But there's no reason to doubt it, Norah. No reason at all.'

Norah suddenly had a bitter taste in her mouth and tried to wash it down with a few mouthfuls of wine.

'What if he forced her?' she said. 'To kill herself, I mean.'

'Norah, I think you're on the wrong track,' Max said gently.

'Why are you so intent on clinging to that theory?' Sandra asked. 'It's almost like you want him to be guilty. I mean, be glad that a murderer hasn't escaped unpunished. It would be pretty hard to pin anything on him now, after all these years.'

Norah heard her swallow.

'Sweetie,' Sandra said, 'it's good news.'

Norah could feel Paul and Max looking at her.

'Okay,' she said. 'Okay, you're right.'

'You still don't sound satisfied.'

'No,' said Norah. 'Because now all the goings-on in my flat make even less sense than before. If my theory was correct, it would all add up, at least. If not, it's just completely preposterous.'

'I don't think the weird goings-on are all that preposterous,' Max said. 'When did you last get a good night's sleep? When did you last eat properly? How many packs have you smoked this week? What if this has nothing to do with Grimm and Valerie?'

'I know what Max means,' Sandra said, 'and I agree. This isn't about Valerie. It's about you. Someone's trying to confuse you, unnerve you, tyrannise you. No one wants justice for your friend or any of that rubbish. You have a particularly nasty stalker, that's all.'

Norah paused to let this sink in.

'Someone put a loaded gun in my flat,' she said.

'Yes,' said Sandra. 'And you'll take it to the police first thing tomorrow.'

'I will not.'

'Excuse me?'

'Where would that get me? I haven't had any valuables stolen. No one can prove that I didn't get hold of the gun myself. I'm not going to the police until I have some kind of proof.'

She thought for a second.

'I still can't believe Grimm reported me,' she added, recalling her embarrassing encounter with the policewoman.

She hadn't heard from her again, but the shock was deep-seated.

'It was clever of him,' Sandra said. 'But don't worry about it. Let me know as soon as the police get in touch with you and I'll take care of everything.'

'Thank you, Sandra.'

Norah lit a cigarette and offered one to Max who refused. Paul got up and opened the window.

'Sorry,' Norah said, 'I should have asked.'

'It's okay,' Paul said. 'Just this once.'

'A nasty stalker,' Norah said, after a few drags. 'I don't know.'

'Don't you trust my judgment?' Sandra asked.

'Yes, I do,' Norah said, and it was true.

'So what's wrong? What's bugging you?'

Norah thought about it. Max topped up their glasses, as if she'd just dropped in for a drink and a chat.

'Something's not right,' Norah said. 'When I confronted Grimm with Valerie's name, he reacted so strangely.'

'Hang on,' Sandra said. 'You confronted Grimm?'

Norah bit her tongue. She'd deliberately left out that part of the story because she could imagine her friends' reactions.

'Jesus, Norah,' Sandra said, and Norah heard her clap her hands to her face.

Max and Paul looked at Norah in horror.

'Have I got this right,' Max said. 'You went up to this guy you think is a murderer—a man who probably has a great deal to lose—and confronted him straight-out?'

Norah was silent.

'Sometimes I have my doubts about your intelligence,' said Max.

'Me too,' Norah said with a shrug.

'And me,' Sandra said. 'But that's not the point right now. What did Grimm say?'

'When I said Valerie's name, he started off pretending he'd never heard of her. But then he said—and I quote—*I didn't do anything to your little friend.*'

Max and Paul gaped at Norah. Norah couldn't see Sandra's expression, but guessed that she, too, was surprised.

'Can you explain that to me?' Norah said. 'Why would he say that if he had no idea what I was talking about?'

For a while nobody spoke.

'It doesn't add up,' Max said. 'It makes no sense at all. It must be some kind of joke. Probably cooked up by whoever's sending you the texts.'

'But shockingly malicious and dangerous,' said Paul. 'A costly, elaborate, totally depraved kind of joke.'

'Psycho terror,' said Max.

'Terror art,' Paul added.

Norah drained her glass.

'You don't look convinced,' Max said.

'I don't know,' she said. 'Who'd go to such great lengths just to wear me down?'

'No idea,' Sandra cried. 'You tell us!'

'We do know one thing about the person who's done all this,' said Max.

'Do we?' Norah asked. 'What?'

'You know him,' he replied.

Or her, Norah thought, nodding thoughtfully.

'It started when I moved to Vienna,' she said.

Nobody said anything.

'I'll send a text suggesting we meet up.'

'No way!' Sandra cried. 'You'll do nothing of the sort. It would be better if you went somewhere else for a few days.'

'I wouldn't dream of it. How would we ever find out who I'm up against if I went away?'

'We wouldn't. You need to keep your distance from this psycho. Don't react to any more messages or calls—not in any way. Keep clear of Arthur Grimm, and if anything seems strange to you, you must call the police at once.'

Norah's eyes fell on Max's British bulldog Lolita who was asleep on the rug, oblivious to the excited buzz of voices filling her territory.

'You're worried,' Norah said.

'Of course I'm worried,' Sandra replied. 'Whoever's behind this story is clearly crazy.'

'Okay,' said Norah, 'I'll take your advice and lie low. But I don't think he or she is going to stop.'

She noticed that she was fiddling with her cigarettes again. She opened the packet and took one out.

'I have this feeling that something's going to happen on February 11. And it's only three days off.'

'Now listen to me,' Sandra said firmly. 'You're not going anywhere on February 11 and certainly not to the Prater.'

'What about my interview?' Norah asked.

'You'll cancel it, of course. Call in sick. If your boss is angry, you'll just have to put up with it.'

'And the gun? I need to get rid of the gun.'

'As a lawyer I have to advise you to do the right thing and hand it in at a police station.'

'And as a friend?' Norah asked.

'Have you touched it?'

Norah shook her head. 'No.'

'Then, as your friend who knows that you haven't had the best of experiences with the police, I would understand if you went and dropped it in a deep stretch of the Danube,' Sandra said drily. 'Provided you wear gloves,' she added. 'But since I'm a lawyer I do of course have to advise you against such a course of action.'

'I see.'

'If you like, I'll come and keep an eye on you,' Sandra said. 'I could jump on the next plane.'

Norah smiled. Sandra was tough—not someone to worry herself for no reason.

'That's sweet of you, but not necessary,' she said. 'But thanks.'

'All right,' Sandra said. 'This is the plan: you keep calm and take care of yourself. Especially on the eleventh. And I'll have a think about how best to deal with all this. And especially what we tell the police. Because there's no question that sooner or later we're going to have to take this to the police, okay?'

'Yes, ma'am.'

'It's not funny.' Sandra sounded severe.

'I know.'

'I'll come up with something,' Sandra said more mildly.

'And we'll hunker down together on the eleventh,' Max said, 'at least in the evening.'

'Okay,' said Norah. 'On one condition. You bring a bottle of this amazing red wine with you.'

'No way,' said Paul.

He grinned.

'We'll bring two.'

47

Norah would have liked to spend the night at Max and Paul's instead of returning to her lonely, empty flat, where she hadn't felt properly safe even before the gun had turned up under her bed. But she gritted her teeth and caught a cab back to Rilkeplatz. Up in the flat, she put the black case in her handbag. Then she headed straight out again, found a lonely spot on the Danube Canal and dropped the gun in the water.

Now, in the semi-darkness of the living room, she was sitting on the sofa in only a sweatshirt, her bare legs pulled up to her chest. The television was on mute; there was something soothing about the moving images. Norah tore a page out of her notebook, picked up a biro, then stopped, the pen hovering over the paper. She didn't hesitate because she couldn't think of any potential ill-wishers—she could come up with a few. But she found it hard to gauge them. How could you tell if someone was vindictive or given to cruel pranks? *Could* you tell? Norah began to doodle.

There had been that stalker, years ago, before she moved to Berlin. He'd inundated her with emails and texts, bombarded her with calls, lain in wait for her—but all that was deep in the past. Who else? Alex was out of the question; he was the least malicious person she knew. And the men before him? None of them had lasted long or been particularly serious—and they were all ancient history. No. None of those men would dream of following her and breaking into her flat just to scare her. Not even crazy Igor, the dancer she'd gone out with before Alex; he was working in Russia at the moment anyway and Norah was sure he had no idea she'd moved to Vienna. No, he may have been crazy, but it wasn't him.

What about women? There must be one or two who held a grudge against her. What about the wife of that doctor she'd dated for a while—Gustav, the one who picked her up in a bar in Kreuzberg and told her he was single? His wife had left a few nasty messages on Norah's phone when she found out—fair enough, Norah had thought and seen no reason to hold it against her. She'd called things off with Gustav and hadn't heard from the woman since. It seemed unlikely that she should suddenly emerge from the shadows.

And work connections? Norah had been working as a journalist for a good fifteen years, mainly freelance at first and then—in Berlin, for example, or here in Vienna—as part of an editorial team. She wasn't an investigative journalist; she didn't uncover criminal activity or political scandals, but worked mainly in culture, interviewing people, writing reviews and the occasional column—sometimes a travel report or a feature. Nothing very controversial, though there could be no doubt that she'd offended the odd person over the years; she'd more than once received nasty letters at the office. On one occasion a theatre director had even turned up at her flat after she'd panned a play of his and told her that *a cunt like her, who didn't know the first thing about dramaturgy, would do best to avoid the subject.* Norah had taken her revenge by sketching the incident in a column. She hadn't named the director, but it was hardly necessary; anyone with any knowledge of the Berlin cultural scene would have known who she was talking about. Norah hadn't heard from him since. Was *he*, perhaps, rearing his head again after all these years? Unlikely. As far as she knew, he was still in Berlin, stuck in the same old rut—starting early on the whisky and getting his kicks out of humiliating his lead actresses.

Norah picked up her phone and reread the texts from the unknown number. She remembered feeling troubled when one of her friends had talked of *him* wanting to do her in, and now she knew why. Without really thinking about it, she had simply assumed that she was dealing with a woman. Yes, it *was* a woman. She could feel it.

'Who are you?' Norah whispered, biting her lower lip, but her mind was a blank.

She put her phone down and ran through the names in her head again, then discarded the pen and tore the paper into shreds. Yes, she'd rubbed a lot of people up the wrong way and caused a lot of trouble. An awful lot. But it was no good rummaging around in the past; all this had started when she moved to Vienna. It had all begun in this beautiful, morbid city. That couldn't be a coincidence.

48

The next morning, the normality of office life seemed almost unreal to Norah. How could two such different worlds exist in parallel? One of them ordered and subject to clearly defined routines—emails and coffee breaks, editorial meetings and deadlines—the other as chaotic as a work of abstract expressionism. Norah buried her face in her hands, ignoring pitying glances from Aylin who, as usual, looked as fresh as a daisy and probably assumed that Norah had boozed her way through the night again.

The day after tomorrow. February 11 was only the day after tomorrow. Maybe the others were right—maybe if Norah lay low, it would all be over after that. But could she lie low? Could she face the prospect of never getting to the bottom of this story? Of course she couldn't. Stories were her life. Or what was left of it. There was no way she could sit around waiting; she had to do something.

There was one more thing she could try. One last-ditch hope. Norah grabbed her phone and wrote:

We have to talk. 10 p.m. tonight in Cafe Jonathan. I'll come alone. Promise.

Norah still hadn't received a reply when she set off through the dark streets that evening, but since that meant no rejection as well as no acceptance, she decided to keep the appointment, just in case. *Aren't the days supposed to be getting longer?* she thought. It didn't feel like it. She had the impression it was always night.

She walked without hurrying in an effort to calm her nerves and slow her racing pulse. She'd be there in five minutes anyway; she was ridiculously early. But she wanted to be the first to arrive; she wanted a table from which she could see everyone who came into the cafe. She wasn't at all sure this was a good idea. It was probably an appalling idea. But she couldn't sit at home and wait. Her friends should have known that.

All the way from her flat, the streets were plastered with the same posters she'd seen in town. They were everywhere—deep black letters on a garish background.

ARE YOU SURE?

The roads were more or less deserted; Vienna was getting on with things, without bothering about her. She could see Cafe Jonathan ahead.

She had been to the cafe once before, with Tanja. Cosy and warmly lit, it seemed to her the perfect place for the rendezvous she had planned. You felt at ease there; it was busy but not bursting, loud enough to prevent eavesdropping, but not so loud that you had to shout across the tables. As Norah walked in, she looked about her to see if anyone stared at her or reacted to her in any way, but apart from two men drinking beer at the bar, who gave her the once-over, she noticed nothing. Certainly, neither of the men—young, well-dressed, dull and attractive—was the person she was here to meet; Norah was sure she was looking for a woman. She found a table tucked away in a corner near the door and sat down on a chair that gave her a good view of whoever came in.

She ordered a glass of wine and waited.

It wasn't long before the door opened. Norah froze, but immediately relaxed again when she saw a small group come into the cafe—presumably students. A glance at her watch told her that it was just gone ten. She sipped her wine and wondered how she would recognise the woman she'd been texting. She had no answer to the question, but felt sure that her instinct would guide her. A couple paid at the bar and left. Before the door had closed behind them, a tall red-haired woman walked in—late twenties, Norah guessed. Her eye caught Norah's for a second, as she scanned the cafe—then she turned away and sat down at the bar. No, Norah thought, sipping her wine, that wasn't her. Too conspicuous. And too young.

Norah kept her eye firmly on the door. Through the buzz of voices, she heard the red-haired woman order a gin and tonic and begin to flirt with the two young upstarts next to her.

Two hours later, Norah called a taxi and went home. Given that she hadn't really expected the woman to turn up, she felt unduly disappointed.

49

Norah slept a kind of hospital sleep—the fitful half-sleep you drift in and out of at the bedside of someone who is gravely ill. She remembered dozing like this, without ever feeling rested, in the weeks before her mother died.

Now she was lying on the sofa, staring into the semi-darkness of her flat. Every now and then the headlights of a passing car threw small illuminated artworks onto the living-room wall. Norah groped for her phone, squinting when the screen lit up in her face. She didn't hold out much hope of a message. She'd checked so many times already it seemed unlikely there'd be anything this time.

There wasn't. Norah made sure that the text-message tone was activated and put the phone back down, then dozed off again. When she woke, the light in the room had changed. She tried to heave herself up, but had been lying on her right arm for so long that it gave way beneath her when she tried to lean on it. How long had she been asleep? Two hours, according to her phone. Better than nothing. Norah massaged her arm and checked for messages. She must have slept deeply; she hadn't heard a thing, but there in her inbox was the text she'd been waiting for when she dropped off.

I don't go to bars.

Norah got up and switched on the lights. Then she sat back down on the sofa. What was the point of that? Whoever wrote that might just as well not have bothered. But she did, Norah thought. Because she wants to communicate with me. The text had been sent only half an hour ago.

What are you afraid of? Norah wrote.

The reply came immediately.

You ask the wrong questions.

Norah almost hurled the phone at the wall, but forced herself to stay calm.

Did Arthur Grimm kill Valerie? she typed.

You've met him. What do you think?

That he has guilt written all over his face, Norah thought.

How do you know it was him? she asked.

This time she had to wait for an answer.

What difference does it make?

We could go to the police, Norah wrote.

No proof. Not enough, after all these years.

Was it you sent me the gun? Norah asked.

No reply. Norah noticed that she had started to pace furiously up and down—probably just thinking about the gun under her bed. She was suddenly livid with rage.

How did you get in my flat? she added.

No reply.

I threw it in the canal! Norah wrote.

A short pause, then:

Doesn't matter.

Norah ran a hand through her hair.

Do you want me to do it? she wrote.

Silence again. Norah put her phone down on the table, finished smoking her cigarette, then went into the kitchen to fetch a glass of water. She hadn't expected an answer—certainly not a direct one—and was surprised to find a reply when she got back to the living room.

Yes.

Why me? Norah wrote.

Who else?

I'm not sure that I can.

The question is do you want to? And you do.

What makes you think that?

The fact that you're still speaking to me.

Norah blinked, stunned. The next message popped up on the screen.

You want to and you can.

Why is it so important to you? Norah asked.

For a while, there were no more texts. Then, once again, Norah saw three dots skipping up and down on her screen.

Because I loved her too.

'Who are you?' Norah whispered. 'Who the fuck are you?'

Why don't you do it yourself? she asked.

I would if I could.

Norah thought feverishly. Who had loved Valerie? Her parents, of course. Her brother. But that was absurd. Who else? Was there someone she didn't know about?

Why February 11? she asked.

It was a test, that was all.

Tomorrow, she thought dully. It's tomorrow.

You know why, was the swift reply.

Of course.

And why the Prater?

The next three messages came in swift succession. A salvo.

He'll be there.

The two of you will be alone.

It will be perfect.

Norah stared at the screen, her anger growing by the second. No way was she going to act as hitman for somebody who was hiding behind an anonymous phone number and obscure insinuations.

I won't do it, she wrote.

Again, the reply came quickly.

It's your decision.

For a long time, Norah sat there, staring at the messages. She was sure the other person was doing the same. Was it possible to get a feel for someone you were only texting? Norah tried to listen to her gut. Man or woman? she wondered. *Woman.* Old or young? *Old.* Older than Norah anyway. Or was she? Already Norah was beginning to feel less certain. Glancing at her watch, she realised that the sun was about to rise.

Don't you ever sleep? she wrote.

Three dots jumped up and down on the screen.

I can't.

Why not?

I'm too sad.

Why? Norah asked.

There was no reply for a long time; then she saw that the other person was writing a message.

I'm lonely.

Me too, Norah thought. She put her phone down and waited for the sun to rise.

50

Rain pelted against the windows and the winter landscape was a never-ending strip of earthy brown, tired green and dead grey. Behind Norah, across the aisle, sat an elderly couple whose old faces looked grimly similar, as is sometimes the way with people who have lived together for a long time. Norah had often wondered whether one changed more than the other—and if so, which—or whether the two met somewhere in the middle. Further up the carriage, Norah could hear a group of teenagers talking in an almost impenetrable dialect. She was glad the train wasn't crowded and that the seat next to her was empty so that she was spared having to make conversation.

Arriving at the station to catch the Salzburg train—it was the day she was to interview the conductor—Norah had heard piano music in the distance and soon spotted a grand piano which had been put there so that passing train travellers could entertain one another. It was something she'd often seen in other cities—at the airport in Rome, for instance, and in various stations in the Netherlands—and she'd always admired those who had the guts to sit down and play in public.

As she hurried to her platform, she saw that in this case the pianist was a young woman. Norah vaguely recognised the pop song she was playing, without knowing what it was, and the tune must have lodged itself in her head because she soon heard exasperated throat clearing behind her and realised she was humming along. She fell silent—and then gave a start when her phone rang.

'Norah?' said Max.

'Yes, hi,' she said. 'How are you doing?'

'Norah? I can barely hear you. Hello?'

'Yes. Sorry. Hello? Sorry, I'm on the train.'

'Ah, now I can hear you,' said Max. 'Can you hear me?'

'I can hear you. What's up?'

Instinctively, Norah glanced over her shoulder at the elderly couple, as if she could feel their disapproving looks on the back of her head. And indeed: the corners of their mouths had slipped even lower. If she hadn't had an alarmed-sounding Max at the other end of the line, she'd have been tempted to smile.

'Okay,' said Max. 'It's a bit weird, and I'm not sure what it all means.'

'Spare me the suspense,' Norah said.

'I've been trying to find out a bit about this woman,' Max said.

Norah felt her antennae twitch.

'What woman?'

'Dorotea Lechner.'

'And?'

'Her name rang a bell,' Max said, 'so I googled her and found out that I saw her in a play not all that long ago. And it seemed strange that she should have turned to begging.'

'Very strange,' said Norah, 'but—'

'I couldn't stop thinking about it. So I asked—a bit. And—what's weird?'

'Max, I can't really hear you.'

'I said: do you know what's weird?'

'What?'

'She—acting jobs until—died. Nothing major—still.'

'What are you getting at?'

'She was engaged by a theatre again soon before she died. And guess—'

The connection broke off. Norah cursed under her breath.

'Max?'

Nothing. A few seconds later, the train entered a tunnel. When it came out on the other side, Norah tried to ring Max back, but without any luck. Never mind. She'd try again after the interview. Dorotea Lechner was dead—it could hardly be urgent.

Some years ago I met a profiler at a party.

I told him I was interested in serial killers and asked him all kinds of questions, which he answered in such weary, blasé tones that I soon realised I'd asked the things everybody asked when he told them what he did. There was only one question he had to think about and I was a little annoyed at my childish pride at having finally managed to pique his interest. After all, I'd already made a name for myself by then; if anything, *he* should have been the one trying to impress *me*.

What I wanted to know was whether there was any way of recognising serial killers. *Good question*, my then-wife said. *What would set your alarm bells ringing?* she asked the profiler.

I'd expected him to laugh and say that he was afraid there were no simple telltale signs. But he had to stop and think, and his answer was interesting. *A lot of serial killers*, he said, *have a desperate urge to talk about what they have done. Of course, they can only talk in hedged and shrouded terms, but the compulsion is strong; there's this hefty great thing in their lives, an obsession that occupies them day and night, but is completely taboo. Many people who unwittingly come into contact with such types report being asked, apparently jokingly, 'Do I look like a murderer?' Or, 'Do you think I'm capable of murder?' So to answer your question*, the profiler said, *being asked a thing like that might well set my alarm bells ringing.*

Since that evening, the question has been part of my repertoire of dinner-party small talk: *Do you think I'm capable of murder?* (My ex-wife was never amused by this, which always rather puzzled the women I was making conversation with.) Of course, the opinion of a casual party acquaintance is of absolutely no consequence, but the answers to the question are invariably entertaining and I always take a well-considered 'yes' as a compliment. What is more interesting is to ask the question of others. There was a time when that was a real fixation of mine— perhaps a professional tic. Would the taxi driver who was giving me a lift be capable of murder? My local chemist? The policewoman on the beat? That photographer setting up his tripod? The man on that park bench over there? The waitress taking my order?

And Norah Richter? Is she capable of murder? I can hardly wait to find out.

51

On the train back to Vienna, the landscape flashing past outside was a dim haze of black shapes against a deep blue background; only here and there lights flared up and went out again like dying stars. The conductor—a tall, slim woman with a cloud of bouncing grey curls—had turned out to be unpretentious and easy to talk to. Given the circumstances, Norah thought, the interview had gone well.

The only trouble was that the woman had talked about her current projects with such enthusiasm and at such length that Norah had got behind schedule and would have missed the Vienna train if it hadn't been a quarter of an hour late leaving Salzburg.

When at last she'd found her seat and settled down, she listened to the message Max had left on her voicemail. He had a business dinner to go to, he said, so just very quickly: not long before she died, Dorotea Lechner had been engaged to act in an *installation in public space*. The role of Cassandra. Max repeated that and Norah could hear the excitement in his voice. 'What I'm trying to say is I don't think Lechner was a real beggar; I think she was playing the part of a beggar. Someone went to some lengths to organise all that. And I don't like that, Norah. I don't like it at all.'

Norah looked out of the window wondering what it all meant. A sense of unease crept over her and for the first time since the strange goings-on had begun, she felt that she had all the pieces of the puzzle in front of her and had only to put them together. But she couldn't get them to join up; there was still something she couldn't put her finger on—a crucial piece of information she couldn't bring to the surface.

She looked alternately out of the window and at a white-haired man who was filling his pipe in anticipation of their imminent arrival. Funny, Norah found herself thinking, pipe tobacco didn't smell as bad as she'd thought. It was actually rather a nice smell.

The driver announced that they would soon be arriving in Vienna. When Norah got off the train, a glance at the display panel told her that it was past midnight. February 11 had begun—and once again, Norah had the feeling she was being watched. She scanned the faces on the platform, but couldn't see anyone she recognised. She suddenly felt as if her body were fighting a disease—viral flu, or worse—and for a moment she thought of getting back on the train and going away, spending February 11 far from Vienna—escaping. But she wasn't like that. She wasn't the kind to run away.

Norah shouldered her bag and took the stairs down to the concourse.

Dank cold and piano music. A requiem, though Norah wasn't sure of the composer. She shuddered, looking about her as she made for the exit, unsteady on her feet as if she'd discharged herself from hospital in defiance of doctors' orders. All she wanted was to get home, but she had to keep dodging lurching drunks and latecomers running to catch trains.

Norah was amazed at the number of people still about at this time of night; more than once, someone bumped into her before she had time to get out of their way. The atmosphere, though, had changed since the afternoon, almost as if the mood in the station had shifted with the music. The pop song that had accompanied the afternoon's buzz of activity had given way to a lugubrious tune for late-night commuters, tired night owls, defeated football fans and a homeless man, rolled up asleep near the left-luggage lockers. Norah approached him cautiously, wary of waking him, and stuffed a crumpled five-euro note in his paper cup. Then she went on her way, advancing slowly, one step at a time, as if battling through a snowstorm. The lingering sounds of the piano drifted over to her, faded and died, and for a moment there was silence. Then a new piece began, sedate and solemn, the 'Moonlight Sonata'. It was a piece she had always associated with death.

The feeling of being watched didn't leave her. When she reached the exit, she stopped and looked about her. Nothing. But then she smelt it—barely perceptible, and yet unmistakable. *That smell.* All at once, Norah knew what it was she associated with pipe tobacco. Not the scent of pipe smoke as such, but a particular old-fashioned aftershave. She had just caught a whiff of it—sweet and bitter at the same time. Nauseating. And then it came to her. She knew who it reminded her of.

The station concourse before her was suddenly red with blood. It dripped from the roof, streaked the ground, covered people's skin, soaked into their clothes, matted their hair. Norah could smell the sweet, metallic smell. She could taste it on her tongue.

It lasted only a moment, then Norah blinked and the station was just a station again.

But *that smell*. She turned away, the taste of blood on her lips, and hurried off.

52

Strange, Norah thought. It's worse than anything I'd expected, and yet I am suddenly completely calm.

Heading home in a taxi, she tried to get the sickly-sweet smell out of her nose. The theme of the sonata she had heard in the station washed over her, seeping bleak and solemn into her pores, as faces and snatches of words flashed into her mind and vanished again.

The sudden grim intuition she'd had as she left the station had cleared her head; she saw everything plainly now. Her doubts were gone; she knew all there was to know.

When her phone rang, over and over, relentlessly, she ignored it. She must act alone now.

Norah went into the bistro on the corner of her street and saw that there was only one customer left, a man at the bar, nursing what looked like a last beer. The barman glared at her as if to say: *Did you have to come now, just as I was about to put the chairs on the tables?*

'Just a quick vodka,' she said.

He nodded, without smiling and set the glass down in front of her. Norah tipped it back; the alcohol stung her parched throat. She swallowed drily, as if to see whether her stomach would take it. Then she fished a note out of her jeans pocket, put it on the counter, thanked the barman and went out.

As Norah climbed the stairs to her flat, she thought of Valerie. She thought of Arthur Grimm and all that Angelika Reiter had told her about him.

Her anger contracted like a mollusc.

She saw herself pointing a gun at Grimm. She saw the terror on his face.

And where, only a few hours earlier, there had been fear and uncertainty, there was now certainty and hate.

When Norah entered the kitchen, there was a revolver lying on the table. For a split second, she thought it must be the same gun as before, returned to her as if by magic—as if attracted, magnet-like, by the mere force of her hatred. Actually, of course, it was only a twin of the gun she had thrown in the canal. Somebody must have brought it round while she was out.

That figured.

Norah stepped closer. Peered at the gun. Picked it up and examined it. There was only one cartridge in the cylinder. She'd have to aim well. But she knew she could.

First, though, she needed proof. Norah put the gun back on the table and went to sit at her laptop. It didn't take her five minutes to find out what she wanted to know. She sat there, stunned. It was so easy, when you knew what you were looking for.

It was exactly as she'd thought.

The bastard.

Norah picked up her phone and saw that she had six missed calls from Coco and two from Max. She closed her eyes for a moment; there was so much to do, so much to sort out. She tried Tanja first. Then she rang Coco, who needed comforting. After that, she spoke to Max. Finally, she made one last call.

When she got off the phone, she had a good, long think. It took her some time to get everything straight in her mind and overcome her resistance. It was suddenly all so final; every action seemed like a ritual. Animal blood, candlelight, white robes.

Norah climbed the stairs to Theresa's and rang the doorbell.

'I've come to say goodbye,' she said when Theresa opened up, her eyes red and glazed as if she'd been asleep.

When everything had been taken care of, she sat down at the living-room table with her phone and tried to calm herself. Talking to Theresa and processing what she had said had left Norah exhausted. But now all was ready.

She couldn't quite believe that it had been so easy. Grimm would come to the Prater and she would get her chance. She had only to be prepared. There was no turning back now.

In front of her lay a loaded gun. Before twenty-four hours were up, she would have used that gun to shoot somebody.

With good reason and of her own free will.

53

After nights of exile on the sofa, Norah had slept in her bed again, the gun beside her. She knew as soon as she opened her eyes. Today was the day.

She looked at her watch—a little before nine. The eleventh. A dark, wet February morning in Vienna. She went into the kitchen for a glass of water, surprised at how calm she was. No more trembling fingers. She longed for the evening to come. She knew what she had to do. The night before, she had prepared everything and then sunk into a dreamless sleep. There would be no sleep tonight. Norah drank another glass of water. When it was empty, she saw that the orchid she had brought from Berlin had wilted.

She decided to have coffee in the corner bistro. On the way there she saw the young woman who had once given her a caramel—Marie. She was standing in a doorway on the other side of the road, talking into her phone and crying. Norah averted her eyes.

The three old ladies were at their usual table and nodded at Norah when she walked in. She ordered a cappuccino and a croissant. When she'd finished eating and drinking, she glanced up and saw that the clock above the door had stopped. Like a watch that stops when somebody dies, Norah thought.

Back in her flat it was, at last, time for Norah to make final arrangements. First she rang Max.

'Hello,' he said.

'Morning. All well with you?'

'Sure. And you? Today's the big day.'

As if she didn't know.

'Are you still on for this evening?' Max asked. 'Still up for hunkering down together? We could get in some food from the Thai restaurant you like. I've already bought the wine.'

'That's why I'm calling,' Norah said. 'I'm not feeling great. I think I might be coming down with something.'

There was a moment's silence.

'You're not just saying that so that you can slope off to the Prater this evening, are you?'

'Have I ever lied to you?' Norah asked.

'No, I don't think you have,' said Max. 'Have you seen a doctor?'

'No, but I really don't think it's necessary. I just need to sleep it off.'

'It's probably the stress of the last few weeks,' Max said, sounding worried. 'Do you need anything? Is there anything we can bring you?'

'No, I'm okay. The fridge is full; I won't need to go out today. I have a feeling I'll sleep all day anyway.'

'Have you got a temperature?'

Norah almost smiled. Max always had loved looking after people. When they were students, he was the one who had held her hair out of her face when she got home so drunk or stoned that she had to throw up; he was the one who'd made sure she ate properly and lectured her when she confessed to having had unprotected sex. He'd make a great dad one of these days—though his mothering did get her down sometimes.

'I don't know. I just feel really knackered and weak. Maybe I ate

236

something funny in Salzburg—I don't know,' Norah groaned. 'But you've no need to come round this evening. I'm not exactly good company and I wouldn't want to give you anything.'

'But it's February 11,' Max said. 'I really don't want you to be alone this evening.'

'That's very sweet of you,' said Norah, 'but don't worry, I'm not going anywhere; I'll stay in and sleep it off. We'll make up for it some other time, okay?'

'All right then,' Max said. 'If you say so. But you're to get in touch if you need anything, okay?'

Norah's heart was suddenly heavy when she realised that this was probably the last time she would speak so freely to her best friend. Maybe even the last time she'd speak to him altogether. She almost said something sentimental, but then the game would have been up. So she just said, 'Okay!' and hung up.

Sandra was trickier, but Norah had expected that. On the other hand, she found it easier to lie to her than to Max—maybe she was getting into her stride.

'I'll be asleep all day anyway,' Norah said, hoping her voice sounded weak and rasping.

'I don't care—you're not to be alone,' Sandra said. 'And if Max and Paul think they can shirk their responsibility, then *I'm* coming round.'

'That's ridiculous.'

'Stopping my best friend from doing something stupid is ridiculous?' Sandra asked brusquely.

'What do you mean—*something stupid?*' Norah asked, feeling foolish because they both knew what Sandra meant.

She sighed.

'Okay,' she said, 'I know what you're thinking.'

She searched for the right words.

'But it's all over,' she lied. 'You're right. Grimm is innocent.'

She took a sip of water.

'I expect it's the stress coming to an end; all I want to do is sleep. I

237

don't want to see anyone or talk to anyone; I just want to leave all this stuff behind me. I'm tired.'

'You sound tired,' Sandra said.

'Believe me,' said Norah, 'the last place I want to be this evening is the fucking Prater.'

Sandra had, eventually, been persuaded that Norah was all right. There was a ring at the door just as Norah put the phone down. The man—forty-odd, thick-lashed blue eyes, Britpop hairstyle—declined to come in, which was probably, she thought, for the best. Just because he'd been recommended to her, didn't mean she wanted him in her flat. He was unassuming—a little taller than her, dressed in black jeans and a blue denim jacket too thin for the time of year. He took a small packet out of his rucksack and held it out to Norah without a word. She took it, handing him in exchange the envelope she had ready. He glanced inside, nodded and vanished silently down the stairs. Soon afterwards, Norah heard the front door swing shut.

She unwrapped the little box of ammunition at the kitchen table and loaded the old-fashioned revolver. She'd decided that a single bullet wouldn't be enough. When everything was ready, she sat down at the window with a cup of coffee and a packet of cigarettes and waited for darkness to fall.

54

Norah looked at the gun that lay loaded on the kitchen table. Soon she would put it in her handbag and set off for the Prater to put an end to things.

She had to. But she wasn't ready yet.

She felt a sudden surge of longing for Alex, a fierce ache between her throat and her breastbone, as if something had been torn from its ligaments and flung against the inside of her ribs. Lying in front of her on the table, her phone suddenly seemed no less dangerous than the loaded revolver beside it. For three years, she had talked to Alex about everything. *Everything.* How could it all be over from one day to the next? How was it possible that what was happening to her was happening—that she was planning what she was planning—and hadn't told Alex? Alex would have listened to her; Alex would have believed her, right from the start. Why hadn't she talked to him?

Because you screwed up, Norah.

Suddenly she had the phone in her hand and was calling Alex's number. It rang. And rang.

She jumped when she heard his voice—closed her eyes for a second.

'Hi, this is Alex.'

Then she realised: it was only his voicemail.

'I can't take your call right now, but I'll get back to you as soon as I can.'

A beep.

'Hey,' she said. 'It's me.'

Her mouth was dry.

'Norah,' she added, realising that a little more was needed, now that they'd split up.

'Hey, I just wanted to say…'

She hesitated.

'I just wanted to say I'm sorry.'

She stopped and would have liked to say something else, but couldn't find the right words and hung up. She pushed the phone away from her and buried her face in her hands, suddenly realising that she had just said goodbye to Alex. 'Fuck it,' she muttered, reaching for her phone again.

I love you, she typed.

It was only as she wrote the words that she knew how much she meant them. Her finger hovered over the screen. Then she pressed *Send*. Even before she could put the phone down, the icon under the message switched from *Sent* to *Read* and her heart leapt to her throat. She stared at her phone for seconds—minutes, even—waiting for a reply. But there was no reply. What had she expected? Norah pushed the phone away again, took a deep breath and waited for the surge of adrenaline to subside.

She looked about her in the cold, empty flat. Cardboard boxes, dust, loneliness. But after sitting quietly for a while, Norah began to hear the music her flat was playing to her. It started softly, almost tentatively, but as she listened more closely, it seemed to surge and swell. The soft creak of the floorboards, the hum of the fridge, the steady trickle of dust, as slow as a glacier, the muffled sounds of the street coming in at the windows. Life.

It had been dark for hours. Norah got up, put the gun in her bag and pulled on her shoes and parka. Her phone buzzed. Her hands trembled as she reached for it, but it wasn't Alex. It was the unknown number.

The Prater, in an hour's time. He'll be there. Please come. For Valerie's sake.

Norah almost laughed. Did the anonymous texter really think she needed reminding?

She went into the bathroom and looked in the mirror. She put on red lipstick, applying it like war paint. Then she took her bag with the gun in it and left the flat. The taxi she had ordered that afternoon was waiting for her outside.

From the back of the cab she saw more of the garish posters; they seemed to have spread through the city like metastases. The background was painfully pink and the big black letters asked Norah the same question, over and over.

ARE YOU SURE?

Norah thought of all the stories that had kept her from sleeping over the course of the years. She recited them to herself, conjuring the faces of war criminals, murderers, thugs. She thought of Leonie's rapist. She thought of the man who had tied his allegedly unfaithful girlfriend to his car in front of the children and dragged her to her death. She thought of all those ordinary bastards who were beating up their wives right now, as she crossed Vienna in a taxi. She thought of the man who had ruined Coco's life—of all the men who had got off scot-free and would continue to do so. She thought of Arthur Grimm.

'Yes,' Norah said softly, ignoring the look the taxi driver gave her in the rear-view mirror. 'Yes, I'm sure.'

She touched the gun in her bag.

She was ready.

55

There was garbled waltz music coming from somewhere, but Norah couldn't work out where. The rides were all shut for the night. Was it one of the fruit machines?

Just before she got out at the Prater, Norah had received an email. More compromising material about Grimm who, if the emailer was to be believed, had twice been reported for GBH and once for attempted rape, but had got off on all counts. The attachments contained photos. Norah clicked on a jpg entitled 'AngelikaReiter1' and saw a woman with short blonde hair, a bruised face and a bloody, swollen nose, who looked as if she'd been photographed for police records. Her eyes were closed and there was a look of shame on her face. Norah felt the blood shoot to her cheeks, she felt her heart begin to thud, her breath quicken. God, she was furious. And God, it felt great. She mustn't give up.

Norah had asked the taxi driver to drop her at the back of the Prater, not at the main entrance. The big wheel rose high in the sky and she couldn't work out whether it was turning extremely slowly or whether she was so overwrought that she was seeing things. She left the road behind her and headed for the fairground. The further she went, the fainter the sounds from the street and the fewer people she saw. At first, she glimpsed the occasional person scurrying along beneath the dark bare trees, but a few minutes from the road she met hardly anyone.

A jogger passed her at the bumper cars, which were shut up for the winter, and a little further on she saw two people out for a walk who seemed to be following her at some distance. Otherwise there wasn't a soul. The closed rides had something almost surreal about them; deprived of their function, they became spooky, sinister. No shining, flashing, twinkling lights, no announcements, no voices, no shrieking people on the roller-coaster, no children laughing on the big wheel or begging their parents for popcorn or candy floss. And no music— except for the elusive waltz melody that seemed to come from very far away, swelling and fading, swelling and fading.

And suddenly there was nothing. The music had died away alto-gether; there was nobody far and wide—only Norah and the darkness and, looming in the distance, the big wheel, turning in slow motion. That was where she had to go. To the big wheel. The main entrance. The place the music was coming from. That was where she would find him—where he was waiting for her.

Norah kept going.

On her right was a deserted swing ride, the swings hanging for-lornly, like the branches of a weeping willow, the bright pastel colours almost completely swallowed by the darkness. A metallic screech came from somewhere, a sound as painful and false as in a bad dream. Norah walked on, all her senses alert. She thought of Valerie and Grimm; of the book in her kitchen cupboard and the gun in her bag; of Valerie's mother and the woman in the photos. She thought of Coco and she knew she wouldn't turn back now, whatever happened.

The big wheel was coming closer and Norah could hear the music again.

The night was cold and crisp, the stars clearly visible over the dark fairground. The wind whistled round the corners and from somewhere came the distressed sound of a hinge that needed oiling. There was a smell of storm in the air.

Norah had almost reached the open space in front of the big wheel when she suddenly had the feeling that somebody was there. She stopped and looked about her, but could see no one. Then, just as she was about to go on her way, she glanced down.

They were small, barely noticeable in the dim light of a distant lamppost, but now she saw them. The path was littered with dead birds.

ART AND DEATH

I am often asked why I do what I do.

Jörg Immendorff once used the brilliant metaphor of a soup bowl to explain his work as an artist. Imagine that you have a soup dish. You know that it is decorated with a beautiful design, but you can only get to that design by eating up the thick soup filling the dish.

That is exactly what I do. I spoon up the soup because I want to know what the bottom of the dish looks like. I do it over and over again, because each time the design is different. Each time it is a surprise. And each time, although I am old, I am as excited as a child.

There is nothing left to do.

Everything is ready. A starry, painfully cold night in Vienna, the strains of a waltz, and black wings.

56

The birds lay twisted on the asphalt, their wings strangely spread. As she picked her way over their small bodies, Norah clung for a moment to the illusion that they weren't real, but then she saw a tiny dead eye catch the light from the lamppost and heard Dorotea's voice, as if she were standing beside her.

Flowers wither. Clocks stop. Birds fall dead from the sky.

Slowly, Norah went on her way. She was now on the central avenue that led through the fair to the big wheel, and she tried to keep to the middle and away from the edges; on either side of her, the fairground was dark and shadowy—anything could have been lurking there. After a little while she heard the waltz music again, clearly audible this time, and far ahead she could see the little statue of Basilio Calafati, the Prater showman. It stood on a plinth, arms outstretched, face frozen in a grimace. That was the place. That was where she would find him. That was where it would end.

She didn't hear it or see it; she sensed it. There was something on her left. Norah wheeled round just in time to see a dark figure slip out of the shadows. It didn't even occur to her that it might be a harmless passer-by; she was all too familiar with his strange way of moving. He was suddenly in front of her, barely two arms' lengths away, standing there as if to block her path. Black trousers, black boots, an elegant black coat—his face almost unnaturally white, his pale eyes grave and alert.

'You've come,' Norah said.

In spite of everything, part of her was surprised that he had turned up.

Grimm looked at her for three or four beats, letting her wait for an answer.

'What do you want?'

Norah suppressed the impulse to imitate him. She wasn't here to play games.

'I want to know what happened back then.'

'And you want me to tell you?'

'Who else?'

For a moment Grimm said nothing.

'Why do I have the feeling you're not going to believe me, no matter what I say?'

'Try me,' Norah said.

'You'll leave me in peace afterwards?' Grimm asked.

'It's a promise.'

Grimm laughed and, in spite of the cold, Norah felt herself beginning to sweat. He was only two or three steps from her, the gun was in her bag, the safety catch was on, the bag was open; all she had to do was slip her hand in.

'You said you had proof,' he said.

She nodded.

'It isn't possible,' he said. 'You're lying.'

He must have noticed that he had raised his voice because he checked himself and added more softly, 'You have nothing.'

His right hand moved to his side, as if to reassure himself of something in his coat pocket.

'So why are you here?'

His eyes flashed in the dark. He moved more quickly than she would have thought possible, reaching her in two steps and attempting to wrest her bag from her. Norah just managed to dodge him; his left hand gripped thin air, Norah stumbled, steadied herself, reached into her bag, tossed it aside. Grimm, too, steadied himself and spun round, ready to attack again. Then he saw the gun in her hands. He looked surprised, like someone who has just woken from a dream and finds himself in unfamiliar surroundings. Gasping, he pulled himself up to his full height. His usually inscrutable mask was now the face of a man who knows he has made a possibly fatal mistake. Norah felt her hands trembling and saw that Grimm had noticed.

'You're crazy,' he said.

'Get back,' she said.

Grimm stared at her.

'And if I don't?'

His shrewd eyes glinted wickedly.

'Will you shoot me?'

Norah said nothing.

'It would be murder,' Grimm said. 'That won't bring your little friend back to life.'

'Get back,' said Norah.

Grimm looked at her challengingly and Norah made a tiny step backwards to put some distance between them. He saw.

'You're not going to shoot,' he said, sliding his hand into his pocket.

Norah shot.

The noise was so loud that it deafened her for a second—the recoil so violent that it sent fierce pain through her hands, arms and shoulders. For a long ghastly moment, Grimm's eyes met hers. Then he fell backwards to the ground and lay there motionless. There was immediate silence.

Above them the stars twinkled.

ON FEAR

Fear is something I think about a lot. Fear is a phantom that holds sway over us, without being real. It is of our own making.

I remember the first time I felt the fear of death. I was thirteen years old and still a child—much less mature than the girls on my road who twisted their hair round their fingers and painted their lips with their mothers' lipstick. It all started in the garden and I still have a clear image of our garden in those days—the lawn that was more moss than grass, the small vegetable patch where my mother grew cucumbers and tomatoes, the gooseberry bushes and, right down at the bottom, the compost heap, which I always avoided because my brother told me there were grass snakes living there—big black snakes with yellow marks on their heads. (I never found out whether he was telling the truth.) Beyond the compost heap, a stream formed a natural border to the garden behind, but could easily be jumped. That must have been how the man got in. I was out in the garden on my own one day, playing football, and when I looked up, there he was, with a knife in his hand. It was all so unreal I didn't even scream. I just stood there, rooted to the spot, staring at him as if he were a still from a TV series or one of the horror films I loved to watch—a still which, by some magic, had found its way into real life—into *my* life. To this day, I haven't understood what happened next. The man came up to me and, with a rapid, almost rehearsed-looking movement, he slashed my face with his knife. Then he turned and ran away. He was never found, but he has fuelled my imagination ever since. Who was he and why did he injure a plump little boy and then steal away? What were his motives? Did he have other plans that he was too scared to carry out? Was he hoping to kidnap me? To kill me? I had nightmares about him for years, and the fear I suffered in those nights was far worse than the fear I had felt in the situation itself. The real horror only set in after the event.

Fear has an aesthetics all its own. A frightened woman, for instance, is almost always beautiful. Hitchcock understood that—though his icons of fear are blonde, while mine are dark. I, for my part, didn't overcome my fear until I began to take pleasure in it. These days, there is practically nothing I am afraid of.

57

A sound she couldn't identify and then dazzling light. For a second, Norah was as disoriented as a newborn baby confronted with the world after months of soothing blackness. She blinked and looked around her. Floodlights—somebody had switched on floodlights. And weren't they footsteps behind her? She turned to look, her arm raised to shield her eyes.

Then she saw him.

Tall. Burly. He was coming towards her from the big wheel, his silhouette emerging in the glare, like an image on a developing Polaroid. Norah stared at him. She had recognised him instantly; his hulking figure was as unmistakable as that of the cruel ogre in the book of fairytales she had read as a child. He was only a few metres from her and very smartly dressed; you might have thought he was on his way to a wedding or the opera. He wore a black dinner jacket and white shirt and carried something tucked nonchalantly under his arm. As he approached, Norah realised that it was a top hat.

Eventually he stepped out into the light. Now Norah could see his face—the coarse features that looked as if they were hewn in rough clay, the large-pored skin, the harsh mouth, and the tiny, disarmingly astute eyes. Professor Wolfgang Balder.

The man who made action art involving electric shocks.
The man who poured pig's blood over passers-by.
The man who tortured women and called it art.
The nastiest man Norah knew.
The man who had destroyed Coco's face, her mind, her life.
The Professor. Big B.
Norah's overwrought brain must have short-circuited; she found herself recalling all the things she'd called him in her article. *A charlatan. A violent criminal disguised as an artist. David Copperfield's brutal brother. A poor person's Houdini.*
And she suddenly understood the meaning of his get-up. He wasn't dressed for an evening at the opera; he was dressed as a magician.

In the cold glare of the floodlights, there was something ghostly about the professor; his face looked as rigid as a death mask. But his eyes were twinkling. He came closer. And closer. Then he raised his hands and, with infuriating slowness, began to applaud. Norah stared in stunned shock. He was only an arm's length from her and now she could smell him too—that sickly sweet smell that was peculiar to him, as revolting as blood; as revolting as pipe smoke.
Norah moved away from Balder until at last he stopped clapping and looked at her calmly. Then his impassive gaze wandered to Grimm and he stared at the motionless body lying in the dark at the edge of the path. He stared for a long time. Then he raised his eyes again.
'The curse has struck,' he said and it took Norah a moment to realise that he wasn't speaking to her, but to someone behind her.
She wheeled round and saw Theresa holding a video camera.
'What the fuck's going on?' Norah asked.
The hulking man with the quick, cold eyes that looked too small

for his face tossed his top hat onto the ground and smiled.

'My dear Miss Richter,' he said, 'have you still not worked it out?'

Norah stared at him mutely. She hadn't seen Balder since their last meeting in Berlin and had forgotten how intimidating he was with his massive form and sinister smile.

'Art,' Balder said soberly. And then, smiling, 'Raw, real, bloody, sweaty, filthy, grim, throbbing art.'

Norah took another step backwards.

'I don't understand.'

That shark's rictus again.

'I think it's only fair that I explain it to you,' said Balder.

Norah glanced at Theresa. Balder noticed.

'Yes,' he said. 'She's one of mine.'

Theresa stared at the ground. Norah was about to say something, but didn't have a chance.

'*Curse*,' Balder cried, 'is my last great work of art.'

'Curse?' Norah asked.

The professor nodded.

'On February 11 you will kill a man called Arthur Grimm,' he said dramatically. 'With good reason and of your own free will.'

'How do you know what the woman said?' Norah asked.

Balder bared his teeth.

'Because I paid her to say it.'

He studied Norah's face, evidently satisfied with what he saw.

'But why?' she asked.

Balder tilted his head, as if waiting patiently for her to work it out for herself.

'Art,' Norah said dully.

'An experiment,' Balder explained.

'But…Valerie…' Norah stammered.

He tilted his head again.

'Do you know what a self-fulfilling prophecy is?' he asked.

Norah stared at him in silence.

'Forgive me,' he said. 'Of course you do. It's not hard, after all. A

253

fortune teller prophesies to a superstitious woman that a tall, dark stranger will soon appear in her life and, unconsciously, that woman does everything to fulfil the prophecy. Her world is suddenly full of tall, dark men; she begins actively to seek their company. Looking back, the prophecy will seem to her confirmed, but in fact, she herself has done all the work.'

Norah still said nothing.

'*Curse* was based on the same principle. As I said, it was an experiment. What happens if we prophesy something completely absurd to someone sane, intelligent and not remotely superstitious? Will it be fulfilled?'

'You wanted me to kill Grimm?' Norah said.

She could hear her voice trembling.

'No, you've got it all wrong,' said Balder, clutching his chest in a dramatic gesture of innocence. 'I never wanted you to kill him, young lady; it was an experiment. Did Jackson Pollock know how his pictures would turn out before he threw the paint at the canvases? All I wanted was to see what would happen. I had no idea how it would turn out. There were thousands of possible outcomes. You might have ignored the whole thing, gone to the police, lain low, gone on holiday, moved to another city. Every step that has brought you here this evening was a conscious decision on your part. You decided to seek out Grimm. You decided you had a reason to kill him. And you killed him. All I did was to plant the words in your head: *On February 11 you will kill a man called Arthur Grimm in the Prater, with good reason and of your own free will.*'

Norah was still holding the gun; she could feel the weight of it in her hand. She looked across at Grimm's lifeless body, rushed over to him and put her hand to his throat to feel for a pulse. It was no more than a gesture. Grimm's pale face was turned away from her so that she couldn't see whether his eyes were open or closed. She took a deep breath and realised that she was trembling, but didn't know whether it was with cold or hatred. She pulled herself up and forced herself to turn back to face the professor.

'I've just killed somebody,' she said tonelessly.

'Yes,' said the professor and Norah saw him bite back a grin. 'How does it feel? How does it feel to destroy a life?'

'That's not how it was,' Norah shouted. 'Valerie. And Grimm. The evidence. The guns that kept turning up in my flat...'

She broke off.

'You're lying,' she said eventually. 'It wasn't just a self-fulfilling prophecy. It was *you! You* did this to me! This is *your* work!'

Balder was silent. He looked as if he couldn't decide whether to look proud or caught out.

'How did you do it?' Norah asked.

'*I* didn't do a thing. *You* did all this.'

Norah laughed mirthlessly.

'There's no point lying to me. I was there. I know it wasn't me who got hold of the gun. I know there was someone in my flat. I know that Grimm knew Valerie and—'

Norah cleared her throat.

'I don't understand,' she said. 'He killed Valerie. He—'

She heard Balder laughing softly and broke off again.

'Do you remember our little talk in Berlin?' he asked abruptly. 'Our first talk. In the Adlon.'

Norah stared at him.

'We talked about magic tricks. You knew that I'd incorporated stage magic into my action art and asked whether I could explain a conjuring trick where someone was made to disappear. Do you remember?'

Norah nodded.

'I told you the key to every magic trick,' said Balder. 'Do you remember?'

'Distraction,' Norah replied automatically.

'That's right,' said Balder. 'All great conjuring tricks rely on distraction.'

He looked at her patiently.

'I'd told you,' he said smugly. 'You should have known.'

'Valerie—' Norah began, but Balder interrupted.

'Everyone has some driving force—an incident, a relationship, a trauma—something that defines them, makes them who they are. And whatever it is, it's like a lever; once you know what's driving someone, you have that person in your grip. I didn't have to dig very deep to find out what was driving you; it was soon obvious that it was the death of your best friend.'

Valerie.

Again, Norah's eyes drifted across to Grimm's motionless form. She felt her gorge rise.

'So this wasn't about Valerie?' she said.

It hurt just to say her name.

'No. Never.'

'Valerie was only the distraction.'

'Precisely.'

Balder nodded, apparently amused at her confusion.

'So, do you mean—' Norah began.

'You're getting there,' he said encouragingly.

'You mean he didn't kill Valerie at all?'

'No, I don't think he did.'

'I don't believe you!' Norah yelled. 'You're lying!'

Balder shrugged.

'I shot him,' Norah said in the same toneless voice as before.

'Indeed,' said Balder deliberately, as if he could scarcely believe it himself, 'you shot him. You weren't exaggerating in that article of yours; you really are a fantastic shot!'

For a moment he said nothing.

'I don't understand,' Norah cried. 'Why him? If he was innocent… Why Arthur Grimm?'

Balder looked at her indulgently as if she were an obtuse child.

'We looked for men who were living near your friend at the time of her death and had since moved to Vienna—men who might possibly have known Valerie. We weren't exactly spoilt for choice; finding Grimm was a real stroke of luck. He was just the job. That face!

Undeniably good looking. But sinister, too, don't you agree?'

'And he had to die because of that?'

'*I* didn't shoot him,' Balder cried in mock outrage. '*You* did.'

He bared his teeth again—his version of a smile.

'In Berlin it would have been Leon Weiss,' he added.

'What?' Norah asked, confused.

'Yes!' said Balder. 'I had it all worked out; you very nearly foiled my plans. The whole thing was originally supposed to take place in Berlin: *On February 11 you will kill a man called Leon Weiss.* And so on. Then you moved away in a rush and that was the end of that. We had to improvise. But in the end, Vienna was the better backdrop. Death is at home in Vienna, don't you agree?'

'And that was what you were aiming for?' Norah asked, pointing vaguely in the direction of Grimm.

Balder was silent.

'You're just as guilty of his death as I am!'

'All I did was make a prophecy. Nobody *forced* you to do anything,' Balder replied calmly.

'You gave me reason to believe he'd murdered Valerie.'

Balder spread his arms, but said nothing.

'Why me?' Norah asked. 'Why do you hate me so much? Because I attacked you in the press? Is that it? Because I took Coco's side?'

'Please! That would be despicable.'

'Then why?'

Balder's look of amusement gave way to a more pensive expression.

'I don't know,' he said at length. 'Who can say why one topic interests us more than another. Why we prefer Mahler to Mozart. Why we're drawn to one person in a room of thirty. I'm an artist; I trust my instincts.'

'You call this art—this sick game?'

'*Sick game*,' Balder repeated, smiling indulgently, like a fond father disappointed by his daughter. 'You say that now because you're so close-up. If you want to see the work as a whole, you have to take a step back. Well worth it, I must say. It's great art.'

He stopped for a moment and considered.

'Hasn't death always been the greatest work of art?' he added at length.

When Norah didn't reply, he continued.

'You once wrote in an article that you wished you lived in a work of art. For three weeks now, I have made your wish come true. Yes, I have documented *Curse*. I have shared my art with the world. But large parts of it were for your eyes alone. Only you felt the pull of the curse; only you saw the birds that had fallen from the sky; only you pulled the trigger. If I'd thought you had no appreciation of art, I would never have chosen you to take part in my performance. My art would have been wasted on a philistine.'

'Bullshit!' Norah shouted. 'Complete bullshit. All you care about is power. Nothing else—except perhaps your wounded ego.'

Balder raised bushy eyebrows.

'I've shot an innocent man because of you,' Norah cried.

'As I told you,' Balder said, and Norah saw him glance at the camera, 'I wasn't interested in the man's death; all I was interested in was what you might call the experimental aspect.'

'Bullshit,' Norah said again. 'That's nonsense, Balder, and you know it. Tell me how you did it.'

She saw Balder glance at Theresa.

'Shall I switch off the cameras?' Theresa asked softly.

Balder nodded.

'Okay,' he said. 'Okay.'

He took a deep breath, evidently wondering where to begin.

'Okay,' he said again. 'We started planning *Curse* about five months ago. We began by casting various characters—notably Cassandra, who was to utter the curse. Then we watched you, Miss Richter—your habits, your preferences. *Amat victoria curam*—victory loves preparation.'

'Watched me,' she repeated dully. She hadn't noticed anything—not in Berlin, anyway.

'Oh yes,' said Balder airily. 'But your social media accounts, your blogs and emails were, frankly, more fruitful. Like most people, you have no idea how much you reveal about yourself.'

Norah suddenly recalled an old blog post she'd written about Valerie's death after the suicide of a Hollywood actor. She felt dizzy.

'We bought the rest of the data,' Balder said matter-of-factly. 'In the end I knew more than enough about you to be able to steer you. It didn't cost much, only a bit of skill and time.'

'You wanted me to kill him,' Norah insisted. 'Because you knew that my worst fear was to be responsible for somebody's death.'

Balder smiled, but said nothing.

'You stole my phone,' Norah said, 'hacked my email account…'

Balder gave a brief nod.

'Your friends' accounts, too.'

'You bugged my phone and—'

He gave a laugh of satisfaction.

'Please, Miss Richter, I'm not the CIA! Only an artist. All it took was ingenuity, chutzpah and a little social engineering.'

Norah said nothing.

'I couldn't resist a few symbols and allusions. The white rabbit in your flat and my top hat here—both part of the conjuror's stock-in-trade. The vanitas still life, the dead birds—I admit that I've always had a weakness for the melodramatic.'

He was crowing.

'I think that's something we have in common.'

Norah stared at him. Not five metres away, Arthur Grimm was lying struck down on the ground—and Balder laughed.

As if he'd read Norah's thoughts, he turned to look at Grimm's motionless body. Then he looked at Norah again.

'I said something similar to you once before, do you remember?'

'What?'

'That we're not so very different, you and I,' said Balder.

He looked at her, sizing her up, and Norah began to feel that she was getting to the root of things.

'Do you remember what else I said to you that day?'

There was a glint in his eyes. Whatever he was about to say, he'd clearly been looking forward to saying it for a long time.

'I said that women like you always try to convey an impression of superiority. You think you're better than everyone else. But you're not.'

He laughed softly, then grew serious and leant forwards to whisper in her ear.

'You're not,' he repeated. 'Just look at yourself.'

He leered into her face. Then he took a step back—and another, and another, and another, as if to view his work in its totality. He wasn't in any hurry, but stood and looked at Norah, who was standing motionless. Eventually, he picked up his top hat and dusted it down. He spread out his arms and took a slow bow. When he'd straightened himself, he set the hat on his head, smiled at Norah and turned to leave, retreating into the darkness beyond the floodlights.

Norah gripped the gun so hard that the metal cut into her hand.

'You made one mistake,' she called after him.

Balder stopped and turned slowly, eyeing her with a combination of curiosity and amusement.

'Oh, did I?'

'Yes.'

'And what might that be?'

'Your brilliant orchestration leaves me standing in front of you with a loaded gun in my hand.'

Norah raised her arm and aimed the gun at him. Balder coughed out a laugh.

'There was only one bullet in the cylinder,' he said.

'How do you know I didn't add more?'

Balder bared his teeth.

'You're bluffing. That revolver is extremely rare. Where would you get hold of—'

Norah shot into the air and the grin vanished from Balder's face.

'You've stalked me, intimidated me, manipulated me,' Norah said. 'You broke into my flat. You made me panic and then pressed a loaded gun into my hand. That wasn't an experiment. You had a clear goal.

You wanted me to kill Arthur Grimm. Here. Today. Supposedly of my own free will.'

Balder raised his fleshy hands placatingly.

'Say it,' she demanded. 'Into the camera.'

'The cameras were switched off ages ago,' Balder muttered.

'No,' Theresa said. She'd been standing in the shadows all this time, listening to everything, her phone pointed at Balder. 'The cameras are on.'

Balder looked at her aghast.

'What the hell—'

'You got me to plant a real gun on her,' said Theresa. 'Fuck you, Balder.'

'You sneaky little bitch,' Balder shouted at her. 'You won't be going anywhere in life, I can tell you. I shall make quite sure of that.'

'If I put a bullet in your head now,' Norah said, 'she won't have to worry about that, will she?'

Balder blinked.

Under different circumstances, Norah would have laughed; there was something comical about his facial expression. You could almost see the cogs whirring. Then his entire face seemed to drop a centimetre. A surprised old man. Only his cold eyes retained their menace.

'Say it,' Norah repeated.

Balder said nothing.

She was still clutching the gun in both hands, the way she'd been taught, pointing it at Balder's chest. Now she raised her arms and aimed at his head.

'Okay,' he said soothingly. 'Okay, nice and calm.'

'Okay, what?'

'Yes, yes, I wanted it,' Balder said.

'*What* did you want?'

'I wanted you to kill him so that the curse would come true,' he cried. 'Death as a work of art. The ultimate artwork.'

'Where did you get the gun?'

'Anton got it for me.'

'Who's Anton?'

'A friend.'

'Did Theresa know that the gun was real and loaded?' Norah asked. Balder took a deep breath, as if Norah were beginning to bore him.

'No,' he said. 'She didn't.'

He glared icily at Theresa.

There was a pause and for a moment all was silent; even the waltz music had died away. Suddenly Norah noticed that Balder was no longer looking at her, but staring past her into the darkness, an expression of bewildered astonishment on his face. Norah lowered the gun a little and, without taking her eyes off him, took two steps back and looked about her. In the darkness, just outside the beam of the floodlights, something was stirring. It looked as if a dark shape were growing out of the floor.

Grimm.

'I think it's all right for me to get up now, isn't it?' he said into the silence.

Norah watched him stand and brush the dirt from his clothes. Then she turned to Balder again.

'Yes,' she said, fixing him with her gaze. 'I don't see why not.'

A whole sequence of emotions came and went on Balder's face.

'He isn't…?' he stuttered. 'You didn't…?'

He gave a bewildered laugh.

'Fuck, I really thought you'd… God, you gave me a shock. I—'

'Get on your knees,' said Norah.

Balder stared at her in disbelief.

'You're not serious.'

'Now!' Norah said.

She jerked the gun a second and Balder began to move, kneeling down ponderously. Beads of sweat glinted on his brow, in spite of the cold.

'This is your chance to apologise,' Norah said.

'I'm sorry,' Balder said quickly. 'Miss Richter, Dr Grimm—I'm sorry. I didn't want this to happen. It was an experiment. That was all. I didn't want anyone to get hurt. It wasn't supposed to be anything but—'

'Quiet!' Norah said. 'God, the man's unbearable. He can't open his mouth without lying.'

Balder looked up at her.

'Anyway, you're not supposed to say sorry to us, but to Nicolette Thiel.'

Balder's mouth fell open and snapped shut again. Then Norah saw the muscles at his massive chin tighten. He looked as if wanted to argue with her.

'Into the camera,' Norah said.

Balder's jaws ground.

'Come on!' Norah said.

'Coco,' Balder said. 'Coco. I'm sorry. I didn't want to inflict pain on you, I swear. All I was ever interested in was art. I always saw it as my duty to sound out the limits and...'

'Shut up,' said Norah, and he did. 'That's the worst apology I've ever heard.'

Balder looked at her like a dog eager to do a new trick for its mistress, but not quite up to the challenge.

Norah was silent for a long time. She had all the answers. Now all she had to do was make a decision. And she did. Balder must have seen it in her eyes because a look of absolute horror spread across his face. Theresa must have seen it too.

'What are you doing?' she asked and there was panic in her voice.

'I'm going to put an end to this.'

'That's not what we agreed! We only wanted to give him a scare!'

'Shut up,' Grimm shouted at her. 'The bastard thought she'd killed me and he didn't give a fuck.'

Theresa ignored him.

'Don't do it,' she said. Her voice was trembling. 'Let's call the police. They'll take care of him.'

Norah didn't reply, but only gripped the gun tighter. She could feel the sweat breaking on her upper lip.

'Norah,' Theresa said, desperately. 'You can't do this.'

Norah ignored her.

She gripped the gun in both hands and aimed.

58

22 HOURS EARLIER

When I get off the train and see the time on a display board, I know that the day I have been fearing for weeks has finally come. I fight my way through the station, a mixture of fear and relief surging through my body—afraid of what the day will bring, but at the same time glad that it will all be over in twenty-four hours. I could jump on the next train that pulls into the station, but I don't; I go to meet the day.

Fucking February 11.

As I approach the station concourse I hear music. I find myself thinking of death and of Valerie and realise that someone is playing a requiem, but I resist the temptation to stop and listen—to let the music swallow me like the dark waters of a pond at night. I just want to get home. I keep going. The lingering sounds of the piano drift over to me and I fight my way forwards as if through a snowstorm, my arms wrapped around my body. Then the music falls quiet and a new piece begins. I know at once that something isn't right. And although I don't know what's troubling me, I stop. I recognise the piece. It's the

'Moonlight Sonata'.

Suddenly the feeling of being watched is back. Then that revolting smell rises to my nose. And all at once I know what it is that I associate with the smell of pipe tobacco—not pipe smoke as such, but a particular old-fashioned aftershave. I have just caught a whiff of it—sweet and bitter at the same time. Nauseating. And then it comes to me. I know who it reminds me of: Professor Wolfgang Balder, Coco's ex. The nastiest man I have ever met. The man who destroyed Coco's life. The man who lost me my job, my relationship, all my old life.

And suddenly it's raining blood. It's dripping from the roof and streaking the ground, covering people's skin and matting their hair. I can smell it. I can feel the sickly-sweet metallic taste on my tongue, and all over the station people have collapsed like marionettes and are lying in their blood in crumpled heaps. Only the pianist and I are left. He is still playing his melancholy little tune, just for the two of us, and everything is drowning in black and red.

Then I blink and the station is just a station again; people are hurrying to the platforms or the exit and there is no blood, only everyday life. The whole thing can't have lasted more than two or three seconds.

I know where I've seen the scene before—or something similar. It was in a museum in Berlin. One of those provocative installations that brought Balder criminal complaints—and world fame. A station, innocent passers-by and gallons of fake blood.

I leave the station, the music ringing in my ears, and suddenly that, too, brings back a memory. I remember when I last heard it. Not something similar, but *exactly the same music*.

It was also in Berlin—in the bar of the Adlon Hotel. Halfway through my first interview with Balder, he got up, sat down at the grand piano and suddenly began to play. And now it hits me: the man sitting at the station piano is Wolfgang Balder.

All at once I know everything. I don't understand, but I *know*. Wolfgang Balder followed me to Vienna. Because the havoc he wreaked in Berlin wasn't enough for him. Because he wasn't satisfied with destroying my job and my relationship. Because he thought I'd got off too lightly.

I think of violent blows. I think of electric shocks and a scalpel.

I think of the way he destroyed Coco. The way he isolated her from her friends and family. The way he seduced and manipulated her, chipping away at her, inside and out—with words, with fists and finally with a scalpel. I think of Coco's face before she met him, beautiful and girlish and innocent—a naïve Alice in a grisly Wonderland.

Professor Balder called such treatment *art. Conceptual art. A performance.* No court was willing or able to prosecute him.

I think of Coco's face today, one side untouched, the other ruined— not only by the ridges of scars left by the scalpel, but also by the deep incision that severed her facial muscles and left her unable to move her face. Two sides. 'Dr Jekyll and Ms Hyde' was Balder's name for this 'work of art'.

That is the man I am up against.

That is the man I loathe more than anyone else on the planet.

Professor Wolfgang Balder.

I take a cab. I drink a vodka. I try to calm down. Then I head for home. As I trudge up the stairs I think of Valerie. I think of Arthur Grimm and the woman who told me about him on the phone. I think of Sandra, the most scrupulous, reliable person I know, who assured me that Grimm was innocent. And I see myself, pointing a gun at Grimm. I see the terror in his eyes and—

Suddenly I no longer feel insecure and frightened; I feel sure of myself. I feel hate.

Grimm is innocent. He did nothing to Valerie. He has probably never done anything to anyone. Sandra was right.

It was all an illusion.

A set-up.

A performance.

Just another of Balder's sick games.

I go into the kitchen for a glass of water and when I see the gun, the identical twin of the revolver I threw in the canal, it seems to me that my hatred has drawn it there, as if by some strange magnetic force.

All right, I think, picking it up.

If my hunch proves right, I really am going to kill a man tonight.

59

Once I have calmed down a little, I open my laptop and google Balder's name. Directly underneath his Wikipedia entry I find his homepage and click on it.

The screen goes black. Then a countdown appears.

20 h 58 min 32 s

A quick sum tells me that the countdown will end at 10 p.m. I scroll up and down, then realise that I have to click on the numbers themselves. Words appear.

Curse, it says. And underneath, *Performance*. And then, *† 11.02.2017*.

I stare at the screen.

Curse.

Next I google 'Balder + Curse' and although I'm not particularly hopeful, I find something immediately: an interview with a German newspaper, less than two weeks old. I quickly scan it and soon find what I'm looking for.

•

So, tell us a bit about your next project. The only information on your homepage is a countdown that ends on February 11 this year—and the sinister title 'Curse'.

WB: *Curse* will be my final performance. My working materials are video, digital space and humans.

Interesting that you class humans as a 'material'. In the past you have often attracted criticism for your treatment of the participants in your artworks. You've even been sued several times for grievous bodily harm and—

WB: And it never came to a trial. Art is free. That tenet, I'm glad to say, still holds true. But it has always been important to me that no one is forced into anything. All the people who take part in my performances do so entirely voluntarily—including those who go on to sue me.

The claimants' argument was that you manipulated them.

WB: What does that mean, *manipulated*? What is manipulation? Don't we all manipulate each other all the time? Where does it begin? Where does it end? Even babies are brilliant manipulators, aren't they?

If the cultural pages of the newspapers are to be believed, you're the master of manipulation.

WB: If that's supposed to be damning, all I can say is: I'm not offended. I've always liked manipulating the way people see, breaking popular paradigms.

So what's the topic of your latest performance?

WB: I don't want to give too much away. But it's basically about free will. And death.

Sounds bleak.

WB: Depends how you look at it. Some people see death as something dark and negative. But isn't it, in fact, the greatest work of art?

Thank you for talking to us.

I have to let it all sink in.

I try to recall my first interview with Balder. I can remember the passages that were printed, but not the in-between banter. What did we talk about? What did I reveal about myself?

It takes me only a few minutes to find the digital recording of the interview on my laptop. I click open the file—not without reluctance—and almost immediately, Balder's deep voice fills the room and I see him before me again, sitting over his coffee in the Adlon (presumably the only place good enough for him), sizing me up with those tiny, darting eyes of his. Later that day he would make a pass at me, apparently failing to notice the dislike I was fighting to conceal behind a carapace of professionalism. But I didn't know that then.

I fast-forward a little to skip the polite clichés at the beginning of the interview, then click on *Play*.

'I read your feature on guns,' Balder says. 'Fascinating.'

'Do you think so?'

'I've *always* been fascinated by guns. Haven't you?'

My reply was fuzzy. In fact, Balder was altogether louder and clearer, presumably because I'd placed the recorder nearer to him— but perhaps also because, unlike me, he made no effort to keep his voice down. He seemed not to care that everyone else in the hotel could hear what he was saying.

'Why did you do the feature if you have such an aversion to guns?' he asked, in response to whatever I said.

'Precisely *because* of that aversion, I suppose.'

'And what makes guns so terrible?'

'You can do such terrible things with them.'

'You mean, you can kill people with them?'

Again, my reply—if there was one—was inaudible.

'Do you think you could do that?' Balder asked. 'Kill someone?'

'No,' I heard myself say with a laugh. 'I don't think so.'

'Then what are you scared of?'

I closed the file; I'd heard enough. After that first meeting in the Adlon I had persuaded my boss to let me write a longer feature on Balder rather than stick to a straight interview format. She had agreed and I'd gone on to interview Balder a second time. That was when I met Coco. And disaster took its course.

I had never put so much work into a feature. Luckily, it went straight to press because my boss was laid up with appendicitis and couldn't check through it. I knew it wasn't balanced; I had sided entirely with Coco and the other women.

Fuck that, I thought. *The bastard deserves it.*

I close my laptop, feeling so calm that I know I haven't yet grasped the full implications of what I've just heard.

The whole thing was orchestrated by Balder.

It would explain so much—the sinister fortune teller's acting career; Sandra's certainty that Grimm is innocent. It's all beginning to make sense. The truth is seeping into my consciousness.

Grimm is innocent.

Valerie killed herself.

That's all.

No, I think. That is not all.

If Balder's behind all this, I was wrong to suppose that I'd had a gun thrust on me by some eye-for-an-eyer. In fact, I'm dealing with a recognition-craving bastard who would do anything to avoid boring his greedy, jaded, overstimulated audience.

He would have let me kill an innocent man.

I hear Coco's voice in my head. *I'm scared he'll do the same to you. I'm scared he'll destroy you—leave you without anyone, not even able to help yourself. He's good at that, you know. He finds your weak spot and worries away at it. You don't notice at first. With me it started when I cut myself off from my friends. I didn't realise until it was too late.*

I think of the way Max and Paul suddenly cut me. I think of Tanja's similarly abrupt cold-shouldering—and I have to know. I take my phone from my bag, noting missed calls from Max and Coco, and ring Tanja. She sounds alarmed.

'Hi, Tanja,' I say, 'it's Norah. Did I wake you?'

'No. But what's so urgent?'

'There's something I have to know,' I say. 'Why did you suddenly drop me? I didn't understand, but I was too hurt to ask you at the time.'

Tanja is silent for a moment.

'Oh, come on, Norah,' she says eventually. 'What are you playing at?'

'How do you mean?'

'I read your email. The one you sent me by mistake.'

She laughs bitterly.

'It happens more often than you'd think,' she says. 'I told a few friends about it and a lot of them had had similar experiences. I guess that people who do a lot of bitching about someone get so fixated on that person that they end up sending them one of their bitchy emails by mistake.'

It's a moment before the penny drops.

'You think I bitched about you in an email?' I ask. 'And sent you the email by mistake?'

Tanja is silent again.

'I'm such an idiot,' she says. 'I really thought you were ringing to apologise.'

'Tanja, please don't hang up,' I say quickly. 'I know this must sound like a pathetic excuse, but it wasn't me. I didn't write that email. My account was hacked a while ago and I'm only just beginning to realise the extent of the damage.'

Silence again.

'Okay,' Tanja says eventually. 'Sure. Good luck to you.'

Then the engaged tone. I stare at my phone. Tanja has hung up. I suppose it does all sound rather far-fetched. I probably wouldn't believe it myself if I were her.

I have to collect myself before I can ring Coco back. I'm not sure how much to tell her and how much to keep quiet. In the end, I decide not to tell her anything, but just to give her the usual reassurance. To be there for her. She picks up on the second ring.

'Norah,' she says, without even saying hello. There's panic in her voice. 'Balder's in Vienna.'

I close my eyes for a moment.

'I know,' I say. 'I've seen him.'

For a few seconds there is only a faint crackle down the line. Coco doesn't ask me what I know or how I found out.

'Do you think it's a coincidence?' she says.

'No,' I say, 'I don't.'

'Do you think he followed you there? Oh, Norah, you have no idea how vindictive he is. He once had this assistant—'

'Yes,' I say, interrupting her, 'I think he followed me here.'

'Holy fuck,' says Coco.

Yup, I think, that's about the size of it.

'Norah, I've heard he's planning something big. Something really big.'

'I know.'

'I'm afraid he's going to kill someone.' says Coco.

Not quite, I think, but all I say is, 'Don't worry about me.'

'What are you going to do?'

She sounds as hopeful as a child.

'I don't know.'

I'm sure I can hear her smiling. She knows I've just lied—at least, I think she does.

'Take care of yourself,' she says, 'okay? I don't want anything happening to you.'

'Course I'll take care of myself.'

'Promise?' she says.

'I promise.'

Two lies within seconds.

As soon as I'm off the phone, I ring Max. He, too, picks up almost immediately, although it's so late.

'Hey,' he says.

'Hey,' I echo. 'You tried to call me.'

'Yes. Oh, God, it's all so completely weird.'

'Max, before you tell me anything, there's something I must ask you.'

'Go on.'

'A while ago you wrote to me saying that Paul was ill and needed looking after so you couldn't go out with me, do you remember? But that evening you were in the Goldfinch with friends. I wasn't spying on you, I swear, but I saw you there. I'm not offended or anything, I just wanted to know...'

'What the fuck?' Max says. 'Paul? Ill? When was this?'

He stops to think.

'I remember the evening in the Goldfinch,' he says. 'But I've no idea what email you're talking about. And anyway, I'd find it a bit strange if *you* were offended, I must say. If anyone has reason to be offended, it's me.'

'How do you mean?'

'Excuse me? I asked you round to introduce you to a few friends and you didn't even reply. Then you didn't pick up the phone for weeks. I thought you were back on drugs or something.'

My brain has gone into overdrive. The more I think about it, the more certain I am: I didn't lose my phone soon after I came to Vienna; somebody stole it from me. And that somebody must somehow have gained access to my emails and texts, deleting messages like the one from Max and sending other messages in my name—including the one that so outraged Tanja.

'And what's all this bull about us being ill?' Max goes on. 'Paul forces freshly squeezed green juice on us every morning. Spinach, celery, lemon—the works. Vile stuff, but it seems to do the job. We haven't been ill all winter.'

So the message wasn't from Max.

275

I say nothing; my head is whirling. If that email was fake, what else was?

'What's wrong, Norah?' Max asks, when I don't reply.

'Forget it,' I say. 'I'll explain some other time. I promise. Tell me *your* news.'

'Okay. Well, I spoke to Dorotea Lechner's agent earlier. And it's true—she *was* engaged for a piece of conceptual art. Her role, like I said, was called "Cassandra". I couldn't get her agent to tell me *who* engaged her—apparently there was a confidentiality clause. But I got a few details out of her.'

I wonder what lies Max fed the woman to get her to talk. Did he flirt with her? One day I'll ask him.

'What?' I ask.

'Lechner found the job pretty strange, but basically didn't care because she was paid well and up front and because the artist who'd engaged her *was famous for some fucking weird shit.* Her words, not mine.'

'Wow!'

'You can say that again, sister. Anyway, I just wanted you to know. It confirms Sandra's findings. Grimm probably didn't do a thing. Someone's got it in for you. Both of you.'

'It's unbelievable,' I say, but my voice is toneless.

'Yes,' says Max. 'It's going to take some digesting. The important thing, at any rate, is that you stay at home. I've no idea *how* that lunatic's going to try and lure you to the Prater, but we can be sure he'll spare neither trouble nor expense.'

'I don't know what to say,' I reply and it's the truth.

'I know, it's all a bit much. But we won't leave you on your own tomorrow, so don't worry.'

'Today,' I say.

'What?'

'It's already February 11.'

'So it is,' says Max. 'Today.'

'Max?' I say. 'Thank you.'

'What for?' he asks, genuinely confused and I love him more than ever.

'We'll talk later,' I say and hang up.

Cassandra, I think. The priestess whose doom-laden prophecies no one believed.

60

go up to Theresa's. Her eyes are red and glassy, as if she's been sleeping.

'I've come to say goodbye,' I say and she asks me in with a look of surprise. As I follow her into the living room, I pull the revolver from my waistband.

Theresa gapes at me as if I'd slapped her in the face and I can't say I blame her. It must be pretty terrifying to have somebody walk into your living room and pull a gun on you—never happened to me, I'm glad to say. Still, there are limits to my sympathy.

'What is this?' she asks.

I shake my head.

'Don't give me that crap,' I say. 'I've no time for any of that.'

She's admirably quick to digest and adapt.

'How did I give myself away?' she asks.

'You didn't. I'm suspicious by nature. Got an old friend to check on you. It was just a hunch.'

'And what happens now?'

'Now you're going to sit down there on the sofa and tell me all I need to know.'

Theresa gives me a look I can't quite interpret and backs away a few paces, as if she's scared I might hit her. She jerks her chin at the gun in my hand.

'I'm not afraid of that,' she says. 'It's a fake.'

I look at her for a long time, trying to read her face. But she's not bluffing. She really doesn't know.

I check to make sure the safety catch is on and then carefully open the cylinder and hold it out to show her.

'Does that look like a fake to you?'

Theresa stares at it.

'I don't know,' she says, horrified.

'You planted this gun on me, didn't you?'

She doesn't reply.

'A fake. You were told it was a fake. Not loaded.'

I watch the colour drain from her face. Theresa suddenly looks younger and more fragile than ever.

'Is it...' She swallows. 'Is it loaded?'

I nod.

'One bullet,' I say. 'But I guess I wouldn't need more than one.'

'I don't under—'

'Sit down,' I say, pointing the gun at the sofa.

This time she does as I ask.

'I know you're an art student and work for Balder,' I say. 'So let's not lose any time. I want to know what your job was.'

'Norah,' she says, as if she hadn't heard me. 'Is that the gun we left in your flat?'

I nod.

'Oh my God,' Theresa says. 'Oh. My. God.'

I decide to give her a moment to let it sink in. She shakes her head and I'm afraid she's going to flip out, but when she looks up, her eyes are clear and alert.

'He said no one would come to any harm. The whole thing was

279

supposed to be an experiment. Someone would speak a prophecy—what effect would it have? Would it be fulfilled? Or would nothing happen? Just an experiment, that was all.'

'Do you really believe that?' I ask.

She stares at me like a deer and I have to get a serious grip on myself to stop myself from slapping her. I can't bear it when intelligent women play dumb.

'Did you really believe that?' I ask again. 'Or is it what you wanted to believe?'

She says nothing.

Somehow I manage not to make a snarky remark. She just admitted that they were in my flat—that they planted a gun on me. How could she think that was okay? But I get a grip on myself. However much I may hate Theresa, I have more pressing problems right now.

'You're an artist,' I say. 'I've seen some of your stuff online. You're good. Why are you working for a bastard like Balder?'

'Wolfgang Balder is one of the most famous action artists in the world,' she bursts out. 'And I'm only a second-year student. For the first months, I felt awed just sitting in his lectures. And then one day he called me to his office and said he wanted me to help him with a new artwork—his biggest yet. I almost swooned. You've no idea what a big deal it was for me.'

The colour has returned to her cheeks.

'And when you found out that he planned not only to maim someone—like in his previous artworks—but actually *kill* someone, you thought: Hey, this guy's the most famous action artist on the planet, it must be all right?'

My voice oozes disgust.

'No,' Theresa says in dismay. 'It wasn't like that. I didn't know!'

I look her in the eyes. I still feel like slapping her—but I believe her.

'Do you know why he chose *you* rather than anyone else?' I ask.

She looks at me steadily.

'Because I'm good,' she replies. 'You said so yourself.'

I almost burst out laughing. Not because she isn't good, but because

I find it so absurd that she can still believe that Balder's interested in her art.

'He chose you because you look so like her,' I say coldly.

'Like who?'

'Valerie.'

I watch to see the effect of my words. Theresa blinks, aggrieved, and for a moment neither of us speaks.

'I want to know what his plans are,' I say, raising the revolver again.

Theresa laughs bitterly at the gesture.

'You don't need to do that,' she says. 'He tricked me into planting a loaded gun on you. I'll tell you whatever you want to know.'

'Okay then,' I say. 'What was your job?'

'To keep an eye on you. Inform him when you left the flat. Things like that.'

But that isn't everything.

'What else?' I ask sharply.

Theresa stares at the floor.

'The first time I was in your flat I took some stuff with me and left a few things behind.'

My phone, I think. That fucking pen.

'Other times, Balder's assistant was in your flat. Whenever you went out or came to see me.'

'Breaking and entering.'

She doesn't look at me.

'Before you changed the lock, it was all quite easy. We had a spare key to your flat. From the previous tenant.'

'What was it all for?' I ask. 'I understand the phone. But the rest? What good was my toothbrush to you? And why did you leave a fucking bunny rabbit in my flat?'

'To unnerve you,' Theresa says. 'Confuse you, disorientate you. Classic gaslighting. To make you feel you were losing your grip on reality, couldn't trust your senses—that anything was possible.'

'How could you agree to all that, Theresa?' I ask tonelessly.

She opens her mouth, shuts it again.

'At first I was proud to be part of it. And then things got kind of…
out of hand. It all started to run away with itself. It was harmless to
begin with; it was only later that things got more and more extreme,
and…'

She interrupts herself, starts over.

'I never thought anyone would get seriously hurt.'

I let this sink in for a moment.

'But what's the idea?'

'What do you mean?'

'What's the idea behind the whole operation? What does Balder
stand to gain? He can't have droves of spectators in the Prater if I'm
not supposed to notice anything.'

'He's going to document everything,' says Theresa. 'For his exhibition. Image, sound, video art—he didn't go into the details.'

I feel sick. I imagine an exhibition about a perfectly normal woman
becoming a murderer. A perfectly normal woman who just happens
to be me.

'That's absurd,' I say. 'That's sick. Even he can't get away with that.'

Theresa only tilts her head to one side.

'Okay,' I say. 'Tell me how he plans to proceed tonight. How's he
going to document everything?'

'We've set up various cameras at the big wheel in the Prater, and
I'll also be videoing it, on my phone.'

'Who is this *we*?' I ask.

'The team?' Theresa says. 'It's just me and Kim 5 on the permanent
team. There were other people involved, too, of course—the actor,
extras, technicians, research assistants. But they weren't told about
the project.'

'Kim 5?' I say.

She rolls her eyes.

'He calls all his assistants Kim—men and women. Don't ask why.
Probably can't be arsed to remember our names. Or just thinks it's
cool. I'm Kim 4.'

My God.

'And Kim 5? What's her real name?'

'Kim 5's a he. Bela.'

'Describe him to me,' I say.

'You saw him. In my flat.'

Things are beginning to fall into place.

'Your so-called ex,' I say, and Theresa nods. 'The one you couldn't decide whether to call Rico or Maurice.'

She says nothing.

'Was the fight real?' I ask and she shakes her head, shamefacedly.

'Just a way of getting closer to you.'

She can count herself lucky that I don't have the time right now to think about the extent of her betrayal.

'He was in my flat. And once I saw him through the spyhole. That was him, wasn't it?'

Theresa nods.

'We made a mistake—thought you were out. You'd promised to join me in Starcode Red, remember? Bela got the fright of his life when you started to chase him. No one had expected you to go after him.'

She gave a short laugh, but her smile fades when she sees my face.

'What was Bela planning to do in my flat when I surprised him?'

'He was supposed to bring you flowers.'

'What kind of flowers?'

'Balder had prepared a bouquet for you—an enormous bunch of dead, withered flowers. Rather beautiful in a morbid way. Bela dropped them when he was running away from you.'

I am beginning to understand.

Flowers wither. Clocks stop. Birds fall dead from the sky.

Dorotea Lechner's words. All part of the plan. I give Theresa a long, hard stare.

'Was it you who hacked my accounts?'

She shakes her head.

'I can't do that kind of thing. Balder has other people for that. At home in Berlin.'

'But there's somebody else involved, isn't there?' I say. 'Here in Vienna.'

Theresa looks at me with a frown, trying to sit up straight, but almost swallowed by the soft cushions.

'Just me and Kim 5,' she says.

'Why are you lying?' I ask. 'What's the point in lying now?'

'I'm not lying!'

'Red-haired guy,' I say. 'Plump, pale—skulked around the place.'

I can almost hear the penny drop.

'Oh my God,' she says. 'Of course. That's Simon. He lives here.'

I close my eyes for a moment, take a deep breath. Of course, I think. Of course this isn't really her flat. It's all a front. God, it probably isn't even her cat.

'He sublet the flat to us for a month,' Theresa goes on, 'but you weren't meant to meet him, of course.'

My eye falls on the bookcase.

'What about them?'

'The books?' Theresa asks. 'Props. Selected by Balder, with a lot of your favourites mixed in. Same goes for the records. I don't really like Arcade Fire.'

'Why?' I ask.

'Why don't I like Arcade Fire?'

'Why did you lie to me about everything?' I yell at her. 'Even books and music.'

She flinches.

'Balder wanted you to like me. He says we like people who resemble us and I think he's right. You saw the books on my shelves and immediately felt comfortable with me.'

I raise a hand and Theresa falls silent. I don't have time to get bogged down in details.

'How did he know I'd be at the station?'

'What?'

'He was sitting at the piano in the station when I got back from Salzburg. How did he know I'd be there?'

'Did you buy your ticket online?' Theresa asks.

I nod.

'Well then. We saw all your emails. *All* of them.'

I'll have to digest this later. Right now I've other things on my mind.

'Who texted me?' I ask.

'Balder. He'd never have left that kind of work to an assistant. But he let me advise him. He wanted the messages to sound as if they'd come from a woman; he thought you'd be more likely to trust him then.'

I close my eyes for a moment. The bastard's good.

'And the woman? The one I spoke to on the phone?'

'Grimm's ex?'

'Yes. Was she real?'

'Norah,' Theresa says, looking me in the eyes, 'we can spare ourselves some time here. *Nothing* was real. It was all us.'

I drop onto a chair. Theresa goes on, unmoved.

'Later today you'll get more emails and calls trying to persuade you to go to the Prater. They won't be real either.'

'Who'll be there?'

'From the team? Only me and him.'

'Sure?'

She nods.

I can't think straight.

'Norah, we should call the police,' Theresa says.

But I hardly hear her. My mind is working frantically. That colleague of mine who suddenly happened to mention a man called Arthur Grimm. The way I found myself at the door of his office, as if led there by fate. How had they done it? I'd chosen the dentist myself; no one had sent me there…

I force myself to abandon these thoughts. I need to work out what to do next.

'Can I ask you something?' Theresa says.

I look at her.

'How did he betray himself?' she asks.

I think about it for a second.

'Vanity,' I say.

Theresa nods as if to say she'd thought as much. Her gaze falls on the gun in my hand.

'We must call the police,' she says, getting up cautiously. 'I'll tell them everything.'

I wonder whether I can trust her. Balder's deception seems to have cut pretty deep. But who knows—she might be pretending, the way she's been pretending for weeks.

'All right,' I say. 'Call the police.'

Theresa gets up, takes her phone from her bag, unlocks it and dials. She takes a deep breath. I grab the phone off her, hang up and put it in my pocket.

'Sit down,' I say. 'We're not going to call the police. If we take this to the police, it won't be Balder who's brought to justice but you. He knows why he left certain jobs to others. Breaking and entering, for example. Depositing loaded firearms in a person's flat.'

Aggrieved silence. Then she says, 'God, I was stupid.'

'You can say that again,' I say coldly.

She falls back on the sofa and buries her face in her hands for a moment before looking at me again.

'What are you planning to do?'

Why does everyone always think I have a plan?

'Stop him,' I say.

'How?'

I don't immediately reply.

'I need to get Arthur Grimm on board somehow,' I say. 'But there's not much chance he'll listen to me.'

Suddenly Theresa is smiling again.

'I think I can help,' she says. 'Dr Grimm and I are good friends.'

61

Grimm takes a little persuading, but it turns out to be easier than I'd thought—I suppose he's come to trust Theresa. I am beginning to realise that Kim 4 is Balder's all-purpose weapon. For me she was the nice neighbour. For Grimm she was an ally.

Some weeks ago she turned up on his doorstep and warned him about a psychotic stalker called Norah Richter who went around (she said) suspecting people of having murdered a certain Valerie. Whenever this woman got it into her sick head that somebody was the culprit, she did all she could to make their life hell. There were indications, Theresa told Grimm, that Norah Richter had fixed on him as her latest target. Nobody knew how she chose her victims. But Theresa, who had herself been stalked for months by this lunatic, saw it as her duty to warn him.

After her visit, Grimm had googled me. Finding a recent photo was as easy for him as it had been for me, and he was even curious enough to wander down my street on one occasion—although, thanks to Theresa's input and my undiplomatic manner, he was soon living in fear and trembling of me, reacting with understandable aggression when I pestered him with calls and turned up outside his house. Eventually an email came from Theresa: there was clearly no point in waiting for the police to do anything about me, and she'd had an idea. If Grimm wanted to know more, all he had to do was come to the entrance to the Prater at 10 p.m. sharp on February 11. By the big wheel.

Not surprisingly, Grimm can't believe his eyes when Theresa and I turn up together at his flat. It's amazing that he doesn't shut the door in our faces, but luckily his curiosity gets the better of him. I like him for that; I know all about giving in to curiosity.

When Theresa has confessed all and Grimm has bombarded her with questions, he asks us in, apparently persuaded by her story.

'Thank you,' I say, as he shows us into his minimalist sitting room. 'It was nice of you to listen.'

At first Grimm says nothing. I find it hard to look at him; my repugnance is tenacious. I've got so used to seeing him as my enemy that I am having trouble readjusting. I can sense that he's experiencing similar difficulties.

'Where do we go from here?' he asks eventually.

'We have two possibilities,' I say. 'Option number one: the three of us go to the police together and tell them everything. I just have a feeling that if we do that, Balder will worm his way out of things while Theresa and Bela get into serious trouble. Because, if you think about it, what's Balder actually done? With a bit of luck we might be able to wangle a fine for him. But it's equally possible that he gets off scot-free.'

'He tried to kill me,' Grimm cries. 'And she helped him. She told me to go to the Prater on the evening of the eleventh. Why are we trusting her when she lied to us both?'

I nod.

'We don't have much reason to, it's true. But I think Theresa knows she made a mistake.'

Theresa stares at the floor.

'The problem is we can't pin anything on Balder,' I say.

'What's option number two?' Grimm asks.

I smile.

'We get our own back,' I say. 'Scare the hell out of him. The way he did with us.'

Grimm's eyes narrow.

'That's too mild a punishment,' he says and I think he's damn right. But I let Theresa do the talking.

'You have to know,' she says, 'that Balder is incredibly vain. He spends hours googling himself and reading articles about himself, and if anyone dares criticise him or even just makes fun of him, he completely freaks out. I once saw him throw a computer at the wall because an art blogger said he was *overrated*. No ordinary person can have any idea how over-inflated that man's ego is.'

'So, what do we do?' Grimm asks.

'Let the air out of him,' I say.

'I've been working closely with him for months,' Theresa says. 'The great Wolfgang Balder. The powerful, the sophisticated, the admired Wolfgang Balder. Larger than life, invulnerable, always in control. The man who baulks at nothing. That's how he wants to be seen. It matters to him more than anything. If there's one thing he can't bear, it's the thought of losing face.'

For a moment Grimm says nothing. Then he nods.

'All right then. We unmask him. But how?'

'We turn his own weapons on him,' I reply.

'A performance,' Grimm says and I nod.

He's quick on the uptake.

'How do we get to him?'

'Oh, that's easy,' Theresa says. 'He always scripts himself into his own artworks. He's not planning to miss the show. He'll be in the Prater, you can be sure of that.'

Grimm gives me a long, hard look. Then he nods and we begin to script and rehearse our own little act. At first, all we can come up with are lines from films we've seen, but after a while we start to develop a feel for the situation.

And when I shoot at Grimm with an outstretched index finger and see how convincingly he falls to the ground, I begin to think we might pull it off.

When I get home, I run through everything in my head. It might work. It really might fucking work. Balder will come—that much we do know.

I get ready—make sure that Max and Paul and Sandra are out of the way. I don't want them getting mixed up in this.

I think of Balder. *Big B*, as the hipsters at the private view called him.

I think of what he said to Coco when she sued him. *This is my world, sweetheart. You only live in it.*

God, am I going to get that Big B talking. I'm going to make him show everyone what a bastard he is.

But that's not all, I think. Grimm and Theresa only know half the truth. Balder ruined Coco's life, he ruined the lives of at least three women before her, and he's been doing his best to ruin mine by trying to get me to do the thing I'm most afraid of. He's trying to make a murderer of me, just because he'd like to know whether I'm capable of it. I feel my heart thumping in my chest, black and bitter.

Yes, Grimm and Theresa and I will put on a little act. No, I won't really shoot Grimm. But I won't be firing blanks either, whatever I've promised Grimm and Theresa.

Oh yes, I think. Balder's plan will come off. Tonight I am going to kill someone. In the Prater. Under a clear, starry sky. With good reason and of my own free will. But the man I kill will not be called Arthur Grimm. He will be called Wolfgang Balder.

62

The waltz music was back. The icy wind smelt of snow, and the metal gun in Norah's hand was so cold it made her fingers ache. She heard a strange noise and opened her eyes. Balder was kneeling in front of her and Norah saw with a mixture of astonishment and disgust that he'd begun to cry.

'Please, don't,' he sobbed.

'What is this?' Norah asked. 'You ought to like this. I mean: *Isn't death the greatest work of art?*'

Balder was whimpering.

'Please... please...'

'Be quiet.'

Balder pressed his fist against his mouth, but the whimpering didn't stop.

'Be. Quiet.'

This time he managed. She saw him swallow his tears.

'You don't have to do this,' he said.

Norah put her head on one side.

'Listen. Listen to me for a moment. You don't have to do this. Call the police. I'll confess to everything.'

Norah didn't react. Then she shook her head.

'If there's one thing I've learnt, it's that people like you get away with everything. You'd even get away with this. Because this is your world. Coco, Theresa, me—we just live here, right? I can only think of one way to change that.'

Norah cocked the gun.

'Don't,' Balder cried in panic. 'You'll regret it for the rest of your life.'

'He's right,' someone said behind Norah and at first she thought it was Theresa. Then she realised it was Sandra's voice. What on earth was she doing in Vienna? Norah glanced over her shoulder and saw that Sandra wasn't alone; Max and Paul were with her. All three out of breath and drenched in sweat.

'We heard a shot,' Sandra said. 'We thought we were too late.'

Norah turned back to Balder and her friends closed in on her, entering her field of vision.

'What are you doing here?' Norah asked them.

'Looking after you,' Max said. 'Put the gun down, Norah.'

Norah was silent.

'You know you're not going to shoot him while we're looking on,' Sandra said. She sounded quite calm.

'What makes you think that?' Norah asked.

'Because you're not like that.'

'Like what? Angry? Oh, believe me, I'm angry. Angry enough for ten people.'

'I know,' Sandra said. 'But you're not stupid. You don't want to spend the best years of your life in prison. Not because of a piece of shit like him.'

Norah didn't reply, but lowered the gun a little.

'Put the gun away, Norah.' Now it was Max's turn to reason with her. 'You're a good person. And you're definitely not a murderer.'

Norah thought of Coco and Grimm and, completely irrationally, unable to separate her emotions of the last few weeks from the present situation, she thought of Valerie.

Norah looked at Balder. Balder looked at her.

Norah raised the gun and pulled the trigger.

63

Like water. Time had frozen like water in a lake. Balder was kneeling before her, his eyes squeezed shut. Sandra and Paul had screamed; Max's hand was clapped to his mouth; Theresa and Grimm just stood there, their arms hanging at their sides.

It was a moment before time began to thaw. The first thing Norah heard was the thud of the gun as it hit the ground. Then she heard someone breathe out and realised that it was her. Then Balder opened his eyes. And then, realising that Norah had shot into the air, high above Balder's head, everyone started talking at once.

Balder blinked as if waking from a nightmare, but he didn't move.

Norah looked down at him.

His mouth snapped open and shut.

'Go,' she said.

He stared at her.

'Get out of here.'

Balder got up awkwardly and Norah knew from the way he moved that he had wet himself. He looked about him. It occurred to Norah that he was scanning the place for the cameras he'd had installed, looking to see if they were on. The world's vainest man wanted to know if he was being videoed. Then he pulled himself up to his full height and set off. It didn't take long for him to leave the bright floodlit circle—only two or three seconds before the darkness began to swallow him up. Grimm watched him go for a moment, clearly unsure whether or not to follow. Norah knew that she wouldn't have the energy to stop him.

And then Sandra and Max and Paul were there with her, hugging her, and no one said anything for a while.

'What the fuck are you doing here?' Norah asked eventually.

'I had a bad feeling,' Sandra said. 'You sounded so strange on the phone. I called Max straight away and he was worried too. I got on the next plane.'

'I don't think you know what an unbelievably bad liar you are,' Max said.

'Lousy,' Paul agreed.

'You have a lot to explain to us,' Sandra said.

'I will,' Norah said. 'Tomorrow.'

They fell silent again.

'Norah?' Paul said when everyone was feeling a little calmer. He pointed at the gun that was still lying on the ground.

'I wonder if anyone heard the shots,' Sandra said.

'I think we'd know by now if they had,' said Max.

'Is it still loaded?' Sandra asked.

'No.'

'Okay,' she said, bending down to pick it up. 'I'll take care of it.'

'No,' Norah said, also reaching for the gun. She snatched it up and slipped it into her bag, which was lying on the ground a few metres away. 'I'll take care of it.'

When she stood up again she caught Theresa's eye.

'Don't forget to send the video,' Norah said.

'I'll do it as soon as I get home, promise.'

Norah gave her a nod and Theresa vanished into the darkness.

Only Grimm was still standing there; he seemed uncertain what to do.

'Okay then,' he said.

Norah didn't know what to say.

'I'm sorry about Valerie,' Grimm said.

His eyes glistened in the darkness. Norah gave him a brief nod then he too turned and left.

'I'm freezing my bum off,' said Paul. 'Haven't we been here long enough?'

'Yes,' Norah said. 'Let's go.'

Norah didn't even wait to get home to ring Coco, but called her from the taxi. Coco picked up at the first ring, but didn't say her name, the way she usually did.

'Coco?' Norah said.

Silence.

'Hello?'

Silence.

'*Hello?*'

Nothing.

'Coco, can you hear me?'

'I can hear you,' Coco said.

'Why aren't you saying anything?' Norah asked.

Silence.

'Hello?'

'I'm speechless,' said Coco.

Norah understood and hung up with a grin.

Theresa had kept her promise.

64

When she opened the door, her flat came rushing towards her. Suddenly she was alone and all was quiet and still again. Her home. No pictures on the walls, no rugs on the bare boards, no books on the shelves. No ghostly memories floating about between floor and ceiling. Norah stepped in, closing the door behind her, and sat down at the kitchen table. She took her phone from her bag—no reply from Alex, nothing. Of course not. She put the phone aside and listened.

There were no footsteps overhead. Theresa must have gone home to her real flat. No other sounds either; nothing was stirring. Norah went over to the window and looked down onto the square. There was a couple snogging on the exact same spot where Arthur Grimm's dark figure had once stood peering up at her.

Really, Norah thought, I ought to look down at the pair of them and smile. I ought to feel a huge burden fall from my shoulders because it's all over.

But it wasn't all over.

Something wasn't right.

Norah sat down again and closed her eyes to think.

Something wasn't right.

Something to do with Grimm.

She got up and was climbing onto the chair to take the book out of the cupboard when she stopped, mid-movement. She knew what was wrong.

She glanced at the clock and thought of calling a cab, but decided it wasn't wise. Was she going to repeat all her stupid, impulsive mistakes? Was she going to go round to Grimm's flat in the middle of the night to confront him—after all that had happened? Of course not. She'd wait until morning and she certainly wouldn't go alone. On the other hand…Was she even right? Or was she just imagining things?

Norah closed her eyes, trying to remember. Grimm had stood before her and seemed to hesitate. Relieved—and yet, at the same time, tense. But then, he was always like that. Like someone about to attack. He had looked at her and said, *I'm sorry about Valerie.*

Adrenaline shot into her bloodstream, leaving her dizzy.

I'm sorry about Valerie. Those were his words. He hadn't said, *Sorry about your friend,* or anything like that—the kind of thing people said when they were talking about someone they didn't know. No, he'd said, *Valerie*—and there hadn't even been any mention of Valerie just then. And the look on his face…He'd had tears in his eyes.

All at once, Norah was certain: Grimm had known Valerie.

She wrestled with herself. No, she thought. She mustn't confront him alone again. Not after all she'd been through. That would be—

She jumped. *Someone was ringing at the door.*

She knew who it was even before she heard his voice over the intercom.

'We have to talk.'

Norah hesitated.

'What do you want?'

'I have to talk to you,' he repeated.

Cursing, Norah buzzed him in and heard him enter the building. She went into the kitchen, loaded the gun and laid it on the chair beside her, covered with a teacloth. Then she hurried back to the door and peered through the spyhole.

I shouldn't let him in.

Softly, tentatively, he knocked at the door.

But I have to know.

Norah opened up to him.

That face. Balder had chosen well.

'May I come in?' Grimm asked.

'Of course,' Norah said, standing aside to let him past. She wasn't going to walk in front of him.

Grimm squeezed past her and Norah realised that his calm was feigned. He was as tense as before, though he was doing all he could to hide it.

'Straight ahead,' said Norah. 'We'll sit in the kitchen.'

Grimm obeyed, sat down at the table.

'So, what do you want?' Norah asked.

'You know what I want.'

'I'm too tired for riddles, Dr Grimm.'

'Ask me.'

Norah felt herself break into a sweat.

'What do you want me to ask you?'

'I made a mistake. And you noticed.'

Norah felt as if something were sticking in her throat, preventing her from swallowing. Something alive.

'You knew Valerie,' she said.

Grimm was silent for a long time.

Then he said, 'Yes. I knew Valerie.'

And when Norah said nothing, 'I hadn't thought about her for years. But when you mentioned her to me, it all came rushing back.'

'Why did you do it?' Norah asked.

Grimm looked at her in bewilderment.

'What do you mean?'

'Earlier this evening, in the Prater. You said you were sorry about Valerie. You must have known I'd find that strange. So why did you say it? You were already off the hook.'

Grimm studied his hands on the wooden table.

'Maybe I wanted to talk about her,' he said. 'I've never talked about her to anyone.'

Nor have I, Norah thought.

'How did you come to know her?' she asked.

'Pure chance,' said Grimm.

And he told her everything. How he and Valerie had become close, how their friendship had developed into an affair. It was all completely legal—Valerie was over sixteen—but they'd kept it quiet because they knew people would have disapproved of the age difference.

'What happened?'

'She fell in love with another man,' he said. 'And left me.'

'Is that why you killed her?'

Grimm leapt to his feet; the chair clattered to the floor.

'What did you just say?'

Norah was silent.

'Are you mad?' Grimm yelled. 'Do we have to go through all this again?'

Norah shook her head mutely.

'Calm down,' she said.

'I have an alibi,' Grimm said. 'I wasn't even in town when Valerie died. Anyway, I'm sure you know *how* she did it.'

He didn't want to say the words either, Norah thought.

'Someone could have done it to her,' she said.

'I don't understand you,' said Grimm. 'I thought you were Valerie's best friend. You must have known what she was like.'

'What was she like?' Norah asked.

'Beautiful,' said Grimm. 'Funny. But very, very moody. And resentful. And seriously unstable.'

Norah said nothing.

'I came here to come clean,' Grimm said. 'Yes, it's true, I knew Valerie. Yes, I had an affair with a sixteen-year-old when I was a young man. Some people may find that reprehensible, but it isn't

300

punishable. Especially as Valerie was—or seemed to me—the more mature of us.'

He sighed.

'Our affair was over a good six months before she died.'

Norah felt him trying to catch her eye, but kept her gaze firmly on the tabletop.

'There's no big mystery, Norah. No shady conspiracy. I didn't murder Valerie. She killed herself.'

Norah raised her eyes and met Grimm's gaze, fighting back her tears.

'I know.'

Norah sat and thought for a long time after Grimm had left. So many of the supposed coincidences of the past few weeks—big and small—had been orchestrated by Balder, but Valerie and Grimm really had known one another. King Coincidence *had* struck after all.

Norah's gaze fell on the kitchen cupboard. She climbed on a chair, took out *How to Disappear Completely*, sat down with it, opened it and pulled out the letter that she had slipped between the pages.

A perfectly ordinary white envelope. Her name in Valerie's school-girl handwriting, like a slap in the face. No address. No stamp. No postmark. The letter had been delivered by hand. For a long time Norah had driven herself half mad, wondering when Valerie had brought it round.

Norah had been at home that evening. She had sat in her room, reading, trying to ignore Valerie's devastating texts and smiling at Milo's messages, waiting impatiently for a suitable time to elapse so that she could reply to him without appearing uncool. She hadn't felt guilty for a moment. For months Valerie had claimed to be in love with some mysterious stranger she couldn't talk about; Norah had sometimes wondered whether it wasn't all made up. But Valerie had insisted. And now, all of a sudden, Milo was supposedly the love of her life again. Norah was, quite frankly, pretty sick of Valerie's moods.

•

She turned the letter over in her hands. When had Valerie written it? And when had she brought it round? What if Norah had seen her posting it? Would she have gone down to her? Would they have made it up? Would everything have turned out differently? Norah tried to avoid stepping on that carousel of *what ifs*. The fact was she hadn't found the letter until the following afternoon; her mother had emptied the letterbox while she was at school and left it on her bed. By then everyone knew that Valerie had disappeared.

Norah ran a finger over the paper—the same finger she had used to slit open the envelope all that time ago. She pulled out the letter. She had read it only once before. Almost twenty years ago.

Norah,

I've called and texted you hundreds of times, but apparently I'm not worthy of a reply. I loved you. More than I loved Milo, more than I loved anyone—even myself. I don't know how you could hurt me the way you did. It's all so fucking unfair. YOU'RE so fucking unfair. You're probably just a bad person, only ever thinking of yourself. First you use people, then you chuck them. I'm sorry for you, Norah. You'll never understand what love is. You'll never find anyone else who loves you the way I loved you, because YOU DON'T DESERVE IT. You'll never have a real home. You'll never marry, never have children. You'll never have any friends and no matter how hard you try, you'll never belong anywhere. You don't deserve that either.

I want you to know that I'm doing what I'm doing because of you. Because of what you've done. Don't ever forget that. You've broken my heart. And I know I should make peace with you, I know I should write something forgiving, but I can't. I'm not a fucking liar like you.

V.

Norah sat there for a long time, staring at the paper—at Valerie's soft, round handwriting, so different from the tone of her letter.

When Norah had read the letter back then, as a teenager, she'd immediately panicked and tried to call Valerie. She was just setting off to look for her when she heard she'd been found. Milo told her. It was the last time they spoke.

She never showed anyone the letter or told anyone about it. She felt too ashamed, too guilty.

But she couldn't bring herself to throw it away either. And now she wondered what would have happened if she'd spoken out back then, instead of keeping silent. If she'd shown someone the letter. Would she have been told what she needed to hear? That it wasn't her fault. That Valerie was sick. That she was probably more unstable than anyone had realised. That a healthy girl didn't kill herself just because one of her friends went out with a boy she'd have liked for herself. Would Norah's life have been different without the burden of her secret?

She thought of Grimm. The rational part of her must have known all along that he was innocent—that Valerie had killed herself.

But there was another part to her. The part that had a *but* for every fact—that was always asking *are you sure?*

Valerie killed herself. *Are you sure?*

She wrote me a suicide note. *Are you sure? How do you know she wasn't forced to write all that?*

And so on.

She had wanted to believe that it wasn't her fault. That there was some other explanation. *Any explanation.*

Carefully Norah folded the letter and put it away. She knew what she had to do. It was time for a confession.

65

The lake was still frozen, like back then, but Norah didn't venture out on it. The ice looked thin and fragile; it wouldn't hold a grown woman. The trees at its edge were dripping.

Norah looked out over the lake.

This must have been where Valerie waited that night. Norah had imagined it so often—seen her standing here, on the ice, or at the edge of the woods, waiting. How long had she waited before she realised that no one was going to come this time—that she was alone. An hour? Two hours?

Norah shivered. How this place had haunted her.

She no longer knew the exact wording of the dozens of texts she'd received that evening, but she remembered the gist. All those big words. *Betrayal, deceit, malice.* And the threats.

We are meeting by the lake, aren't we?

If you don't come you'll see what I'm capable of.

For the first time in her life, she didn't answer. She knew what Valerie could be like and she decided she'd had enough. She wasn't going to put up with it anymore—wasn't going to follow that girl's every command. It wasn't as if anything dramatic had happened. Okay, so she'd fooled around with Milo. And yes, Valerie had fancied him since primary school—but then, so had Norah. And if he'd suddenly fallen in love with Valerie, would Norah have flipped out like that? No way.

Then there were the threats. Norah hadn't even thought of them as threats until one day, when Katharina happened to see one of her texts from Valerie. *Tell me,* she'd asked casually, *does Valerie often threaten you?* Norah was thrown into confusion. For her, that was just the way Valerie was. A bit of a drama queen, that was all. Valerie was never thirsty; she was always *dehydrated.* Valerie was never bored; she was always *dying of boredom.*

If I fail maths, I'll throw myself in front of a train.

If my parents split up, I'll jump off the dam.

How was Norah to know that she really meant it this time?

Norah hunched her shoulders and thrust her hands deep into her coat pockets, but she shivered all the same. She strode out, walking fast to warm up. It had taken her four hours to drive here. Strange, she thought, that something she'd been putting off for twenty years should suddenly be so urgent. Now that she'd made up her mind to do it, she felt compelled to get it over with as quickly as possible.

She had called in sick. Her friends would have to wait till she was back in Vienna; she'd tell them everything then. She'd had a quick word with Sandra, promising to go and see her soon, and she had taken Sandra's advice and spoken to the police and to a lawyer she'd recommended. Then she had rung Max and asked him and Paul for dinner at the weekend.

About twenty minutes later, Norah had reached her destination. Valerie's parents' house was just the way she remembered it: a pretty terraced house with a well-kept front garden. Of course, there was no longer a family of four living here with their dog; Monika was on her own now. But it didn't feel any different. Norah had at the very least expected it to seem smaller, like most childhood places she revisited. But only the smell had changed. The smell of cooking that used to fill the house was gone, replaced by a hint of parquet cleaner.

Norah sat on the pink sofa opposite Monika. Since Norah had last seen her, Monika had lost a lot of weight, but not in a bad way. She looked radiant and fit—a woman who had reinvented herself.

'You look stunning,' Norah said awkwardly, taking a sip of her milky coffee.

It was true, but she'd been expecting the soft, motherly woman of her memories. She still had to get used to this new Monika.

The new Monika smiled and Norah knew that any second now she would ask her how she was, what had brought her to the area and so on. She knew, too, that she'd probably reply evasively to avoid having to broach the subject she had come here to broach—and end up leaving for home without having achieved anything.

'There's something I have to tell you,' Norah said, before she could change her mind.

'Oh?' Monika said, sipping her tea.

'It's about Valerie,' said Norah.

Her bag was next to her on the sofa. On a chest of drawers, behind Monika, stood family photos from happier days. Norah tried not to look.

'I don't know if you knew,' she went on, 'but in the class above us at school, there was this boy all the girls were crazy about. Including me. And Valerie.'

Monika smiled.

'I remember. What was his name again?'

'Milo.'

She gave a loud laugh.

'Milo, that's right. Goodness, he thought he was cool, didn't he, with his gelled hair and his mirrored shades.'

She smiled.

'It's sometimes hard for parents to relate to their daughters' tastes.'

Norah ignored this remark, determined not to let Monika distract her. She felt her fingers start to tremble and pressed them against her thighs.

'I was going out with him back then,' she said. 'Valerie really resented it.'

This time Monika said nothing, but she was still smiling.

'Do you remember how amazed we all were that Valerie didn't leave a note?'

A shadow passed over Monika's face.

'That wasn't actually true. There *was* a letter. And…'

She had thought carefully about what she would say, but now she couldn't find the words.

'I should have said something. I should have told the police. I should have told *you*. But I couldn't. I couldn't bring myself to do it.'

She reached over to her bag, took out the envelope and held it out to Monika.

'I'm sorry.'

Valerie's mother looked at it without moving a muscle.

'This was from Valerie?' she asked.

Norah nodded.

'She must have brought it round before she…'

She couldn't say the words.

Monika took the letter from Norah, slowly, cautiously, as if it might snap at her.

'It was my fault,' said Norah. 'She killed herself because of me. And I didn't even have the decency to tell her family—'

She broke off, feeling Monika's eyes on her.

'You've had it all this time,' Monika said. 'Almost twenty years.'

'I'm so sorry,' Norah whispered.

She looked up and saw Monika running her fingers over Valerie's writing on the envelope.

'You can read it, if you like,' Norah said and then neither of them spoke for a long time.

Norah sat there with lowered head. She heard the rustle of paper as Monika took the letter out of the envelope and unfolded it, and she closed her eyes while Monika read. Then she heard the soft rustle of skin on paper again and didn't dare look up. She heard a gentle click in Monika's throat as she swallowed; she heard a car drive past outside; she heard the metallic tick of Monika's watch.

'I'm sorry,' Norah said. 'I don't know what to say.'

For a long time Monika sat frozen on her chair. Then she got up and left the room without a word. She was gone some minutes; Norah began to think she wasn't ever coming back, but then she heard footsteps and Monika reappeared with a book in her hand. As she came nearer, Norah saw that it was the first Harry Potter. Monika sat down. She seemed slower than before—older, more fragile.

She looked calmly at Norah.

'Do you remember how much you girls loved this book?' she asked.

'Of course. Gryffindor forever!' said Norah, laughing dully. 'But what—'

Monika blinked a few tears away.

'There's no good place for a thing like this,' she said. 'I mean, cutlery belongs in the cutlery drawer, insurance documents belong in a folder in the study. Holiday photos belong in an album. But where do you keep your daughter's suicide note?'

Norah didn't understand what Monika was trying to say. Monika hesitated for a second, then opened the book. It fell open in the middle and there was an envelope between the pages. Monika took it out and hesitated again for a moment before holding it out to Norah. The handwriting was instantly recognisable—that big loopy M. But it didn't say *Mum* or *Monika*; it said *Mother*.

Norah felt sick.

'You got one too,' she said tonelessly.

'Me, my husband, Sven…Probably everyone she loved.'

Norah felt her mouth hanging open.

'But the police said—'

'It was none of their business,' Monika said firmly, pressing her lips together.

'Do you know what borderline personality disorder is?' she asked at length and Norah nodded, although the words sounded very far away.

'Valerie was undergoing treatment, Norah,' Monika said. 'She didn't talk about it and neither did we. Not to anyone, not even to you. Maybe that was a mistake. I'm sure people deal differently with these things nowadays. But that's how it was back then.'

Carefully, very carefully, she slipped the letter back into the book and put it down beside her.

'It wasn't your fault, Norah,' said Monika. 'It wasn't mine either. Not just mine, anyway. Valerie was sick.'

She sighed.

'People with borderline suffer from unbearable feelings and anxiety. A lot of them harm themselves or attempt suicide.'

She was silent for a moment.

'There's a common pattern in the relationships of people with borderline. Do you know what it is?'

Norah shook her head.

'First they worship their friends and partners. Then, at the slightest provocation, they start to demonise them. For them there's only black or white, good or evil.'

Monika sighed again.

'If you'd talked to me,' she added, 'I could have told you eighteen years ago.'

Norah didn't reply. Something in her chest had come adrift and was fluttering around wildly.

'Have you ever spoken to anyone about it?' Monika asked.

Norah shook her head.

'No,' she said, 'never.'

'All these years, you've thought you were to blame?'

Norah didn't know what to say or feel. She said nothing.

Then she said, 'Valerie was a wonderful girl.'

'Yes,' said Monika. 'She was.'

'I ought to be going,' Norah said, getting up. Monika got up too.

'May I give you some advice?' she asked and Norah looked at her.

'Answer the letter.'

66

When Norah arrived back in Vienna late that evening, it was mild, almost spring-like. She had spent the best part of the day on the motorway and was so tired she felt numb all over. Luckily there was an empty parking space right outside the flat. As she parked the car, a loud beep announced an incoming text. She registered with annoyance that part of her was still hoping for a reply from Alex, but it was only Monika, thanking her for coming. Norah wrote back and texted Sandra, too, to let her know she was home safe and sound. (Sandra's dad had died in a car crash and she didn't like to think of her friends on the road.) Then she unlocked the front door and began to trudge up the stairs. Someone was coming down. Norah stopped when she realised who it was. Theresa.

Theresa froze too.

'Oh,' she said, embarrassed. 'Hi.'

Norah gave her a nod.

'You're moving out,' she said.

'Not exactly,' Theresa replied.

'True,' Norah said. 'I guess you never really lived here.'

Theresa nodded, avoiding Norah's eyes.

'Have you…' Norah began.

'Heard from Balder? No. No one has. But I spoke to Bela. You know, Kim 5. He went to Balder's studio the morning after to pick up some stuff he'd left there and it was so loud, he didn't dare knock. He said it was terrifying—shouting and crashing, as if someone was on the rampage.'

Norah said nothing.

'I've asked around a bit,' Theresa went on. 'He'll lose his professorship. And the video went viral. The whole net's laughing at him. Wolfgang Balder, King of the Memes.'

She grinned.

'And that comedian, you know the one I mean, the ginger guy who does that late-night show? I don't actually like him—too malicious for me. But Balder loves him. Never misses him. Anyway, he did a sketch about Balder last night. Something about geriatric nappies. I'd love to have seen his face.'

Norah didn't comment.

'Was it you posted the video?' she asked.

Theresa shook her head. Norah smiled in spite of herself. *Coco.*

'Okay then…'

She pushed past Theresa.

'Norah?'

Norah turned to face her again.

'I'm sorry. I don't know what else to say.'

Norah looked her in the eyes.

'It's all right,' she said.

They nodded at each other and Theresa turned to go, clearly uneasy.

'One more thing,' said Norah. 'No, two.'

Theresa looked at her almost fearfully.

'My colleague. How did you get her to mention Arthur Grimm?'

'I don't remember involving a colleague. There was Balder, me, Kim 5, Cassandra, the woman who played Grimm's ex, a passer-by we hired to speak to you on the street, a few video technicians, some research assistants and Balder's theatre-director mate who agreed to give you an interview to get you to the Prater. I think that was all.'

Norah nodded slowly.

'Maybe it was a coincidence?' Theresa suggested.

Yes, Norah thought.

'And the second thing?' Theresa asked.

'How did you lead me to Grimm's office? I chose the dentist myself—completely by chance. No one recommended it to me and no one knew I was going. Nobody.'

Theresa's face brightened.

'Your emails,' she said. 'You were sent an email to remind you of your appointment.'

'And?'

'That wasn't Grimm's office.'

'I don't understand.'

'We knew you had an appointment in that building. So we went round a few hours before you were due and put up the plaque. Arthur Grimm actually works somewhere else.'

She grinned.

'It was risky. But it worked.'

'Your idea?' Norah asked.

Theresa nodded reluctantly, half contrite, half proud.

'Goodbye Theresa. You're damned clever. Don't waste it.'

Again Norah turned to go.

'Why aren't you angrier?' Theresa asked.

'Oh, believe me, I'm angry with you. Angrier than you can know.'

'So why don't you show it?'

'Maybe I think you've earned a second chance,' Norah said. 'Or maybe I'm just too tired.'

'Why are you still nice to me?'

Norah shrugged.

'Someone once said, *There's a special place in hell for women who don't help other women.*'

'Madeleine Albright,' Theresa said. 'I think.'

'Told you you were clever,' Norah said.

Her eyes narrowed.

'You got away this time, Kim. Make the most of it.'

'And if I don't?'

'A contract killing costs about twenty thousand euros,' she said. 'It's an urban myth that you can have someone murdered for two or three grand; I've looked into it. You have to put up twenty thousand.'

Theresa stared at her, not sure if she was joking.

'I'll be honest with you,' Norah went on. 'I don't have that kind of money.' She pushed her hair out of her forehead. 'But a shot in the kneecap starts at about three and a half, and I think I could manage that.'

Theresa grinned.

'I mean it,' Norah said.

'I know. After all, you are the High Priestess of Evil.'

'Exactly. So don't disappoint me.'

'I won't.'

Norah turned to go.

'Norah?'

'What now?'

'The other night in the Prater,' Theresa said and then hesitated.

Norah looked at her patiently.

'If your friends hadn't turned up,' she said, 'would you have…I mean, were you really going to…?'

'Of course not,' Norah replied.

And the women looked at each other, the way two people do when they both know that one of them has just told a lie.

'Didn't think so,' Theresa said.

Back in her flat, Norah wandered through the rooms. The cardboard boxes had begun to gather dust and for the first time she realised why she hadn't unpacked them: part of her had thought she wouldn't stay in Vienna—that she'd end up going back to Alex. But that door was closed now. Alex had found a new girlfriend and although she hadn't expected it, although the thought hurt like hell, a small part of her—a decent, grown-up part of her—was pleased for him.

First thing tomorrow, she'd start to unpack. She'd manage somehow, though she knew it wouldn't be easy. But first...

Norah put her keys on the table, went over to the window and lit a cigarette. She looked down at her car. Tomorrow, when she'd finished unpacking, she'd drive somewhere nice. To Prague, maybe, to visit Kafka's grave. Or to Hamburg, to surprise Werner. The possibilities were endless.

Her eyes came to rest on the kitchen table. She sat down, opened her notebook and began to write.

Dear Valerie,

It's strange. You've been dead for eighteen years, but if someone asks me who my best friend is, you're always the first person to come to mind. Eighteen years. A child born on the day of your death can drive a car now—tear around the place in a beat-up VW like the boys in the sixth form, or show off in Mum's BMW like your cousin. Those kids are older than you ever were.

Eighteen years. Although I know you've been dead for so long, I still think of us as being the same age as each other. Isn't that funny? You're sixteen and always will be. I'm in my mid-thirties and I'm writing to a teenager.

I'm writing to say goodbye. I'll keep it short, because it isn't easy for me. Your mum's well, so is your brother.

I'm okay, though I've had a weird few weeks. I've been thinking of you a lot again lately. I suddenly got it into my head that you might not have killed yourself. But you did. You killed yourself. You really did. I must accept that.

Maybe your mum's right. Maybe nobody's to blame, including me. Either way, I'm sorry.

When you went... it was like a shadow falling over my life, like perpetual night.

For eighteen years I was sure I was to blame for your death. But that has to stop now, Valerie; it's time I returned to the light.

I am going to try to think less of you in the coming months—try to let you rest. It won't be easy, that's for sure.

And maybe what you wrote is true—maybe I am just a bad person. I've thought about it a lot lately. I have so many fucking flaws. And yes, the world is fucking unfair and it's not often that I feel it in my power to change that. But I do try. And tomorrow I'll try a little harder.

That's it, I think.

Norah

P.S. You were wrong about one thing. I do have friends. (You'd like them.)

Norah read the letter through, then went into the bathroom and undressed. Her tattoo was healed; the new skin beneath the scab, fragile and translucent as parchment, no longer hurt when she touched it. Some primeval instinct drove her into the shower to wash; it was like an ancient ritual.

When Norah was finished and had put on clean clothes, she returned to the kitchen and took out the heavy crystal ashtray that she had once bought at a flea market, but never used. She tore the letter out of her notebook, folded it up and put it in the ashtray. Then she took the envelope containing Valerie's suicide note from her bag, put that in the ashtray too and set fire to the lot.

To her surprise, she suddenly felt weightless. And perhaps, she thought, that was all right. Perhaps she was allowed to be happy. Even after all the mistakes she had made.

Norah watched the flames swallowing the paper.

There was a curse in those flames. There was her guilt, her pain.

There was a letter. There was burning paper.

Then there was ash.

Then nothing.

Epilogue

That night Norah slept deeply and dreamlessly and when she woke in the morning, she felt more refreshed than she'd felt for a long time. She got up, made herself an espresso and drank it standing at the window with a cigarette. Then she set to and unpacked the boxes.

Twice, tears came to her eyes when she found herself holding things Alex had given her—both times, she wiped them away, blew her nose and carried on. When she had finished, she collapsed, exhausted, on the sofa and put on the TV.

The world hadn't improved overnight. Greed, blood, splinters of bone. Norah felt the old fury rise inside her and was reminded of something Wolfgang Balder had once said to her. *I bet that if I were to take a scalpel and cut open your chest I'd find a heart that's every bit as black as mine.*

The TV showed images from a civil war zone, then cut to a devastating oil slick. Balder was right, Norah thought. However much love there was in her heart, there was also a hell of a lot of anger. Images of a killing spree flashed up onto the screen. Norah finished her coffee;

it had gone cold. Maybe, she thought, it's okay to be angry. Maybe it makes sense to be angry. Maybe I have a right to my anger.

Maybe the question isn't what I feel, but what I do with my feelings. She switched off the TV.

When she picked up her phone and opened her inbox, she found an email from Werner with the subject line *Special Mission*. At last—the information she had asked for, address and all. Norah wrote back, thanking Werner. She immediately felt quite different; now she could do something useful. She took an envelope from her desk drawer and wrote:

From a friend.

Then she got dressed and went out into the evening light.

The beauty of Vienna hit her with full force; she walked through the streets, drinking great gulps of the wintry city. The Karlskirche, the little florists, the sumptuous opera house, the horse-drawn carriages clattering past the old hotels, the cakeshop windows. And the charm, the elegance, the beauty of the people. It was as if she were seeing it all for the first time. On a sudden impulse, Norah went into a newsagent and asked for a packet of Gauloises.

'You're smiling like you've won the lottery,' said the man who served her, a little man in an old-fashioned suit.

'The city's so beautiful,' Norah replied. 'I hadn't noticed until now.'

'A wise woman once wrote: *We don't see the world as it is, we see it as we are*,' he said, handing her the cigarettes.

Norah nodded thoughtfully. There was probably something in that.

The next cash machine was only two streets away.

What had she read? *A thousand-euro fine.* Norah took out five hundred euros, added the five hundred she'd brought from home, put the notes in the envelope and sealed it. Thanks to Werner and Google Maps, she found the building where Marie T. lived and rang a bell at random. When she was buzzed in, she slipped through the door, sending up a quick prayer that the names would be on the letterboxes.

Her prayer was answered. She dropped the envelope in Marie T.'s letterbox and went out again.

Back in her flat, she saw how nice and homely it looked now that the boxes were gone. It had cost her a lot of strength to unpack them, with all the memories they contained, but it had been worth it. Norah collapsed on the sofa.

A second later, her phone announced the arrival of a text. Probably Max, wanting to know how—

Alex. Her heart began to beat faster. She shut her eyes for a moment, steeling herself, then clicked open the message. It was only six words long.

I love you too, damn it.

For a few minutes all Norah could do was sit and stare at the text. Then she got up and went over to the window. Her car was parked just across the road; the tank was full.

As she left the city that evening, she decided against the motorway; she'd take the country roads.

Darkness. Woods. Norah smiled.

She lit a cigarette and stepped on the accelerator.

Silence. New moon. Stars.

Before her, an empty road and behind her, the night.

Acknowledgments

So many people contribute to the making of a book. Some directly, some indirectly, some without even realising—by inspiring me or encouraging me or simply being there.

First of all I should like to thank my wonderful family. I am unbelievably lucky and I know it.

Huge thanks also go to my brilliant (and incredibly patient) publisher and editor Regina Kammerer and to all those I have been lucky enough to meet at btb and Random House over the course of the years. It is a pleasure to work with you. Thanks to my agent Georg Simader and to everyone else at Copywrite: Caterina Kirsten, Lisa Volpp, Vanessa Gutekunst, Felix Rudloff and my 'canaries in the mine' Laura Kampf and Ursula Waldmüller.

Two artists have accompanied me during my work on this novel. Firstly, Soap&Skin whose songs I have listened to very intensely. And secondly the incredible Karen Köhler and her unforgettable short story collection *We Were Fishing for Rockets*. Thank you.

Thanks, too, to all those who love literature as much as I do. Those who make books or contribute to their success by buying them, talking about them, writing about them, recommending them—and reading them. What a good thing you exist.

And…Jörn? I hope you didn't think I'd forgotten you. The swift (I don't need to tell you) is, as always, for you. Thank you for everything.

Melanie Raabe, February 2018

© Christian Faustus

MELANIE RAABE is the internationally bestselling author of *The Trap* and *The Stranger Upstairs*. *The Shadow*, her third novel, spent eighteen weeks on the *Der Spiegel* bestseller list when it was published in 2018. She lives in Cologne, Germany.

IMOGEN TAYLOR is a freelance literary translator based in Berlin. She is the translator of both *The Trap* and *The Stranger Upstairs*, as well as *Truth and Other Lies* by Sascha Arango and *Fear* by Dirk Kurbjuweit.